Advance praise for Rolando Hinojosa's
new Rafe Buenrostro thriller,
ASK A POLICEMAN

"Rolando Hinojosa, the master weaver of tales about the legendary Klail City, has created **a hard-edged, unforgiving police procedural** . . . *Ask a Policeman* is a ride on a bullet through the windswept, heat-scorched badlands of the Texas-Mexican border."

–Manuel Ramos, author of *Blues for the Buffalo* and other Luis Montez mysteries

"Those of us awaiting the return of Rafe Buenrostro have much to cheer about. *Ask a Policeman* is **a fast-paced story of intrigue,** replete with fascinating characters, murder for revenge, dope-smuggling, and just enough sex. **Hinojosa's style is at its best**, and sure to garner new readers worldwide for this old master."

–Rudolfo Anaya, author of *Bless Me, Ultima*

(please turn the page for more rave reviews)

Praise for Rolando Hinojosa's
previous Rafe Buenrostro mystery,
Partners in Crime

"Like Dashiell Hammett with a Texas twang . . . A brilliant technical achievement . . . It can be read both as a compelling story in its own right and a sort of summary piece within [Rolando Hinojosa's] 'Klail City Death Trip' series . . . Combines gritty realism with a yearning for justice . . . As the story of how one intelligent and human person deals with outright evil, it is a compelling and incisive book."

—*The Dallas Morning News*

"Bewildering murders challenge the amusing and erudite Rafe Buenrostro of the Belken Country Homicide Squad . . . A pleasurable, intelligent novel revealing the South Texas-[Rio Grande] Valley cultural milieu . . . The plot meanders with the narrator's digressions and intrusions, reminiscent of nineteenth-century English novels. Hinojosa writes with humor." —*The Review of Texas Books*

"American and Mexican police officials cooperate to solve a horrible crime. What moves *Partners in Crime* are the essential ingredients of good detective fiction . . . Hinojosa has learned well from the masters of detection." —Charles Tatum, *World Literature Today*

Praise for the novels of
Rolando Hinojosa

"Every sentence of every paragraph is clean, clear, and unambiguous . . . I am neither a Chicano nor a Texan . . . But I know the people of [Hinojosa's] *Klail City* and *The Fair Gentlemen of Belken County*. They are my uncles, and cousins, and friends . . . Hinojosa's characters have moved beyond the role the political writers of *La Raza* would assign them. Like the Armenians in Saroyan's *Human Comedy*, they are far too alive to hold still for an ethnic-racial label . . . They are simply fellow humans. He loves them. So do we."

–Edgar-winning mystery novelist Tony Hillerman

"Rolando Hinojosa is one of Texas's most remarkable writers. The 'Klail City Death Trip' series is one of Faulknerian dimensions."

–*The Dallas Times-Herald*

"Just as surely as Yoknapatawpha County, Macondo, and Lake Wobegon belong to other literary settlers, Klail City, Texas, down in the Rio Grande Valley, is Rolando Hinojosa country . . . Although Hinojosa's sharp eye and accurate ear capture a place, its people, and a time in a masterly way, his work goes far beyond regionalism. He is a writer for all readers."

–*The New York Times*

Ask a Policeman

By Rolando Hinojosa

Estampas del valle

Klail City y sus alrededores

Korean Love Songs

Mi querido Rafa

Rites and Witnesses

Claros varones de Belken

Dear Rafe

The Valley

Klail City

Partners in Crime

Becky and Her Friends

Los amigos de Becky

The Useless Servants

Ask a Policeman

Ask a Policeman

Rolando Hinojosa

Arte Público Press
Houston, Texas
1998

This volume is made possible through grants from the National Endowment for the Arts (a federal agency), Andrew W. Mellon Foundation, the Lila Wallace-Reader's Digest Fund and the City of Houston through The Cultural Arts Council of Houston, Harris County.

Recovering the past, creating the future

Arte Público Press
University of Houston
452 Cullen Performance Hall
Houston, Texas 77204-2004

Cover design by James F. Brisson

Hinojosa, Rolando.
Ask a Policeman / by Rolando Hinojosa.
p. cm.
ISBN 1-55885-226-3 (alk. paper)
1. Mexican Americans—Mexican-American Border Region—Fiction.
I. Title.
PS3558.I545A94 1998
813′.54—dc21 98-10316
CIP

♾ The paper used in this publication meets the requirements of the American National Standard for Information Sciences—Permanence of Paper for Printed Library Materials, ANSI Z39.48-1984.

Printed in the United States of America

2 3 4 5 6 7 8 9 0 1 12 11 10 9 8 7 6 5 4 3 2

To my parents

My father,
Manuel Guzmán Hinojosa

He was the policeman.

And my mother,
Carrie Effie Smith

The policeman's wife.

One

By nine o'clock on that hot, humid, first day of August, Chief Inspector Rafe Buenrostro of Belken County Homicide had finished his third cup of coffee. He looked at his watch, placed the empty cup on his desk, and headed toward the elevator. Waiting for the elevator, County Judge Servando Garza and two homicide detectives, Peter Hauer and Sam Dorson, chatted for a moment as Buenrostro led the way into the elevator. They were on their way to the final hearing for Lisandro Gómez Solís, a/k/a Lee Gómez, a Mexican national and former government official, recently convicted of homicide and now bound over to the federal government on drug charges. The four men looked straight ahead.

Downstairs, in the first basement of the county courthouse, a chunky, balding, middle-aged man with a two-day growth of beard, and dressed in gray electrician's coveralls, struggled with a dolly as he stepped out of the service elevator. He motioned to the officer guarding the holding cells. The guard waved back and put his hand to his ear when the electrician yelled something at him.

As the man approached, the guard came around his desk and said, "I'm sorry, I couldn't hear you."

The man in the coveralls waved him off and said, "I just said the third floor shorted out again."

The guard shrugged and then said, "Well, we got no shorts here."

The electrician nodded and said, "Can I use that phone? It'll only be a minute, my partner's upstairs in some judge's chambers. Think it'll be okay?"

At that moment, the basement elevator opened again and another electrician came out. He waved at his partner and then clenched both fists making a breaking motion.

"Like you said, Al. It's the damned wiring. It's old."

"Yeah, that's what I was telling the guard here."

The guard was heading back to his table when the electrician closest to him rammed a handgun to his spine.

"No trouble, now."

The second electrician ran up and stood by the cell occupied by the prisoner Gómez, who rose from his cot.

"You'll be out of there in a jif, mister. Okay?"

The guard, as ordered, kept his hands down and looked at the floor. "Now, if you don't have a key to that cell, you're in bad trouble. Do you have the key?"

"Yeah. Right-hand shirt pocket. It's a special key reserved for the feds."

"Good boy." The man called Al unbuttoned the pocket, grabbed the key, and tossed it to his partner, after which he taped the guard's mouth.

Unlocking Gómez's cell, Al said, "Too bad about the mustache, mister. You got to shave it off if we're to get out of here peaceful-like. Got something?"

Gómez showed him an electric razor, plugged it in, and went to work.

The first man turned to the guard again. "We're putting you in that cell, that's all. We've got to use those bracelets you got hanging there. No need to worry, we're not interested in shooting ourselves out of here."

Gómez stepped out of the cell and rubbed his upper lip. He looked questioningly at both electricians as if to say, "What's next?"

One of them said: "The federal marshals will be here in forty-five minutes to take you to the hearing." Reaching down to the dolly, he took out another pair of gray coveralls.

"Here, this is your passport."

Gómez quickly slipped on the coveralls on top of his prison garb and zipped them up. One of the men then walked to see the guard, who was sitting on the cot, staring at the floor.

"Hey." When the guard looked up, the man said, "Don't worry, you'll be out of there right quick."

The three took the service elevator to the main floor. With the clean-shaven Gómez leading the way, the two others pushed the dolly into a hallway closet.

As they reached the hall lobby leading to the nearest exit, the trio froze momentarily when they saw half-a-dozen county patrolmen running through the hallway. They waited a moment, looking around as more policemen came scrambling out of the building and into their cars parked in front of the courthouse. The three turned to the nearest exit, walked leisurely out of the building and into the main parking lot. Gómez climbed into the back portion of an old VW van and sat down.

They drove slowly toward the toll booth, where the parking lot attendant took the two dollars and checked off the van's license plate. The driver waved at the attendant and turned right, away from the downtown area.

As they did so, the driver checked the time: "We've got a thirty-five minute head start."

Gómez looked at him and then at his partner but said nothing. The second man smiled, pointed to a corner of the van, and said: "You'll find a pair of jeans and a beige guayabera shirt in the bundle there. Just your size, mister. I think the cowboy boots will fit, and that goes for the Stetson, too. Brand new, just got them this morning. Here, your brother said you might need this," and he handed Gómez a loaded nine-millimeter Browning automatic and two extra clips.

With this, he then joined Gómez, who had started removing his gray coveralls. The second electrician tapped the driver on the shoulder and said, "I'll spell you just as soon as I get out of these things."

The driver turned his head slightly and nodded. Gómez stared at the man giving the order. The man smiled at him. "We got ten thousand dollars from your brother to get you out. You don't know us, and we don't know you. Our orders are to drive to the first highway junction cutoff heading east. After that, we're to follow your directions."

Gómez nodded.

Ten minutes later, the van came to a stop at a roadside park, the driver got out, opened the side door, and climbed in the back. His partner got behind the wheel and drove off.

The first electrician pulled off his coveralls. "You'll read about it in the papers tomorrow, but you may as well know now. At the time we were getting you out, there was a shooting somewhere in the downtown area. That got the county cops out of the courthouse, just as we figured."

The man then stuffed Gómez's prison clothes and shoes and the three coveralls inside the laundry bag. He took out a pack of Mexican Raleigh cigarettes and handed it to Gómez.

"We figured you'd want a smoke. Keep the lighter."

The three drove in silence. Twenty minutes later, they were on the old Military Highway and drove to the first road junction heading east again, closer to the Rio Grande. The driver slowed the vehicle, moved to the shoulder of the road and then drove straight into a cane field, gunning the motor as he did so.

The two men took their lead from Gómez. He led them across the highway, they clambered up a small irrigation levee, walked down to a clearing, and the three sat on the ground under a shady mesquite tree and waited.

They'd been there some five minutes, and Gómez was lighting his second cigarette, when they spotted a 210 Cessna flying in from the south. Snuffing out the cigarette, Lee Gómez motioned for the men to follow him; they walked toward the landing strip half-hidden by a healthy sorghum crop.

Once aboard, the pilot, quickly and expertly, veered the plane sharply to the right, revved up the engine, and pilot and passengers headed for the Gómez ranch across the Rio Grande, some ten miles south of Klail City, Texas.

Within a few minutes, the plane circled the main house. Gómez looked down and saw his station wagon. Next to it stood one of the family's two navy blue Jeeps. As the plane prepared to approach the landing strip, he caught a glimpse of two figures running toward the second Jeep.

The twins, he said to himself.

The plane stalled somewhat as it banked but straightened itself again, and Lee Gómez saw Deaf-mute Farías, one of his farmhands, operating a backhoe near an irrigation ditch.

The pilot went easy on the throttle, and the Cessna glided in smartly as the two Jeeps headed for the plane. The electricians shook hands with Gómez as he slipped out of the plane. Arms akimbo, he waited for the Jeeps. Lee's brother, Felipe Segundo, was driving the one to his right, and he waved as he drove.

A workman in the back seat held on to his straw hat as the Jeep sped toward the lone figure. Lee Gómez then looked at the second Jeep and recognized the driver, his nephew Juan Carlos; the other twin, José Antonio, took off his wide-brimmed straw hat and waved at him.

Within seconds, the pilot taxied out, revved the engine again, and was airborne by the time the Jeeps came to within twenty feet of Lee

Gómez. His brother glanced up at the airborne plane then jumped out of the Jeep. Suddenly, he pulled out a nine-millimeter Beretta and fired. The shot hit Lee Gómez above the right elbow and sent him spinning to his knees. The second shot struck him on the shoulder and this drove him to the ground, spread-eagled. As Lee Gómez turned his head, he saw his nephew Juan Carlos approaching, gun in hand. Conscious but going into shock, Gómez reacted instinctively and reached for his own nine-millimeter.

He never heard the third shot, nor did he hear the Cessna overhead lose speed, stall again when it banked to the right, and dive sharply into a plowed field. The plane crash was muffled somewhat by the surrounding sorghum and sugarcane fields as Felipe Segundo fired the fourth shot into his brother's face.

He turned the body face up, ripped open the guayabera shirt and pulled the bloody automatic from its holster. He shook some of his brother's blood off his left hand, released the automatic's spring mechanism, and caught the clip in mid-air. After this, he checked the firing pin. Sheared off, just as he'd ordered.

Juan Carlos Gómez pointed with his chin toward the body; Felipe Segundo then turned to the workman in his Jeep. "Morales, get out the tarp and roll don Lisandro in it. Juan Carlos, help Morales with the tarp."

His second son waited in the Jeep.

"José Antonio, remind Farías I want that plane ground to pieces. And Toni, shoot the pilot and the other two twice just to make sure." The youngster drove off.

Felipe Segundo Gómez turned to his other son. "Juan Carlos, I'll go see what the Texas TV stations are saying about the shooting at the parking lot."

The youngster grinned. "Maybe they'll have something to say about the daring escape, too."

He placed his hand on Juan Carlos's shoulder. "They'll have a time explaining that one, won't they? Well, on your way now."

The youngster laughed again and headed the Jeep toward the smoke rising out of the sorghum fields.

Two

Shortly after eleven a.m., while the escaping Lee Gómez was pulling on the coveralls provided by the two fake electricians, Homicide Detective Ike Cantú took a call to the squad room.

"There's been a shooting, a terrible thing. Right here, at the parking lot . . ."

"Slow down. Where are you?"

"Watson's cafeteria, the parking lot."

"Your name?"

"What? Oh. Rick Barrera. I'm a night cook, and I seen the whole thing."

"Be right there. You wait."

Cantú pressed the intercom button to the desk sergeant and asked for the chief inspector.

"He's meeting with the county Commissioners' Court, Ike."

Cantú's phone rang again. This time it was a woman who had called 911 and alerted the Emergency Service, which in turn called the technical squad headed by its medical examiner, Henry Dietz. This phone call galvanized the county patrolmen, who dashed out of the courthouse in all directions, much like Lord Randal's horse.

Five minutes later, as Cantú was about to drive out of the parking lot, Detectives Sam Dorson and Peter Hauer caught up with him, and the three rode downtown together as Hauer and Dorson checked their .38 Police Specials.

Dorson: "Cut the light and the siren, Ike." A few minutes later Cantú turned into the cafeteria parking lot.

EMS was already there when county patrol cars streamed in to begin blocking off the parking lot. Soon after, the technical squad drove in. Dorson, Hauer, and Cantú walked toward a shiny, black Lincoln. The passenger's side was riddled with bullet holes along parallel lines from left to right and from right to left again. The car, the pavement, and the two bodies were covered with broken glass and spent shell casings. The dead men wore identical black jumpsuits and lay awkwardly across each other.

The detectives looked intently at the bodies, saw no sign of life, and stepped back as the technical squad began its work.

The gathering crowd was being moved out of the way, and two of the uniforms started stretching the familiar yellow tape.

Wheezing a bit, Medical Examiner Henry Dietz stood next to the detectives as the technical squad went about its business. A woman police photographer circled the bodies and took shots from several angles. This took but a few minutes, and the photographer put her equipment away.

After this, two men wearing plastic gloves and plastic covers on their shoes stepped gingerly around the glass and the bodies as they bagged the personal effects. Three other technicians, baggies in hand, scooped up the empty cartridge shells, most of which lay scattered around a fifteen-foot area; some of the shell casings had been run over by a wide-tire vehicle.

One of Dietz's assistants nodded a greeting to Dorson.

"What's that smell?" asked Dorson.

Dietz answered. "Bug killer, and I'm allergic to it. One thing, though, that ought to keep the flies away for a while."

Dietz asked the technician, "What'd you find?"

The man held up two plastic baggies full of empty shell casings. "Automatics, most certainly, and Uzis, most likely. The current weapon of choice around here."

"Don't miss a one, Sparky."

Arms crossed, Dorson said, "Here comes the rest of the courthouse group, with Narcotics leading the way, as usual."

Peter Hauer grunted, as did Ike Cantú.

Cantú then raised his hand and called to a senior uniform. "Keep everyone away. That includes the Narco Squad. This is a homicide, and we don't want people tracking all over the place. Tell Narco to send one of their men over here. We'll send them a full report later on. When the taping's done, start on names and witnesses."

Dorson gave the policeman the name of the first caller and told him to ask for the other person who later called 911.

The dusting for prints was being done methodically back to front, in and out of the car. As usual, blood from the victims was sticking to the plastic shoe covers. Dietz looked around and said, "We're just about through. The EMS body bag men will stay here until you give the word. See you, Sam."

The crowd began to move away to make room for the cars that began pulling away. Another shooting. Drugs, most likely, some were saying.

Sam Dorson asked Peter Hauer, "What've you got?"

"First off, the Linc's a rental. Two passports on my man, one Mexican, one Guatemalan. Both made out to one Julio Salas. Alligator wallet and shoes. Credit and bank cards, American and Mexican. Two pants pockets full of American money. All hundreds. A nasty looking Beretta M-92, 15-shot and three extra clips. My man's a clubfoot."

"Ike?"

"A nine millimeter Browning MKIII. Two clips here. Two passports here, too. One Mexican, one Guatemalan. Name of Gustavo Rocha. Must be payday; he's got two thousand American in hundreds wrapped in a Farmers Trust money band. Fancy tailored denims. A Rolex, a gold ID chain, and a plain gold ring, third finger, left hand. That's it."

Pete Hauer called for the body bags. "Wrap 'em up."

Dorson said to the nearest county patrolman, "Go with the body bags, Villarreal." Turning to Hauer and Cantú, he said, "Let's go talk to the witnesses."

The caller, Rick Barrera, turned out to be an assistant cook at the cafeteria. He was on his way home after his night shift when he noticed a gray-maroon Silverado drive into the lot and come to a sudden stop. Two men got out and walked toward the men leaning against the Lincoln.

"The guys from the Silverado opened up on 'em, just like that. And it happened fast, I'm telling you. They kept firing when the guys hit the ground. Then, back to the Silverado, and phfft, they was gone. Fast."

"Wasn't there a driver?"

"Oh, yeah, but I didn't see his face."

"Which way'd they go?"

Barrera hesitated for a moment, "Headed east and stopped for a light, yeah."

"You call EMS too?"

The youngster shook his head and said, "Not me."

Presently, a slim middle-aged woman came up. "My name's Myrlene Moy, and I saw it all. I'm the one who called EMS." Pleased with herself for doing her civic duty.

Dorson thanked her. "Detective Cantú here will take your statement, ma'am. Here's my card."

Hauer took additional notes from Rick Barrera as Dorson walked around the shot up Lincoln on his way to his patrol car. He picked up his cellular phone and dialed the chief inspector's office.

The desk sergeant answered the phone. "Yeah, Sam, he knows. Just came down from the meeting, and he's on his way. We also got trouble here. Gómez escaped."

Dorson looked at the dead men, the Lincoln, and at the number of county patrolmen. A diversion. How like Lee Gómez, he thought.

He then thought on the man with the clubfoot. Well, there can't be too many of those. He looked at the four baggies Hauer passed to him. Jewelry, gold chains. The usual. The wallets and the passports were also bloody affairs. He checked the names on the credit and bank cards. The cards matched the names on the passports and they were issued by Farmers Trust in Edgerton and Bancomer in Barrones, Tamaulipas.

Locals, Dorson thought. That would call for close work with Lu Cetina de Gutiérrez, the new Director of Public Order in Barrones.

"Mark this stuff, Pete."

A patrolman came up to Dorson. "Just got a radio report that Lisandro Gómez got away, Sergeant. Escaped. The courthouse was all ajumble with this shooting here and it looks like that's when he got away. You imagine that?"

"Yeah, I just heard."

The patrolman said, "Your phone's ringing."

"Get it, will you?"

Looking up from the spot where the bodies fell, Dorson saw Chief Inspector Buenrostro driving into the parking lot. The body bags removed, the EMS people stood by waiting for orders.

Ike Cantú: "Straight to the morgue, gang."

A wrecker from Belken Southside Service rolled in, and Hauer made the man circle around the Lincoln. Hauer pointed to the car and said, "Pick it up from the front."

Cantú fell in with Hauer, and both walked to where Buenrostro and Sam Dorson were waiting for them.

Three

When Dorson walked in, Henry Dietz was finishing the autopsy on a man's corpse that had recently washed up on the Texas side near the mouth of the Rio Grande.

Dietz's voice, dry and monotonous as he spoke into his lapel microphone, didn't break stride as he nodded to Sam Dorson. An assistant looked on uninterestedly at the dead man as she put away the various saws and scalpels into a Hommer sterilizer.

Dietz called across the room. "Sammy, want to see what fresh alligator gar bites look like?"

"Not interested."

"Sam, have you noticed how many more bodies have washed up on our side since the last flood?"

Dorson looked across the morgue, sat down, and said, "Haven't kept count."

"Well, we gained some two thousand acres from Mexico on this last flood and hurricane, and my guess is that the new channel now forces the current closer toward the Texas side."

Dorson wasn't paying attention.

"Almost through here. These are your two," pointing to lockers four and five, "and we'll start on them right after lunch. Irene here volunteered to help me out."

Irene Paredes nodded much like any soldier who's been volunteered.

Dorson held the door open for Dietz and Irene Paredes who handed him a folder. "Ballistics reports. Uzis, all right, courtesy of our friends from Israel. What a break, eh?"

"Thanks. We'll be in the squad room. Call us when you've a complete report."

When Dorson walked into the squadroom, Buenrostro was leaning against a file cabinet next to his office. Hauer and Cantú sat behind their desks.

Cantú spoke first. "The three of us were at the site within seven minutes after I took the call. And we'd been at the cafeteria parking lot ten to twelve minutes when Al Contreras called from the desk and told us of Gómez's escape."

Hauer: "I alerted the two bridges at Jonesville, the two here at Klail and the one in Flora right after that."

Dorson stifled a yawn, and asked: "Anybody check with the *Migra* guys?"

Hauer: "I called them. No record of a Silverado crossing any bridge. I touched base with Art Styles at Amity bridge. Same thing, no Silverado."

A second later, the desk sergeant called: "This may be something for you, Chief Inspector. Tommie Nakamura just phoned from your brother's farm. One of the hands called him and said a VW van had been driven into a cane field and left there. Got something to do with what we're working on, you think?"

"No idea, but thanks anyway." Buenrostro turned to Dorson: "Sam, call Lu Cetina in Barrones. Tell her about Lee and the parking lot. We'll send her the prints from the Lincoln, and from the two dead nationals at the parking lot. Ask if a VW van's been reported missing on her side of the river. After that, check with our parking attendant. He's bound to have a record of a van parked in the lot this morning.

"Ike, call Joe Molden at Auto. Ask him if there's been a stolen report on the VW and the Silverado and have him send a wrecker for the van. After that, call my brother and have him give you the VW's plate numbers and pass them on to Auto.

"Pete, call the Jonesville airport and run a check on the Lincoln at the cafeteria lot."

Hauer: "Right away."

Ike Cantú was back in the squad room within five minutes. He read from his note pad. "Joe Molden says no stolen report on a VW van in the last six days. He's checking on the Silverado. Seven were stolen this week alone. The canefield van's got a Tamaulipas Frontera plate. Six-Three-Nine Y Y Two."

"Go over the statements you got at the cafeteria parking lot, Ike."

Ten minutes later Dorson walked into the squad room as Hauer cradled the phone.

Hauer read from his notes. "The Lincoln at the airport was rented at nine-twenty this morning. Not Texas Mexicans, but Mexican nationals with passports, according to the clerks. As a courtesy, the Lincoln was brought directly to them. The clerk thinks the two men left the rental desk around nine-thirty or so.

"I figure it's a fifty-five minute drive from the airport to Watson's Cafeteria."

Buenrostro: "All right, we'll say the dead men got to the cafeteria parking lot around ten forty-five. The killers were either there or waiting for them."

Ike Cantú: "I got the call at ten to eleven."

Dorson looked at his notes. "That checks with what the cafeteria cook said. Got off the late shift about that time. The parking lot keeper gave me the VW's plate numbers: Tamaulipas Frontera plates Six-Three-Nine Y Y Two."

Buenrostro: "That's a match, Sam. Anything else?"

"While I was downstairs, the desk sergeant gave me a copy of his phone log. He transferred the Barrera kid's call to me at ten to eleven. The log also shows the Myrlene Moy call to EMS shortly after that."

Cantú asked, "What's the log's time on the woman's call?"

Dorson answered, "Three minutes later. I also got hold of Lu Cetina at her office. There's a VW van missing, all right. A Mexican insurance agent reported it to the Barrones police two days ago."

Cantú: "So Lee Gómez walked out of here any time between ten forty-five and ten fifty-five."

Hauer: "The papers are going to have a good time on this one. Gangland execution. No clues. Police baffled."

Buenrostro: "Lee Gómez was lucky, that's all. We'll go with Sam on the diversion angle. Pete, call Auto again. Tell them we'll have the technical squad check the VW, and make sure Lu Cetina gets a fax when the van's prints are ready."

Peter Hauer dialed Joe Molden at Auto on the interoffice phone. Dorson yawned rather loudly. He walked to the slightly ajar office door, closed it, and said, "We got the times pretty well covered, and we've got both the Lincoln and the VW pegged. Anything on the cell guard downstairs?"

Buenrostro: "I checked with the feds as soon as we got back. The guard says they were two men dressed as electricians pushing a dolly. He said they said the word *out* kinda funny. Said it sounded like *oot*."

Dorson looked up. "Some Southerners talk that way, don't they?" He followed this by saying, "It may not mean anything."

Buenrostro: "Ike, get the basement guard to tell you exactly what happened, what was said, and what Gómez's reaction was to all of this. Ask him how the electricians came in, how they left and so on. It should be fresh on his mind. Anything else comes up, call me at the hospital or at home."

Cantú carried his suit jacket and unloosened his tie as he headed for the elevator.

Dorson walked into Rafe Buenrostro's office.

Dorson asked, "Anything else?"

"Call the Jonesville private airport. We want a fax showing the names of the pilots, owners, operators, whatever, and the type and number of planes that flew out yesterday and today, before noon."

Dorson got an outside line and began dialing the Jonesville private airport. Just then, the desk sergeant came in: "Sorry to bother you, Chief. Thought I'd warn you, though. D.A. Chip Valencia's in the hall."

"We're not here, Contreras."

Dorson looked up, but Buenrostro waved him off as he measured out a fresh pot of coffee. He rinsed two cups, sat down, and waited for Dorson to finish his phone call.

Dorson: "Appreciate your help. We needed this yesterday, right?" He replaced the phone and said, "What's with the D.A.? Does it have to do with this morning's meeting?"

"Most likely, and Gómez's escape, I imagine." Buenrostro stared at the parking lot. "He wants the county to buy a tank."

Dorson: "A tank? What else? A Howitzer? I don't even trust our guys with the .38s we issue them. Good Lord."

Buenrostro looked at some darkening clouds. More rain, he thought.

"How'd the airport go?"

"They're faxing the stuff. Should be coming in soon."

Dorson poured two cups of coffee. "How do we stop Chip Valencia, Rafe? Can we stop him?"

"Judge Ochoa's against it, and that's a help. Sounds like the fax out there."

"The airport manager, probably."

Four

Dorson picked up his cup and walked into the squad room as the fax machine clacked away. Buenrostro followed him and waited at Cantú's desk.

"No flights three days ago due to the storm up the coast in Nueces County. Ah, here's today's list." Dorson placed the sheets on Cantú's desk.

"Go ahead."

"As of one-thirty today, half an hour ago, they'd registered nine small planes flying south out of Jonesville. Three Pipers and six Cessnas. Four of the Cessnas and a Piper don't fit the time schedule we're working on."

"Is that the manifest, Sam?"

"Yep. Plane numbers, pilots' names, addresses, the works."

"Any names familiar?"

"Not to me. Take a look."

The names were listed alphabetically:

– *Grayson, Randolph Jason*
– *Herrera, Juan Carlos*
– *Vásquez, Alberto Emilio*
– *Wimsatt, Anson B.*

Buenrostro handed Dorson the Valley-wide telephone directory. After a short while, Dorson said: "Grayson's from Edgerton, both Herrera and Vásquez are from Klail, and Wimsatt hails from Flora. They're all due back tonight by six. All four are mechanics as well as pilots. Nothing new."

"Type a note for Pete and have him phone these guys tomorrow morning. You get hold of Packy Estudillo tonight. Have him meet you at Wilkins's Garage early tomorrow. Maybe our reformed car thief's heard something."

Dorson chuckled.

"From there, drive on over to Barrones. Talk to Lu Cetina. She's bound to have something for us on the van prints by then."

Dorson yawned again.

Buenrostro: "My car's in County Maintenance, and I need a ride out there."

As they approached Dorson's car, a uniformed policeman ran toward them. "Chief Inspector, the District Attorney says he needs something for the press right now. He said it was urgent."

Before Buenrostro said anything, Dorson cut in. "Here. Tell him everything is being done to recapture Gómez and we're looking for the ones responsible for the killings at the parking lot. That we need the public's invaluable help as always. That they're to call the D.A.'s office if they see or hear anything suspicious. As to the murders, several clues have come up that Homicide's not at liberty to discuss just yet. The full force of the district attorney's office and that of the sheriff's department is being brought to bear on this for timely results."

The young patrolman nodded and said, "I'll get right on it, detective."

As they watched the young policeman hurry away, Buenrostro said, "You sound like a handout from Kenny Breen at Public Affairs."

Dorson laughed. "Well, that ought to hold District Attorney Chip Valencia for a while."

They put on their sunglasses. The rain clouds disappeared and the sky, white with heat, held a blistering sun beating down on the sticky tarmac. They sought the shade of a *huisache* tree.

"That was a break on the VW," said Dorson.

"It may help us explain the missing Silverado."

Dorson thought for a minute. "Yeah. Let's say the driver of the Silverado and the killers go on out to Nakamura's farm to pick up Lee and the electricians. The farm fronts the Military Highway, and the river's, what? Two hundred yards away? Okay, say they picked up Lee and the electricians. If it's one of the fancy Silverados with the half seats in the back, they'd be cramped with the six of them inside, but yeah, they could make it."

"We'll see," said Buenrostro, in a neutral voice.

Dorson adjusted his sunglasses and fanned some gnats away.

"And what was that about a tank?"

"A mini-tank. Chip saw a video demonstration in New York, someplace. He says we can get a lot of money from the feds."

"Good Lord. What does the sheriff say about all this?"

Buenrostro shrugged. "Norm Andrews goes along with it."

"It's the fed money, isn't it? AK-47s, right?"

"And Uzis."

"Those idiots'll wind up killing each other, Rafe."

At this, Buenrostro burst out laughing. "Come on, I need a ride."

Dorson changed the subject. "How's your father-in-law?"

"Restless. Wants to go home today. I'll look in for half an hour or so, and then I'll go home and rest a bit myself. I'll be back later this afternoon."

"Been a busy morning, Rafe. You sure your shoulder's okay?"

"Yeah, it's getting there."

Dorson dropped him off at County Maintenance and from there, Chief Inspector Rafe Buenrostro drove to the Klail City hospital.

Five

Buenrostro opened the door to his father-in-law's hospital room quietly. He sat down and began reading from his Penguin edition of Euripides.

"What're you reading?"

Surprised to find the old man awake, Buenrostro held up the paperback. "It's a Greek tragedy, Noddy."

Half-awake, red-faced Noddy Perkins sat up and said, "Me, I'm a Welsh tragedy." He scratched the gray stubble on his chin, and asked, "Is there any ice water around here?"

Buenrostro rose from his chair and poured him a glass.

Perkins drank half of it as he ran a freckled, liver-spotted hand through his scraggly hair. "Those damned doctors tell me I'm coming along nicely. I sure don't feel like I am, but I'm going home anyway. How long have I been asleep?"

"I don't know. I got here twenty minutes ago."

Noddy Perkins reached over to the end table and picked up his wrist watch. "Two-oh-four, hmph."

He then looked around the room and asked, "How's the weather out there?"

It wasn't like his father-in-law to attempt small talk.

"I think it'll rain tonight. When's Sammie Jo coming by to pick you up?"

"She's not. My car's downstairs." Buenrostro glanced at him.

The man fidgeted again and scowled. "Now, you don't have to babysit me, you got that? If you got business to do at that courthouse of yours, go to it. When do you go back on full-time duty, anyway?"

"Started today."

"You really okay to go back, are you? How's that arm?"

Buenrostro glanced at it. "Still there. Why don't I go get us some coffee?"

"Don't want any." The grumpiness was back; a good sign.

In deep thought, Perkins had made up his mind about something. He reached out to Buenrostro.

"Boy, lock that door. I've got something to say." He started to cough and pointed to the water glass. Buenrostro handed it to him.

Noddy Perkins drained the rest of the glass, and Buenrostro returned it to the serving tray.

Perkins pointed to the door again. "Lock it, I gotta say something."

The old man sat up, turned around and planted his fists on the bed. The short light-blue gown revealed two bony legs. The left one was gnarled from a ranching accident many years ago.

The next time he spoke, his voice sounded strong. The old Noddy.

"I'm going to ask a favor from you, but first, I got to say something, I want to clear something up between us."

Buenrostro asked him if he wanted another glass of water.

Buenrostro waited, as he usually did with reticent witnesses, those who were nervous, unsure of themselves. They were the ones who often revealed more than they intended.

"Straight off, Rafe. I want you to know I was never against your marrying Sammie Jo. And neither was Blanche. I want you to know that. I want you to get that straight from me."

Buenrostro's face was noncommittal.

"I'm not a racist. I also want you to know that."

Buenrostro chuckled. "Does that mean some of your best friends are Mexicans?"

"I'm a banker, goddammit, I don't need friends."

Buenrostro laughed aloud this time. "How long've you been carrying that little burden with you, Noddy?"

"Since you two married four years ago."

What a waste of time, Buenrostro thought.

"I told Jehu, but I don't imagine that cousin of yours ever said anything to you, did he?"

"No. That's not like Jehu."

A sigh. "I know." Perkins lifted his legs, laid back on the bed, and sighed again. In a rather awkward motion, he sat up again and ran both hands across his face as if washing and drying it at the same time.

Perkins cleared his throat as he looked at his son-in-law with some suspicion. "No recriminations?"

"No."

"Well, all I've got to say is that you're making this easier for me. I thought it was going to be a whole lot harder. You get me?"

"You said something about a favor."

Once again Noddy Perkins looked with some uncertainty at the younger man sitting comfortably and relaxed in the straight-backed chair.

"You do have a way of putting the ball on the other side of the net, don't you?" A short laugh. "This doesn't get any easier, son."

He looked around the room for a while. "Well, I guess it's not your job to make things easier, is it?"

There was a knock at the door, and Noddy Perkins raised his hand as he whispered, "Don't say a word, maybe they'll think I'm in the bathroom."

The knocking stopped after the fourth rap, and the swish of the rubber heels and soles faded away.

"It's a big favor. A personal one. You're the middle son, and I know about those things. Aaron's the youngest, and he can't make this decision. Israel is the oldest, but in your late father's family, it's the middle son, right?"

Perkins pointed a shaky index finger at his son-in-law. "Old Esteban Echevarría told me that about you Buenrostros."

He cleared his throat again. "Here, move your chair over. What I've got to say won't take a minute. I've been thinking on this a while and not just because I'm in the hospital, got that?

"I want you to know that what I'm about to ask is something I haven't discussed with anyone. Not Sammie Jo, not Blanche, not Jehu. No one."

Noddy Perkins took a deep breath.

"Son, I want to be buried in the Old Families cemetery by the Carmen Ranch, on your brother's land."

Rafe Buenrostro nodded.

"Is that a 'yes'?" The voice was insistent, not cranky.

"Yes, of course it is."

"Oh, Jesus Christ, you ever show how you feel? You ever lose your goddamn temper? You got one, don't you?"

"Where are we going now, Noddy?"

"You probably think it's crazy, but you're not about to say anything like that, right? But it isn't crazy. You and Sammie Jo are going to be buried there. Well, I want to be buried there too."

"And Blanche? What's she going to say about all this? Doesn't she have a say-so in this?"

A longish pause. "No need to ask. She'd want to be buried with Sammie Jo and me. She's her baby. And I'd want Blanche there too."

"It's not too much to ask, Noddy."

Oh, God, don't start crying now, thought Buenrostro. And the old man didn't. What he said, in a half-whisper, was thank you.

"I'm tired, Rafe. Here, ring that nurse, find out what she wanted. Go. Go on. I'm okay. Go do your work."

"Hah."

Startled, the old man looked up and his ruddy face showed a mixture of suspicion and incomprehension. "Now what was that all about?"

"Our cemetery's a state-designated landmark. That means the state of Texas takes care of it. That also means you'll be a ward of the state for eternity."

"You find that funny, do you? Go away. I'm going to sleep now." He pointed to the water and suddenly looked older than his seventy-five years.

After a short sip, Noddy Perkins sank his head on the pillow and closed his eyes. Buenrostro picked up his book and watched his father-in-law try to sleep. After a few seconds, Perkins's breathing became regular, and he soon started to snore softly.

Buenrostro began to read.

Some fifteen minutes later, a soft tap-tap on the door. Buenrostro remembered he'd locked the door and tiptoed to the door. The nurse.

"How is he?"

"Resting."

A nod from the nurse, and he followed her out the door.

Six

i

The next morning at six-thirty, Sam Dorson folded the *Klail City Enterprise News* and placed it on the kitchen table. He then walked to the hall bedroom, pushed the door silently, and took a peek at his sleeping wife. After this, Dorson returned to the kitchen, prepared a fresh pot for her, and then drove to Wilkins's Garage.

The owner, Butter Wilkins, a retired Army sergeant, had spent most of his military career as a maintenance mechanic. After his retirement, he ran a successful repair shop and, out of friendship to Dorson, had hired a former car thief, Packy Estudillo.

Packy, with the assiduousness of the weak in nerve and heart, made himself almost indispensable in the garage. He came early, left late, was handy with all manner of tools, and helped out as a dependable mechanic. He said, and not as a brag, that he knew all there was to know about cars from the thirties until now. Even those, he humphed, with the latest computer gadgetry. The last five years had been the only honest ones in a life of car thievery dating from forty years ago in 1949, when, as a youngster of ten, he had stolen his first car.

As Dorson drove into Wilkins's garage, Packy was waiting for him in one of the bays. The little man opened the car door and said, "At your service, Detective." He then led Dorson to one of the small air-conditioned offices, offered him coffee, and poured himself a cup.

"Here it is, barely seven o'clock in the a.m., Mr. Dorson, and the humidity's already at eighty-seven percent."

Dorson hung his seersucker jacket on the nearest nail.

"Need your help, Packy."

From the former car thief, Dorson learned that a young Mexican national named Daniel Varela, working as a fry cook down the block from the garage, had approached him recently about the car-stealing profession. That the young man had also said he was ready to join a gang across the Rio Grande and that he'd soon be doing a job for them.

"When'd you talk to him?"

"Three weeks ago, but I ain't seen him the last two, three days."

"Who owns the cafe where he works?"

"The Pecten? An ex-shrimper named Pete Richard, a Cajun. Came to the Valley back in the fifties when shrimping was hot here. It's a two-man hamburger and fry place, Mr. Dorson. Richard waits on tables and cleans up, while the kid cooks. But, as I said, I ain't seen the boy in a couple of days."

Dorson thanked him and walked to the cafe. Three booths and a table faced a short counter, on which stood an old Burroughs cash register. A small thing, but his own, thought Dorson. Two regulars sat at the counter and talked in low tones.

The man sitting closest to Dorson, a commercial fisherman from the smell of him, was complaining about Mexican gunboats drifting over to Texas Gulf waters, and muttered, "By God, that ain't right, Sorley." The man called Sorley glanced briefly at Dorson and went back to listening to the litany of complaints.

The owner came out of the kitchen, a dirty towel on his shoulder and a dirtier one on his hands which he used to wipe grease, water, something. Dorson couldn't tell and didn't care.

"Mr. Richard, my name's Dorson, and I'm with County Homicide." Sam pulled out his half-wallet and flashed the gold shield.

"So?" Unimpressed.

"I'm looking for Daniel Varela. I understand he works here."

Richard gritted his teeth. "Well, I'm looking for him, too, goddammit. He ain't been here since day before yesterday. Don't tell me the little shit's got himself in trouble across the river?"

"I want to talk to him, that's all. Know where he lives?"

"Across the Rio, that's all I know. Been working for me three years straight and never missed a day. Always on time, and a good cook. Reliable. Well, he was, until he didn't show up last Monday. What's this about?"

"I need to see his health card. Maybe that's got his address."

A shake of the head from Richard. "Naw, he uses my place as his mail drop and address. I'll tell you what he looks like, though."

Dorson listened to a description which could have fit almost any young Mexican or Mexican-American, for that matter.

"He's a neat one, though. After we clean up here, he goes to the john, washes up, takes his time, gets his hair just so, puts on his street duds, and out he goes to conquer the world."

"Friends?"

"On this side? I don't know. As I said, he works here, but he goes home to Barrones. He don't drink, like I said."

Dorson said thanks and handed Richard his card. In his car, Dorson turned east on the way to the international bridge and called the courthouse.

Sergeant Al Contreras answered the call.

"Al, patch me through to Director Cetina in Barrones."

Within seconds, the patch went through and Dorson asked for the Director of Barrones's Public Order. The woman's predecessor in her position had been Lee Gómez–the fugitive, as the Mexican papers were now calling him.

She came on the line. "Well, Sam."

The top federal cop in Barrones. A graduate of Villa María Catholic High in Klail City; two surviving sisters, also graduates of Villa María, had married Mexican-American businessmen and lived on the Texas side of the river. After law school in Mexico City, Lu Cetina worked herself up the federal civil service ladder, and, after Gómez's indictment, the governor of the state of Tamaulipas appointed her to the job.

There'd been a sense of urgency in the appointment, since the mayor of Barrones had been beset by businessmen from both sides of the river to do something about hiring a new director. An honest one, was the unstated request. Among the first actions when she took over was to fire, phase out, and retire fifty city, state, and federal officers who, as the Barrones newspapers put it, "had been on the take since Christ was a child."

That had been eighteen months ago. She settled in, making sure that aside from the regular civil service salaries, Mexico City's additional cost-of-living to cover living expenses on the border were equitable for her special police force. Knowing some local and state and federal cops remained on the take was galling, but she meant to keep the new feds honest.

As far as discipline and morale were concerned, she ran eight-month evaluation reports on each of her agents, and this wasn't paperwork to be filed away. Wisely, Lu Cetina had courted the border newspapers on both sides of the river. After Gómez's indictment, it had taken her a year to establish a trusting relationship with her opposites on the Texas side.

As Dorson drove across the river, he relaxed somewhat. As early as it was, he knew the Barrones streets would be crowded with a mix of American tourists and street vendors. He breezed through Mexican Customs and didn't bother to turn in his gun. He turned toward downtown, six blocks away, and grinned at the sight of the throng.

Life on the streets in Barrones was filled with tooting horns and the leaden smell of diesel fumes spewing out of the Gillig buses. The yelling of the kids darting in and out of sidestreets mixed with that of the high-pitched voices of the shoeshine boys who doubled as lottery vendors. One had to be careful since the tickets sold by the sidewalk vendors could be old ones picked from some garbage barrel or other. As always, some pedestrians stopped to chat in the middle of the street, and the legitimate lottery ticket vendors stopped the motorists, causing traffic to come to a momentary halt. Life on the streets.

Dorson grinned as he took in the familiar state-run sidewalk stores laden with gimcrack toys made in China or in the Tamaulipas state prisons; stores which stood next to flashy bars catering to tourists and Mexican businessmen. Next to the bars were haughty upper-class residences with ten-foot high red brick walls, topped with broken beer and soda pop bottles set in cement to discourage forced entry. Grinning still, Dorson pressed on the horn and added to the noise and the sense of Barrones's vitality in its daily fight to earn a living.

A brown-shirted cop waved to him in recognition, spread his hands to the immediate crowd in a gesture of cooperation, and this allowed Dorson to make his way downtown. A school boy made a *verónica* bullfighting pass with his book bag at Dorson's car. Dorson waved at the kid as the traffic cop continued to prod people out of the way.

Five minutes later, he parked in the visitors' slot directly across the street from Lu Cetina's office. A policeman in the blue uniform of the *federales* walked over to Sam and asked him his business. Dorson identified himself and was escorted across the street.

"The *directora* is expecting you, sir."

ii

The usual formalities of a warm handshake, a comfortable seat, and the offer of coffee over with, Lu Cetina said, "We got your fax on the van's license plate, the prints of the driver, and those of the two dead men at the parking lot. Since the *Enterprise* published their names, I've been contacted by their families. Think your chief will release them soon?"

Dorson said yes. As early as tomorrow, he added.

"Well, the van's owner isn't in town. We heard he was down in Tampico, and I've men checking on that too."

"It's the car thief we're after, Lu. We think he's a kid named Daniel Varela. You have the van's driver's prints on file here?"

A smile. "We do now. Sent 'em off to Mexico City as soon as your lab faxed them to us. Mexico City, with Interpol's help, says the driver and his friend are French-Canadian. In their fifties, and they've been partners since childhood. They move around: Montreal, Marseilles, Paris, and so on. It's all in the folder, here."

She pressed a button and in walked the young policeman who'd escorted Dorson to the office. She told the young policeman to bring her the file on one Daniel Varela. The young officer saluted and walked out with a greeting to Sam Dorson.

She coughed slightly and made a face. "Allergies," she said. "Varela's not a northern name, by the way. Can't be too many in Barrones. My man there will come up with the name and address in a minute."

Dorson asked, "You mean you've got everybody in Barrones on computer?"

"Just about. It's a program devised by that whiz kid who just left. Have you guys set one up already?"

"Invasion of privacy, Lu, but we use telephone and city directories. Tax rolls, of course. And the suspect files, but nothing like this. When'd you start on this grand project of yours?" Smiling easily.

Another slight cough. "Soon after I took over, we discovered that Lee Gómez had erased some two hundred names from our field files. I decided we needed an update, and the kid there said it wouldn't be much trouble to put our hundred-thousand population on disk, and there it is."

After a moment, she said, "The Napoleonic Code gives us some leeway, Sam."

A polite knock and the young federal officer walked in, greeted both of them again, and handed each a computer printout.

Varela's full name was Alfredo Daniel Varela; he was nineteen years old, and his home address was listed as Granados Avenue, Number 3A. Occupation: Student. Well, Dorson thought, that needs updating.

"Is that our van thief?"

"Four different prints: Varela, the Canadians, and the owner is my guess."

"Think we could talk to Varela?"

She pressed the button again and another policeman entered the room. "Call me on the cellular when you get to this address. I need to know if Varela is home or not. Tell whoever answers the door that this is federal business."

Ten minutes later, the expected call came through. Varela had not been home the last four nights. According to his mother, the family had no idea where he was. He'd gone to work in Klail City and hadn't reported him since he would stay across the Rio Grande from time to time. The mother reported that her son was a good boy, that he worked six days a week, and that he brought his mother his paycheck every two weeks.

"Sounds like a model child, Sam. By the way, the van was taken from the owner's driveway some two blocks from Varela's home, on Granados Avenue. That's the one-way street which leads to the Amity Bridge. Handy, don't you think?"

"What do you mean?"

"It could've been planted there for the kid to drive off."

Sam Dorson thought on that one a while. He asked for another cup of coffee.

"He may have joined a gang. He told a snitch of mine he was going to steal a car for them. A sort of initiation rite.

"His prints, on the wheel were smudged, but we found a good number on the window, the door . . . We also found Lisandro Gómez's prints and those of the two Canadians. The kid may have stolen the van, dropped it off somewhere for the Canadians to drive off." Lu Cetina then pressed the interoffice button.

Another young officer came in. "Sergeant Dorson needs copies of the prints we got from Mexico City this morning."

Looking out the window, she said, "We also get the prints from school records, whence Varela's. We're not a police state, Sam, we're just different from you, that's all. The French invade us, and they leave us the Napoleonic Code. Tit for tat."

Dorson then asked about the Mexican and Guatemalan passports found on the men at the parking lot.

"Three years ago, there was a break-in at the Guatemalan consulate down in Tampico. Aside from petty cash, the thieves also made off with a dozen blank passports.

"Ramos and Rocha, the dead men at the parking lot, were released from Victoria Prison two weeks ago. Up for extortion and known to have done side jobs for Lee Gómez. The other passports've been turning up here and there for a couple of years now."

She opened the office safe and showed Sam the recovered passports.

They walked outside. Out in the bright sunlight, the two shaded their eyes and crossed the street where another brown-shirted traffic cop stood by the Belken County patrol car.

"We'll find young Varela for you. By the way, there's a noonish float parade starting about now. You better skip Amity and take the old railroad bridge."

As they shook hands, Lu Cetina said, "Tell your boss I'm meeting with someone called Hackett at the Fed building tomorrow morning."

"Who's he?"

"New FBI chief in Klail and just got in yesterday, straight out of D.C. headquarters. Aren't you lucky?"

She made a face and Sam Dorson laughed.

Seven

i

By nine o'clock the next morning, Peter Hauer had already talked on the phone with three of the pilots listed on the airport's manifest. He dialed Randolph Grayson's number again, and this time a woman identifying herself as Grayson's wife came on the line.

No, he wasn't home yet, and it wasn't like him not to call her. Would she come to the courthouse? Yes, and she'd be there as soon as possible. Hauer then double-checked with the airport as to the times the other pilots he'd talked to had logged in and out.

He talked to Buenrostro briefly and told him of the Grayson woman's concern. "I asked her to come in."

Thirty minutes later, a Mexican-American woman in her late thirties, wearing high heels, and clad in a smart white-yellow-orange floral print and a sensible hat to ward off the blinding sun, slid from the driver's seat of a newish-looking Audi and strode up the courthouse steps. She stopped at the information desk in the wide, marbled foyer and asked for Chief Inspector Buenrostro's office.

Given directions, she then asked for the women's restroom and went there to freshen up. Five minutes later, and looking as striking as ever, she walked through the door which read DON'T KNOCK. COME IN. As she entered, she looked into the sharp eyes of the morning shift's desk sergeant, Art de la Cruz.

"I was told this was the chief inspector's office."

"It is. Your name and business, please."

"My name is Laura Castañón de Grayson. I'm here to see Mr. Buenrostro about my husband. He's missing."

"I'll have to examine your purse, ma'am. I'm sorry, but those are the rules."

The woman shrugged, said nothing, and opened the purse for the sergeant's inspection.

"We nearly lost the chief inspector some time back," the desk man explained, "and we have to be careful."

"That's sensible." Her tone was neither sarcastic nor irritated.

De la Cruz handed her the purse. “I’ll tell him you’re here.”

“Can I smoke in this building?”

He nodded and spoke into the intercom.

“Chief Inspector, you have a visitor.”

De la Cruz opened the front door for her and pointed to the left. “Keep going past the water cooler and then turn right. You’ll see his name on the door.”

The woman stepped into the squad room and found Peter Hauer at his desk assembling his material from the airport.

“I’m Laura Castañón de Grayson, are you the chief inspector?”

Hauer looked at the names on the list and then at the woman. A looker, thought Hauer. At that moment, Buenrostro stepped out of his office, stood behind Dorson’s desk, and motioned to a chair across from the desk.

“Good morning, Mrs. Grayson, what can I do for you?”

Her husband had been gone for two days, she explained. He was self-employed, and his chief business was flying hunters and fishermen to the northern states of San Luis Potosí, Tamaulipas, and Coahuila. He was well known, and his ferrying business, going on ten years now, was a familiar one to sportsmen on both sides of the river. He also flew machinery south of the river on occasion.

She showed Buenrostro a cigarette pack, and he pushed an ashtray toward her.

“Well, two days ago, we had an early breakfast, and he said he’d be going to Ciudad Valles for a few days. A hunting trip. He said he’d call when he got there. He always calls me when he gets to where he’s going. This morning, I called some of our friends in Ciudad Valles, but they said Randy, that’s his name, that Randy hadn’t been there or in Taninul either. That he wasn’t expected for another week or so.

“I then called La Pesca Fishery in case he flew out to do some tarpon fishing. Nothing. I also called some of the private airports in Soto la Marina, Tampico, and Tamazunchale. Same thing.

“Well, after I showered, I saw I had a message on my answering machine. It was from this office. I got a second call from a policeman who told me to come here.”

“Have you called the Barrones police?”

She shook her head and looked at the floor. “I don’t trust them.” Buenrostro made no comment on this. “I’ll need names and telephone numbers, Mrs. Grayson. I'll send your information to Missing Persons. I need to know when he left, how long he's been gone, any information to get us going here. This is Detective Hauer, he'll see you now. Meanwhile, I'll call the other sections here at the courthouse."

Buenrostro first called Missing Persons and then placed a call to Narcotics. They'd heard of Randolph Grayson, all right. Nothing to pin on him, but he'd been suspected of smuggling ever since he started flying. Natural enough, thought Buenrostro. The man's a pilot. The policewoman at Narcotics added that so far there'd been no arrests and thus no convictions, but his name kept popping up often enough. Yes, there was a file, but a thin one.

Ike Cantú walked in and went straight to his desk. A moment later, Dorson, back from his trip to Barrones, came in through the side door. Hauer circled Grayson's name and handed the list of pilots to Dorson, who passed it on to Ike Cantú.

Hauer: "Anything on the guard downstairs, Ike?"

"Not much. Tell you in a minute."

The woman opened her purse and handed a card to Peter Hauer. "If I'm not at home, you can leave a message on the machine."

Buenrostro heard himself using the same old line: "We'll try to have an answer for you as soon as we can." As he rose from his chair, she began to sob, and Cantú led her out of the room.

ii

Buenrostro leaned against one of the cabinets and the other detectives sat down as they waited for Ike Cantú.

A short while later, Cantú stepped back into the squad room. "The guard says Lee Gómez was kinda surprised. Like he wasn't expecting to be sprung like that. No violence. Smooth, he said."

Hauer then opened his folder and ticked off the names on the list, saving Grayson's for last.

"Ten years ago, Grayson registered at Jonesville airport as a pilot and shop foreman for a local air service and was authorized to fly to Mexico, Central and South America." Hauer laid a copy of the registration form to one side.

He popped a Hall's lozenge in his mouth. "Grayson's business consists of flying sportsmen down south, but he also contracts for flying plane and farm machinery parts mostly into Mexico. Small-plane pilots are listed with DEA and Secret Service as a matter of course; the FBI gets a bite of this too. So far, no evidence of smuggling. But gossip among the airport mechanics is that all pilots are engaged in smuggling of some kind, despite what the feds' records show."

No reaction from the group, and Hauer continued. He'd also checked Grayson's logs for the past five years and found no entry of business with the Gómez farm and ranch.

At this point, Cantú interrupted. "In five years, not one flight for them for tractor parts, water well-digging equipment, irrigation pumps. That sort of stuff?"

Hauer read on. "Last flight out was two days ago." He paused for a moment. "A day before Lee Gómez's escape."

Buenrostro: "Was there a return date?"

"Yesterday."

Dorson. "Did he report in from Mexico or wherever?"

"No, no record of it. And his wife just told us Grayson hasn't called her either. That's it."

"Sam?"

Dorson gave an account of the van, its missing owner, and of Lu Cetina's suspicions that the VW was planted to make it handy for Daniel Varela to steal.

"I brought back two faxes from her office. One has Varela's prints and the others are those from Lee and the escape men who drove the VW."

Dorson went on: "They're French-Canadian, according to Mexico City and Interpol. Old hands. Mexico City has no recent news on them. By the way, Lu has been asked by the relatives to have the parking lot dead men returned to Barrones for burial."

Buenrostro said he'd sign the release order.

Ike Cantú passed out the laboratory reports and said, "Nothing new. The dead men have been identified and made ready for release. We've got prints from the wallets and the passports. And here's a set of photographs taken at the parking lot as well as statements from Rick Barrera and Myrlene Moy. The other witnesses were a washout."

"Pete, you and Ike, make a list of the people involved so far. Sam, phone Joe Molden again. See if Auto's got anything new on the Silverado as yet.

"It's going on ten-thirty. I expect I'll be done with the Commissioners' Court at one, and I've a lunch date with Sammie Jo. See you at three."

EIGHT

After a quick lunch, Peter Hauer drove across town and parked behind the Amity Bridge U.S. Immigration Service headquarters. The car's interior heated up as soon as he turned off the air conditioning. He pulled out his note pad and rolled down the window. The traffic noise coming from the mob of oil trucks, cars, pedestrians, and street hawkers on the Texas side was deafening. Not much different from across the river, thought Hauer. He rolled up the windows, started the car again and read his notes in air-conditioned comfort.

The time was two p.m. He spotted a senior Immigration officer walking across the parking lot and asked about Art Styles's new office.

"Styles? They're remodeling. You have to go around the building to get to his office."

They shook hands and Hauer finished reading his notes as he walked to Immigration's main building, a fortress-like structure. Some of the older citizens referred to it as Fort Jones, since it had served as a fort when the U.S. cavalry first came to the tip of the Texas-Mexico border in the middle of the nineteenth century.

Hauer himself had been raised on Fort Jones, and the old polo field where his father, a sergeant major, had played for the Fort Jones polo team, was now a massive, white-lined, black-topped treeless parking lot. He glanced at the heat trembling across the black top.

The officers' quarters which once lined the west markers of the polo field had been razed by the city shortly after World War II. The old neighborhood across from the fort, dating back to the 1850s, was now a crowded block of cheap stores and fast-food places catering mostly to the Mexican nationals who crossed the bridge daily. Many came to shop and spend American dollars, and more came to earn their dollars as maids, store clerks, gardeners, painters, carpenters, janitors, and still others to serve as pick-up day laborers paid for work done on the spot.

Art Styles' office stood in the middle of the east wing of the first floor complex. Hauer passed through U.S. Customs, DEA, and assorted offices before coming to Immigration itself. He looked at the bulletin board and noticed there were some twenty different offices and administrations that were stationed along the border. One of the bureaus was that of Indian Affairs; Hauer wondered where the nearest Indians were. Probably up in Eagle Pass, he thought, some two-hundred-fifty miles up river. He smiled as he remembered Sam Dorson's oft-repeated adage: "The federal trough is longer than the Rio Grande. Trouble is, the trough doesn't wash out into the Gulf."

Hauer showed the receptionist his gold badge and picture ID, and then saw Art Styles himself come out to greet him.

"Welcome to the hub of activity where we who serve are proud to hold off the hordes of hardened criminals and thus protect the citizenry from Mexican banditry."

Hauer, raised on the border, and as fluent in Spanish as Styles, said something in Spanish which caused the two Mexican-American secretaries to laugh aloud. He winked at them.

'Where'd you get that little speech?"

Styles told him he'd merely quoted, word for word, from what a visiting U.S. congressman from North Dakota had said at that morning's meeting.

"North Dakota?"

"Go figure."

He, the congressman, said he was well-acquainted with border problems since his own state bordered with Canada. This last, obviously said for the benefit of those Immigration officers deficient in fourth-grade geography. The border businessmen from both sides of the river had looked at each other and rolled their eyes.

"And where's the guardian of our Canadian borders?"

"Across the river, shooting at some white-wing predators to prevent their crossing the border illegally."

"White-wing hunting in the off-season?" asked Hauer in mock surprise.

"The man never rests. This morning he told us how he logged over one-hundred thousand air miles in the past two years busily gathering material for eventual presentation to his colleagues in the House. The trips, he said, took him to many borders in the world."

"A tireless servant of the people."

The banter went on as Styles signed vacation requests, arrest orders, requests for transfers to another border area, office equipment requisition forms, and progress reports or the lack of such on pending cases. When he finished, Art Styles pulled out a cigar, put his feet on the desk, and said, "Well, Peter, planning to attend St. Joseph's reunion-night next month?"

"Beats going to Mass every Sunday," laughed Hauer.

Styles flipped a lever on his intercom and said, "We're not to be disturbed, Polly."

Hauer began. "I talked to the guard at the courthouse. You got anything on him?"

"My men know him. He's no conspirator. The man's just putting time in for his retirement. Of course, the FBI will conduct a full field investigation with the help of Frick and Frack, the two federal marshals who weren't in the basement, where they were supposed to be in the first place."

Frick and Frack: Tony Molina and Willie Cervera, who, as Art Styles pointed out, finished tied for eighth in a graduating class of nine at St. Joseph's, the Marist school.

Hauer reached for one of Styles's cigars. "When you worked on the Canadian border did you have any run-ins with Canadian hitmen, narco-guys, anything of that nature?"

"Very few and all small time. I mainly covered Maine, New Hampshire, and Vermont. Wooded country, and pretty, not many people, but those I did see had bad teeth. Why'd you ask?"

Hauer told him of the Canadians' prints in the van. "We need extensive background on them from the Secret Service and the FBI both."

"Buenrostro can get this stuff from Washington himself. Why doesn't he?"

"We want to localize it."

"To keep that new FBI guy Hackett out of your hair, right?"

"Can you put in a request?"

"Right now." Styles flipped a lever again.

"Polly, come in for a minute, will you."

The door opened and Art Styles said, "Polly Cuevas, meet Detective Peter Hauer. An old friend from our St. Joe days. Need an extensive ID and criminal activities on these two names. What the latest info the Bureau has on 'em, and we needed this information yesterday."

On her way, Polly Cuevas nodded at Peter Hauer.

As they went to the door, Hauer said, "Coffee's on the County, Arturo, and I need something else. Our Mexican friends don't have a lead on Lee Gómez's whereabouts yet. Would your people keep an ear and an eye open for us? And on his brother, Felipe Segundo, and those twins. The usual."

"Well, we've got nationals who work for our Department of Agriculture across the river, you know. Some are bound to work near the Gómez ranch and farm at Soliseño. You all have jurisdiction in this?"

Hauer explained that Buenrostro considered Gómez a state prisoner on temporary federal custody and thus County Homicide's responsibility.

Styles paused for a second. "That's kinda weak, Pete."

No argument from Hauer on this. "Rafe says Gómez's conviction for murder gives Homicide authority since he was the County's prisoner at the time of the breakout."

This time, Styles laughed aloud.

"Is your boss talking about a point of law, or is that some theory coming out of the Homicide Section?"

Hauer laughed, calling it a field theory.

Looking straight ahead at the slow moving traffic surrounding the international bridge, Art Styles said: "You guys are up against it. You've got a double murder and no suspects. Plus, you've got an escaped prisoner. Added to which, there's the two guys who got him out."

"Maybe three, Art. We found the van at Israel Buenrostro's cane field. We think someone had to pick them up at the Military Highway."

"Wheels within wheels," said Art Styles.

Peter Hauer drove carefully, making a right turn to Cooke Boulevard, a wide one-way thoroughfare that took them away from the usual crowded mess near the bridge.

Styles, in his usual dry monotone: "Well, I've always thought it's easier to find four or five villains than one lone criminal. Find one of the bunch, and he may start thinking about cutting a deal, right?"

Hauer, thinking on something else, nodded absently. He then mentioned Randolph Grayson's name. Styles shook his head.

"Never heard of him."

NINE

A Route 15 bus stops at the corner of Hidalgo and First in front of the Belken County Court House every thirty minutes or so. At five thirty on the second of August, two Mexican women, one, gray-haired and a younger one, got off the bus and asked directions from two city policemen sharing a strawberry snow cone.

The women were looking for La Sección de Homicidios del Condado de Belken. One of the cops escorted them to the top of the stairs and pointed in the direction of the County Patrol's main office. "Just take a right at the news stand, you can't miss it."

The woman opened her purse and attempted to pay the officer for his help but was stopped by the young woman who put a hand on the purse. The young woman smiled at the cop. He nodded, and gave them a military salute.

The courthouse hall, with its marble walls and pink granite floors, enjoys a noisy atmosphere. People walk around with folders, briefcases, pieces of paper, cups of coffee, worried looks and apprehension, all on their way somewhere. Some of them walk briskly, others amble by seemingly in no hurry. For most of the employees, the courthouse job is the only one they've ever held, and, as far as work is concerned, the motto on their banner reads: IT'LL BE HERE TOMORROW.

One also sees people standing around the soft-drink stands sharing gossip, a hot rumor, the latest promotion. Some are on break and this usually calls for shop talk. Off in some corner, hands in blue-jean pockets, sullen youngsters stand around with well-dressed types who may or may not be accredited lawyers. A notary public zips by looking for his misplaced authorization seal. One hears men and women asking for the probation officer to explain why Ronnie, or Cindy, or Velia, or Joey have missed the weekly reporting date.

City cops may wander in once in a while, but this is county territory. A judge, robes flying, crosses a hallway with his bailiff in tow. Two young, well-dressed, high-heeled secretaries are laughing at a joke told by their overweight supervisor. Since they are attractive, the secretaries laugh and whoop and holler. It's the homely ones who usually work quietly as they go about their chores in the beehive, Sam Dorson's name for the courthouse.

The young woman with the old lady is just as pretty as the two secretaries, but she's not in high heels and she envies, but not overly much, the two self-assured women holding cigarettes in well-turned, manicured hands. A paper boy shouts for attention and the regulars come by to pick up the copy of the late-afternoon edition of the *Klail City Enterprise*.

The two Mexican women find the news stand, turn right as directed, and come to the County Patrol's main office, which acts as a sort of clearing house.

In this, the main section of the courthouse, one asks for a person, a division, a section, or a squad, and then the desk sergeant, in this case, a woman, usually pulls out a map of the floor and marks the section with an X.

"This shows where we are at the moment. You want to go here, to the first basement," and she draws a circle. "See that arrow there? Follow it until you come to the end of the hall. Take the two flights of stairs, okay? The walls are painted green. When you turn right, you'll see that the walls are now painted brown. Okay. Go straight ahead. Homicide's the first door to your left. Go in, there's no need to knock. Any questions?"

The women look somewhat confused, and an off-duty patrolman standing by volunteers to show them the way.

Inside the long front office of the Homicide Section, the noise abates somewhat and, as the women are escorted inside, the noise disappears as if by magic save for the steady drone of the central air conditioning that fights off the Valley heat and humidity.

Ike Cantú is alone in the squad room. He has been reading yesterday's transcripts so intently that he barely hears the door close as the two women stand and look his way. Not meaning to interrupt an officer of the law, they remain by the door until Cantú smiles at them, rises, and then, palms up, points to the chairs nearest his desk.

"Soy el detective Isaac Cantú."

The young woman says, "My name is Celia Varela at your service. She is my mother, doña Margarita Mata de Varela, and she works as a maid for Mr. Teodoro Crixell, the attorney who is a very honest man." Said in a rush, as if memorized.

Ike Cantú smiled and remained standing.

He knew business wouldn't start for a few minutes. First, there would have to be some sort of small talk not connected with the matter at hand. After this, the unfolding of the story. Usually highly detailed but always on point.

When the feds and the state guys, thought Ike Cantú, learn to relax, to consider each call as a visit first and then as business, then, and only then, will they begin to get a feel for what the border and the Valley are about. Some of the Old South gentility lives on in the Valley, and this, coupled with Spanish and Mexican graciousness, means that some time will be spent on small talk, whatever the occasion.

Cantú sat up straight, a mark of respect, and listened carefully. What they had to say was important, obviously. If not, why the personal visit to La Casa de Corte?

The girl, Cantú noted, was to carry the ball with occasional corroborative looks at her mother, who sat with folded hands. An offer of coffee was rejected but, yes, ice water would be appreciated.

They had brought, explained Celia Varela, a set of photographs of Daniel Varela, her older brother. He worked on this side, she explained, but he has not returned home. A police captain in Barrones had recommended they cross the river to see if the Belken police could help.

Ike Cantú glanced at Lu Cetina's fax; the name of Daniel Varela appeared on the first line.

They were worried, she said. Daniel was a hard worker and he gave most of the money to his mother. He spent little money on clothes. He chose carefully at the place where they sell clothing by the pound, and Celia and another sister mended cuffs, shortened sleeves, replaced missing buttons, and then washed and ironed the clothes for him. His mother saw to it that Daniel was always neatly dressed.

Daniel is not a drinker. (This was singularly stressed.) He has a steady job on this side of the river, at the Pecten Cafe. He has friends, sure, and he belongs to two dancing clubs, the Barrones Dancing, on Madero and Pino Suárez, and the Tropicana Dancing, across from Abasolo Park. Everybody knows him.

Cantú nodded in recognition of the Barrones neighborhoods and asked about any new friends.

Well, yes, there were two, but doña Margarita did not approve. Neither did Celia, as it turned out. The boys, about Daniel's age, did not come back to the house after the first visit. Pardon? Oh, yes, they came to the house only the one time, and that had been four weeks ago. Their names?

The young woman frowned for a moment. Looking steadily at Cantú, she said the names they used were not their true names. One had called himself José González and the other one Juan García.

Cantú thought on this; he nodded since he knew a dozen or more Josés and Juans last-named either González or García.

And this then brought them to a set of pictures taken at Washington Beach with the new friends. The detective took them. No, we don't have copies, Celia said, but Cantú reassured her he'd have some made and return the originals via registered mail.

Could it be that Daniel had crossed the river to do his work at the Pecten Cafe and had then decided to stay on this side of the river for a week or so? No, he always tells us when he'll stay on this side for a day or two. He has the new pink-orange card that replaced the green one. The old *mica*, she said, and showed her own new border crossing card to Cantú.

Cantú handed them one of his calling cards and took down their home address. As he wrote, Mrs. Varela spoke to her daughter and then directly to him with Celia translating.

This was another personal matter, and with all the confidence in the world as to Detective Cantú's abilities and good sense, they were now seeking his advice on a more personal matter.

Lawyer Crixell had advised her she could retire on Social Security at any time after age sixty-two. Fourteen years before, he had gone with her to the Social Security office to register for the card. And now, at age sixty-one and six months, she would soon be eligible for retirement benefits. She showed Cantú her card, wrapped in a plastic cover tucked inside a baggie.

Cantú said that was a federal matter. Yes, Celia had explained all that to her mother, but the government officials had pointed out that the nearest General Consulate was in Monterrey and that, once eligible, she had to go there once a month to pick up her check. Celia Varela went on: As the detective knows, Monterrey is in the state of Nuevo León, and this means an eight- to ten-hour bus ride each way. Did Detective Cantú see a solution for this so that her mother did not have to go to Monterrey every month?

Ike Cantú pursed his lips in deep thought. After a short while he said there might be a solution.

Could she, he suggested, could she talk to Mr. Crixell about using his Texas address for her checks? She could, with Mr. Crixell's permission, use his house address as hers. Would that be a solution?

Mrs. Varela rose gravely and took his hand in both of hers. She whispered to Celia. "My mother says she will also pray for you tonight when she says her prayers for Daniel."

Was there anything they could do for him, and the old woman's hands went to her purse again. But Cantú, gallantly, said that his service to them was the greatest pleasure he could have had that morning.

He went around the desk, walked them to the door, and asked a patrolmen to escort the ladies to the bus stop. There were assurances of an investigation on the missing son, and he assured them that Director Cetina in Barrones, although a very busy official, was taking a personal interest in this case.

And how, thought Ike Cantú.

At his desk, he studied the photographs showing Daniel Varela and his two new friends. Three of the pictures were out of focus, but the remaining one was on the button. He focused on Varela and then placed the photos in an envelope, wrote Varela's name on it, and dialed Buenrostro's car phone to let him know of the women's visit and concern about Daniel Varela.

Ten

i

After his call to Buenrostro, Cantú returned to his desk. He tapped at the word processor, reworking the chronology of the parking lot murders and the Lee Gómez escape. Cantú began with the list of names he and Hauer had drawn up; he included the interviews at the scene, at the airport and the various contacts made with Lu Cetina, including Dorson's visit. Cutting and pasting the information, Cantú began assembling other notes.

He was at this when Peter Hauer walked in, fresh cup of coffee in hand. Hauer read the chronology over his partner's shoulder.

Together, the two went over material concerning the French-Canadians which Hauer supplied after his meeting with Art Styles. Ten minutes later, they agreed that that was that as Buenrostro entered the squad room carrying an armful of ads in a copper-colored accordion folder.

Cantú printed a copy of the chronology and he and Hauer went over it a second time.

Buenrostro plopped the folder on Dorson's desk. "Ads for AK-47s, Uzis, Magnums, Glocks. You name it," he said, in resignation. Cantú and Hauer glanced at the ads without much interest.

Buenrostro then asked for the chronology and Hauer handed it to him. A quick scan and he placed it on Dorson's in-basket.

"Sam back yet?"

Both men said no, and Buenrostro went to his office to call his wife. He took a rain check on lunch. Supper at home? On time, he assured her. As he hung up, Sam Dorson called in.

ii

Dorson's story: After he returned from Barrones, he had called Joe Molden at Auto and was told Molden had gone on a call to Palmer Heights Estates to see about an abandoned pickup in someone's driveway. The pickup had turned out to be a Silverado, and Henry Dietz's lab people were dusting the Silverado now, looking for traces of prints, clothing, cigarette butts. The usual.

Dorson took a sip of limeade. "Well, I hung up the phone, and who do I see stopped at the outdoor Custom bins on Amity Bridge? Felipe Segundo Gómez, that's who. There was a man in his twenties with him. Probably one of the twins. I decided to follow them, just in case."

Cantú and Hauer looked at each other and smiled. Yeah, sure, just in case.

"A busy boy, Felipe Segundo," said Dorson, matter-of-factly.

He was on them for two hours: first to Klail's Merchants' Bank, from there to Bishop's S&L, from there to an auto-parts store, a farm implement place, and finally to the GMC truck dealer on Bascom Road. This was the longest stay. At the end of it, Felipe Segundo drove out in a brand new Jimmy with the boy following. No trade-ins.

They'd crossed the river via the Jonesville bridge. And no, Dorson didn't think he'd been spotted by either one of the two.

"Business as usual for the Gómez family," said Ike Cantú, with slight irony.

Buenrostro: "We've got nothing on him and neither does Lu. The man's free to come and go as he pleases." He rubbed his nose with index finger and thumb.

"Sam, here's the chronology so far. Write in Felipe Segundo's name when you've finished with it." Buenrostro poured himself some limeade and leaned on a filing cabinet.

Hauer, to Buenrostro: "You look tired."

"Long meeting with the Commissioners, and I missed lunch. Let's send out for something."

A patrol car was called for.

Buenrostro ordered a beer and a Swiss cheese sandwich; the others passed on the sandwich but ordered a beer each.

The interoffice phone rang and Dorson picked it up. Cupping the mouthpiece he said, "Dietz. Says he's got the prints off the Silverado. Daniel Varela's and a whole bunch of others."

Buenrostro looked up. "He's to send copies of them to Lu."

Dorson went back to the chronology and added Felipe Segundo's name to it.

Buenrostro: "Let's run it. Lee Gómez escaped yesterday morning. We've come up with a list of people who have one thing in common:

They haven't been seen since the shooting and the escape. If the pilot Grayson's involved in this, he fits the pattern, since his wife says she doesn't know where he is. So who's missing? Lee, the Canadians, Daniel Varela, the two hit men at the parking lot, and Grayson. Seven men gone missing.

"We need to get Felipe Segundo to come to the courthouse."

He called Dietz. "Henry, that corpse you worked on two days ago, in pretty bad shape, is it?"

"I'll say."

"Don't dispose of it."

"Drop by anytime," said Dietz, laughing at his own joke.

Buenrostro looked at his watch. "Felipe Segundo should be driving into his ranch about now."

He looked around the room for a moment. "Ike, call Lu and tell her we've got a new corpse downstairs. That she's to call Felipe Segundo at the ranch and ask if he can come over to identify the body for us."

Dorson asked, "What's up?"

"It's a long shot, but I think he'll come. He'll be curious to see what we've come up with. If he's heard from Lee, then he'll come, and just-maybe-perhaps he'll identify the body as Lee's to get the heat off his brother.

"We'll wet some hundreds, crinkle 'em up, tear some, and put 'em in an envelope under John Doe with the notation that the money was found stuffed in the corpse's mouth. No credit cards, no clothing, no shoes. Nothing personal."

Cantú: "The corpse's mouth. A snitch?"

Buenrostro. "I think Lu's call will appeal to Felipe Segundo. He's got that romantic streak in him, you know. He's just like Lee. And anyway, all policemen are fools, right?"

Hauer laughed: "Ask a p'liceman."

Dorson: "What's the rest of the plan?"

Buenrostro shook his head. "I don't have one. I want to see Felipe Segundo here. I want him to see the corpse and the money. I want one of us to read him and see his reaction.

"I also want him to think Lee's in the clear after he makes the ID."

Buenrostro then picked up the ads folder; a booklet, showing an armed man in a camouflage suit, fell on the floor. He picked it up.

"Just got all this junk from Chip Valencia. He says there's enough here for the county to come up with an army the size of Costa Rica's."

Ike Cantú said, "Costa Rica doesn't have an army."

"Chip doesn't know that," said Buenrostro who then threw the ads in the wastebasket.

"Pete, we need an article on the corpse. Have Kenny Breen from Public Affairs fax a news release to the *Enterprise*. The body washed up at the mouth of the river just this morning. He's to mention the partial prints, and that we're working on the ID. Have him describe the body as pretty beat up, give him Lee Gómez's measurements. Breen knows what to do. See that he gets the story on both the evening and the morning editions."

Cantú said, "How about the Barrones *El Norte*? Breen can put the same story in Spanish and fax it to them."

"Good. And Pete, as soon as you get through with Breen, call that new editor of the *Enterprise*. Take her out for coffee. We need publicity on the unneeded budget increase and the high risks in the use of the AK-47s, Uzis, the lot. How much this would cost the taxpayers. Mention the mini-tank, the county budget, the need for improvement of county roads, pour it on."

Peter Hauer nodded to Buenrostro and went up to the Public Affairs office.

"I saw the body that first day," said Cantú, placidly. "You can forget the face. Somebody tore off a good part with a shotgun blast, according to the lab people. Of course, the alligator gars also worked on it."

"All to our favor," Dorson, grinning.

"Ike, call Lu now and get the ball rolling."

To Dorson: "My bet is Felipe Segundo won't come running in tomorrow to ID the body, but that he'll do so in a day or two."

Buenrostro said he'd call Art Styles and ask him to station men on the four area bridges beginning tomorrow.

"Sam, it's phone time. Call the Merchants' Bank and Bishop's S&L. Tell them it's a homicide case; we want to know what transactions took place with Felipe Segundo when he went there this afternoon. If it's a withdrawal, I think that's what he used for the new Jimmy.

"If that's the case, call the GMC dealer. Ask him how his customer paid for the Jimmy. If the dealer received cash, he's duty-bound to report it under federal banking laws.

"Lean on 'em, if you have to."

He stood in the middle of the squad room, hands in pockets, as the desk sergeant came in.

"Beer and sandwich, Chief Inspector. I took it out of petty cash."

Dorson opened the beers all around, and Buenrostro ate his sandwich at Hauer's desk.

Dorson: "I'll call Joe Molden and see if he's got anything else on that Silverado."

Eleven

Dorson finished his beer and skimmed through the *Valley-wide Yellow Pages*. A bright voice came over the phone on the first ring, and Dorson identified himself. He then asked for the bank's vice president and cashier.

Another voice came on and said Mr. Perry was busy, and could Mr. Dorson talk to one of the loan officers? No, he couldn't. Well, Mr. Perry was awfully busy at the moment. Dorson said he was investigating a murder and that he was driving over to see Mr. Perry in person. Sam Dorson heard a slight gasp and was told to please wait.

Perry came on and asked, "This is Billy Ed Perry, I'm the cashier. Now, what's all this about a murder, and what do I have to do with it?"

"I'm Detective Sergeant Dorson of Belken Homicide. We need your help by way of information. Would you check with your chief teller and find out if a Mr. Felipe Segundo Gómez withdrew some money this morning, and if he did, how much?"

Flustered a bit, Perry recovered soon enough. "What? What was that?"

Perry's voice was one of those designed to unnerve the hired help or some poor bastard with shaky collateral. "See here, sergeant, what's your name again?"

Sam spelled it for him.

"Well, see here, officer, that's confidential information."

"I imagine it is, but let's cut the crap, Mr. Vice President. Will you cooperate or not? It's as simple as that. I can come by with a subpoena and a federal banking officer, and I wouldn't be above bringing a reporter from the *Enterprise*."

"We run an honest bank here."

"I take that to be a *no*. I'll be there in half an hour with the subpoena and the bank officer."

Perry broke in. "No, no, no. It's just that we're busy here, you must understand that. What's the customer's name again?"

"Felipe Segundo Gómez Solís. He's from Soliseño, with business interests here in Klail and in Barrones as well."

A softer Perry asked if that would be a business account, a personal account, or both, perhaps? Dorson told him to check all the accounts.

Would the sergeant wait? No, he couldn't, and Dorson gave him Homicide's number.

Dorson cradled the phone and redialed. The woman at the Savings and Loan was just as horsy. She would have Sergeant Dorsey–That's Dorson, lady, Sam said. Whatever, she replied. She would have the sergeant know that what he was asking for was privileged. Sam smiled. Just my meat, he thought.

"Your name, please."

"My name is Petra Schilling, and I'm one of the vice presidents." Sam smiled into the phone again and went through the business of a subpoena, a federal bank officer, and a reporter in tow all over again.

That took both the fight and the wind out of her. Sam gave his telephone number, spelled his name slowly out of nastiness, and hung up.

He then took out the Klail City business directory and looked under car dealerships. Ah, Jimmie Van Hooft's Friendly GMC Truck Inc. Dorson asked for the chief salesman. That would be Ernie Zamora, the voice said.

"My name's Dorson, and I'm with Belken Homicide."

The "yes" on the other end of the line was hesitant, but after a pause, Sam could hear a voice on the dealership's loudspeaker calling for Mr. Ernie Zamora. A few seconds later, Zamora picked up the phone.

No greeting and straight to the point. The detective meant to rattle Mr. Zamora. "My name's Dorson, and I'm with Belken Homicide. This morning, you or someone there sold a brand new Jimmy to a customer from Mexico. His name's Gómez Solís. Have I got that right?"

A hesitation and then: "Well, detective, lemme check on that." A rustling of paper, hand cupped over the phone but the muffled sound came through anyway.

"Well, yes, here it is."

"Paid cash, did he?"

"Pardon? Oh, cash. Yes, yes. Cash." The voice trailed off.

"How much?"

"Well, he got the top of the line. Lemme see, with delivery charges, final inspection . . ."

Sam's "excuse me" stopped the man in his tracks. "How much money did he give you?"

A slight cough, followed by a clearing of the throat. "Twenty-four thousand five."

"And that was cash, wasn't it?"

"Yes." Reluctantly.

"Did he come alone?"

"Alone? Well, lemme see. As I recall, there was a young man with Mr. Gómez."

"Who drove the Jimmy?"

"Oh, he did. Mr. Gómez."

"You've been a big help. Thank you." And Sam Dorson rang off.

In his office, Buenrostro finished his beer and threw half of the sandwich into the wastebasket. The phone rang, and he picked it up on the first ring.

"Homicide, Buenrostro."

A subdued Mr. Perry from the Merchants' Bank. Could he please speak with Detective Sergeant Dorson, please.

Buenrostro came out of his office and held up one finger. Sam Dorson picked up Line One.

"Dorson."

"Ah, you were correct, sergeant. Mr. Lisandro Gómez Solís did come in this morning, but he didn't withdraw money from any of the three accounts he has with us. We checked further, however, and his signature appears on today's safety deposit ledger."

Dorson held the phone away from him and stared at it.

"Did you say Mr. Lisandro Gómez Solís?"

"Yessir. Officer Longoria verified the ID and the signature."

"You have no way of knowing how much he withdrew?"

"Oh, no. A safety deposit box is–"

"Thank you, Mr. Perry. I won't take up more of your time. You've been most cooperative, and I'll see to it that District Attorney Valencia hears of your bank's willingness to serve the cause of justice. Now, will you please put Officer Longoria on the phone? Thank you."

A moment later, a questioning "Hello?" came on the extension.

"This is Sergeant Dorson of Belken Homicide. You admitted Mr. Gómez into the safety vault this morning?"

"Yessir."

"Read the name off the ledger for me."

"Yessir, here it is: Lisandro Gómez Solís."

"You ever seen him before?"

"Before today?"

Dorson rolled his eyes. "Yes. Before today."

"No, 'fraid not. I've only been here three months, and I don't know all the customers yet."

"Thank you."

Buenrostro had walked into the squad room in time to hear Dorson's ringing endorsement of Merchants Bank's willingness to serve the cause of justice.

"What was that all about?"

"Oh, that. That was bull crap. But have I got news for you. According to Mr. Billy Ed Perry of Merchants' Bank, Mr. Lisandro Gómez Solís walked into their bank this morning to check on his safety deposit box."

"Say again?"

"Yeah. Seems as if our boy Felipe Segundo is passing himself off as Lee."

Sam Dorson drummed out "shave and a hair cut, two bits" on the top of his desk. "I'm expecting a call from a barracuda at the S&L. Would you call the GMC place for me? A salesman there said Mr. Gómez bought the Jimmy and paid for it in cash. Find out what name Felipe Segundo used to buy the Jimmy.

"Here's the salesman's card and number, Rafe. By the way, drawing money from someone else's deposit box is robbery, isn't it?"

"Not if he's got power of attorney. We'll let it go for now. I've got another idea."

Buenrostro sat on the edge of Hauer's desk and dialed Ernie Zamora's number at the car dealership.

A few seconds later, the light blinked on line two and Dorson picked it up.

"Mr. Dorson, my name is Richard Baroja. I'm in charge of the safety deposit boxes here at Bishop's. Mrs. Schilling said for me to give you our fullest cooperation. So what can I do for you, sir?"

Fullest cooperation? Did she now? "I want to know if Mr. Lisandro Gómez Solís made a withdrawal from his account or accounts."

It turned out that Mr. Gómez Solís had three sizeable accounts with the S&L, a personal account, a business account, and a joint account.

"Who is on the joint account?"

"Mr. Felipe Segundo Gómez Solís."

"And the first name on the accounts is?"

"Yessir, right here. Mr. Lisandro Gómez Solís. And we have three home addresses for him. One in Soliseño, that's the ranch, right? The second is at Padre Island, and the third one is over in Barrones."

"And how old is the application with the Padre Island address?"

"It's four years old."

That condo is fed property now, thought Dorson.

"But no withdrawals from his checking account?" Pleasantly.

"No sir. He came in earlier today to check his safety deposit box, and his name appears on today's safety deposit ledger. Our security guard verified the photo ID from a Texas driver's license, from a Tamaulipas license, from the signature on file, and from the one he signed to open his box."

"Pretty thorough."

Proud of himself. "Yes, we try to be."

"Would you put the safety-box guard on the phone?"

"Right away." The terrazzo-tiled floor rang out with the security guard's heavy tread.

"Who's this?"

"Charles Regan, security guard."

Dorson laughed aloud when he heard the name. The old man was a retired Belken County patrol officer. "Why, Chuck, how long you been there?"

"Is this Sam Dorson? Ha! Well, I've been here two years now. What can I do you for?"

Dorson explained his business and Chuck Regan said, "That's right, Sam. Here it is: Lisandro Gómez Solís. You know him? A Mex, good-looking. Had a boy with him, but I made the kid wait in the lobby area." As an old cop and out of habit, Regan asked: "What's this all about, Sam?"

Dorson, also out of habit, evaded the question. "You know, the usual."

"Murder, for sure."

Dorson let him think so and thanked his old friend. When he rang off, Buenrostro said, "Zamora made out the Jimmy's title to Lisandro Gómez Solís. That means Felipe Segundo passed himself off as Lee and bought insurance from the GMC place. They took care of filing the title, the registry documentation, the license plates, and so on.

"What do you think, Rafe?"

"First off, we didn't even know he had active accounts in the local banks, let alone the safety deposit boxes. I'll call the D.A.'s office to issue some search warrants. Since Lee's a fugitive from justice, we'll also request a sequestration of funds order.

"I'll call for the warrants right now. And Sam, call the other two banks in town. Maybe Felipe Segundo has accounts there. too. We can't touch those accounts, but we can sure as hell nab Lee's."

Dorson opened the *Valley-wide Yellow Pages* again. A whistle from Dorson.

"For a place that ranks as the one of the poorest in the U.S., the Valley has fifty-two banks. It's a regular Panama."

Buenrostro dialed the District Attorney's office, and asked for Gwen Phillips, the D. A.'s executive assistant.

"It's me, Gwen. Just stumbled onto something, and I need your help."

Gwen Phillips listened, made notes, and then read the notes back to him. "That check out on your end?"

"Sure does."

"I can get the warrants and the orders in your hands in forty-five minutes, starting now."

"One more thing, Gwen, can the patrolmen serve the warrants at the bank officers' homes tonight?"

Gwen Phillips laughed. "Piece a cake, handsome. Anything else?"

Buenrostro thanked her and hung up.

Dorson turned around and said, "Looks like we're in business."

Rafe Buenrostro, hands in pockets again, stared at the walls. "Norm Andrews called a while ago."

Dorson smiled and shook his head. "What does Belken County's finest sheriff want this time? Another photo op?"

"He called to assure me that he's with me on the heavy-armament thing. But that, as sheriff, he has to get along with Chip."

"Typical," Dorson, wryly. "What do you think?"

"I think both Norm and Chip Valencia have too much time on their hands."

Dorson laughed.

Buenrostro sat down, staring at the recent file. "And speaking of Chip, he's called for a hurry-up meeting at five."

Dorson checked his watch. "It's twenty till. I'm going home to that good-looking wife of mine."

Buenrostro picked up the file. "I'll go over this again before going upstairs."

Dorson, at the door, said: "I'll call Joe Molden at home tonight regarding the Silverado. He's bound to have something for us."

"It's coming around. See you *mañana*, Sam."

Twelve

i

Earlier that same afternoon, a slim, thirty-year-old Mexican national sat with his mother on one of the back benches of the Magic Valley Transit bus depot in Klail City. His mother fingered a wooden-beaded rosary while he read the Barrones newspaper. His stylish, high-topped brown shoes had been shined to a gloss. They went well with his short-sleeved, tan guayabera shirt of pima cotton. The intricately embroidered shirt was obviously handmade. The tan gabardine trousers rounded out the outfit. He wore no jewelry save for a Swiss Army watch. His mother, although not a widow, wore black, and sat placidly running through another set of prayers, as she had been for the past two hours.

The buses arriving in the Valley from the Gulf Coast that day were running late. The static-riddled public-address system came on again with the same recorded message announcing that the heavy rains south of the Houston area produced by Hurricane Ella had flooded many of the coastal towns and highways south of Houston and Corpus Christi. The recorded announcements ran first in Spanish and then in English, and had done so every fifteen minutes with monotonous regularity. The visitors and passengers excited earlier at the prospect of a trip or an arrival ignored the announcement and remained seated in quiet resignation.

Half an hour later, the static toned down and the harried station manager announced the arrival of that afternoon's first coastal bus coming in from Houston via Corpus Christi. At this point, the young man whispered something to his mother, handed her the newspaper, and walked to their station wagon parked directly across the busy street. He opened the back door of the station wagon, moved aside a gift for Chief Inspector Buenrostro, and unwrapped a bouquet of red, orange, and purple bougainvilleas sheathed in green crepe paper. Upon his return, mother and son walked to one of the islands on the incoming traffic lanes.

Enrique Salinas, husband and father, recently released from one of the units of the massive Huntsville Prison, was coming home to die. Evidently, Buenrostro's letter of recommendation to the Texas Parole Board three weeks earlier had helped effect the early hardship release.

Now, after hours of boredom in the crowded depot, Eduardo Salinas and his mother waited expectantly as the air-conditioned Gillig Phantom bus pulled up to one of the receiving bays.

The baggage seen to, Enrique Salinas embraced wife and son and clutched the flowers grown in the family garden. The three walked slowly and in silence to the son's station wagon.

"To the courthouse, Eduardo."

Only when the car pulled away did Mrs. Salinas begin to cry. Enrique Salinas, also known as "El Camarón" (The Shrimp) to his associates, reached over and patted her hand.

ii

Buenrostro stopped at the desk sergeant's desk and told de la Cruz he was on his way to the Commissioners' Court for a meeting.

In the hallway, Buenrostro ran into three other divisional heads. Bob Vela of Vice muttered, "It's that damned mini-tank business again."

Five minutes later, Florencio "Chip" Valencia, a smile directed to each section head, entered the room with five young aides.

Thirty minutes later, a disappointed D.A. thanked them for their time and left the meeting room without his smile.

Jorge Manrique of Narcotics was the first to speak. "Small-arms fire, men. He'll bring in the big guns later on."

Tolliver Brand from Missing Persons added, "Coming to see us means he hasn't convinced the Commissioners just yet."

The section heads shook hands all around as they entered the elevator. Not one of them considered this meeting to be the end of the matter.

Back at his desk, Buenrostro went back to reading the current file for a third time. He concentrated on Lee Gómez and thought on the most likely places the former Barrones Director of Public Order would have chosen as a safe haven.

Buenrostro dismissed Mexico City; it lay eight hundred kilometers to the south. Besides, Lu Cetina's *federales* would have covered the airport disguised as transients, vendors, and tourists.

He also dismissed the rumors of Gómez having been seen in Acapulco, Puerto Vallarta, or Hermosillo. The distance to the west coast ports was over eleven hundred kilometers from Barrones.

Closer, though more closely watched, were the eastern port cities of Veracruz and Tampico, plus the tourist spots of Cozumel and Cancún.

The city of Barrones, just across the river from Klail City? Why would Lee Gómez take a chance?

The ranch? A possibility, since this would appeal to Gómez's romantic side, he thought.

The Gómez ranch was also the safest, he concluded. The house lay some ten kilometers from the main gate, a distance designed to alert the family in case of curious visitors. The other buildings on the ranch, three large barns and three sizeable sheds, stood a football field away from the main house and were thus even more inaccessible. Buenrostro drew an arrow from Lee Gómez's name to the ranch and underlined it. Too risky, he concluded.

The phone rang.

The desk man: "A family named Salinas to see you, sir."

Buenrostro called his wife and said he'd be home soon.

The phone rang again. It was Peter Hauer.

"I'm in Barrones, Rafe. One of Lu's men made the two guys in the picture with Daniel Varela. The Gómez Solís twins, Juan Carlos and José Antonio. Lee's nephews. The photos are smudgy, but he swears it's them. I also talked with the new editor at the *Enterprise*, and I'll see her tomorrow. Going home, Rafe."

Buenrostro told him of Enrique Salinas's impending visit and rang off. He pressed the interoffice phone and told the desk man to usher in the Salinas family.

Thirteen

i

It had been a pleasant meeting with Enrique Salinas, his wife, and his son, Eduardo, albeit a scrap uncomfortable at the beginning with the son acting as translator.

But the ice broke when Buenrostro spoke Spanish to them. They were delighted and said so.

"My parents want to know if speaking Spanish is not an imposition to you?"

Buenrostro smiled. Was his Spanish that bad, he'd asked.

On the contrary, they were as pleased as they were surprised.

Well, then, Buenrostro had said, why not stick to Spanish; and Spanish it had been until the conversation ended some ten minutes later.

The old man, made older by his four years in prison and older still by the debilitating disease, sat with a gift-wrapped foot-square box and held it in both hands. He sat with it during the conversation and then, standing with the help of his son, he presented it to Buenrostro.

The chief inspector had not known whether to open the box or not; their faces showed he was expected to open it right there and then. He did so and discovered that the present wasn't for him, it was for his wife.

A lace mantilla, yes, but not just a mantilla made of lace. It was something special, black and white and hand-embroidered.

"¿Es de España?" he asked.

The woman smiled. *"Directamente, señor inspector. ¿Es usted casado, ¿verdad?"*

Buenrostro smiled and replied, *"Sí. Cazado y casado."*

Not only married but hunted down as well. The Salinas family smiled at the old pun, and then the son again helped his father rise from his chair.

There was a bit of additional formality as the son, in English this time, said, "My father wants the chief inspector to know he is at his disposal. And I too. Forever."

This was followed by a firm handshake from the son.

Before they left, Buenrostro accepted their card and he gave them two of his. It had been a social call to thank him personally. He wondered how long the old man would be around.

After they left, Rafe Buenrostro thought back on the grisly murder at the Kum Bak Inn, a farm to market road beer joint. El Camarón Salinas had been the driver of the murder car.

He looked over some telephone calls placed on his desk earlier in the day. He read them with little interest and then threw them in the wastebasket. Nothing to do with the case at hand, he said to himself and walked to his car.

A few minutes later, he drove into the Red Bull Supermarket parking lot. He picked up four six-packs of Beck's Dark, and placed them in his basket before going to a pay phone.

Sammie Jo picked up the phone on the first ring.

"Four four five, seven three seven nine."

"Hi, I'm at the Bull, need anything?"

"Need some fresh chicory. I'm in the backyard."

"Oh?"

"We're having a spot of split-pea soup, hard rolls, a bit of salad, and some barbecued heart chunks with freshly made corn tortillas. How's that?"

Buenrostro smacked his lips, and a woman waiting to use the pay phone gave him a surprised look. Smiling, he nodded to her and signaled he'd be off the line soon.

"I'll be there in about fifteen. Bye."

The woman stepped up to the phone and kept her eyes on him. As he turned to go, she said, "I know who you are. You're the chief inspector, and you're married to that pretty redhead. The banker's daughter, right?"

Smiling, he said, "How do you do?"

"We've not met before. My name is Marcia Ridings. Ring a bell?"

"No." Smiling easily.

"I'm the new editor for the *Enterprise*."

"A pleasure."

"I've a coffee date with one of your men tomorrow afternoon. Sounded bright over the phone. Is he?"

"Yes, he is. His name's Pete Hauer, and he's a good man, too."

At five-feet eleven, she was as tall as Buenrostro, but chunky; what his Spanish great-grandparents would have called *jamona*: Marcia Ridings shook hands with a firm grip. Her dark auburn hair was short and combed back. She was dressed in a loose fitting multiflowered print dress, something that Buenrostro thought had been called muumuus at one time.

"I've not met an anti-gun cop before," she said, smiling and showing some slightly crooked teeth, which looked good on her.

"Anyway, I received two faxes from the D.A.'s office today. One for increased armament and one against. But you do carry a gun, don't you?"

"Yes, I do." And then, "You find that contradictory, do you?" he said lightly.

She thought on that a moment. "I find it interesting."

"A neutral word." Pleasantly.

They both laughed at this. Looking at his basket, he said, "You must excuse me, dinner's waiting. Come by the office and visit, anytime."

Marcia Ridings thanked him and began depositing money into the coin slots.

On his way home, he unloosened his tie and turned the air conditioning vents upward and toward him. The sky ahead showed new thunderclouds out in the Gulf, remnants of the hurricane that had hit further up the coast. This took him to his planned fishing trip the coming weekend. He'd invite his cousin Jehu.

ii

But first, he thought, dinner. He drove to the carport, walked around the house and straight to the backyard.

The diced ham in the soup was as crisp as the French rolls Sammie Jo had bought that morning. The soup's smoky tang meant she'd browned the ham in the barbecue barrel. The salad, raw spinach sprinkled with fresh chicory, carried a whiff of apple vinegar.

The tasty barbecued heart chunks had spent the night in a marinated solution of olive oil, white pepper corns, and freshly ground cumin. Homemade tortillas rounded out the feast for two that evening.

They both passed on coffee, and Buenrostro rose, cleaned up the table, and after lightly rinsing the dinnerware, loaded the dishwasher. His wife, allergic to any kind of alcohol, made herself some orange-leaf tea while Buenrostro, finished with his kitchen chores, went upstairs for a quick shower.

Ten minutes later, he walked downstairs pulling on a St. Joe's football jersey.

"Work tonight?"

"Two calls. The first one's to Jehu to see if he and Becky can come fishing with us out in the bay this weekend. By the way, did you notice the last time how good little Sarah was getting at dropping a line?"

"And Becky's no slouch, either," Sammie Jo Buenrostro said.

"The second call's to Theo Crixell. Business."

She showed him an official envelope, from the federal district's Attorney General's office, which had been hand-delivered to their home that afternoon. He asked her to read it while he went to the fridge and got himself a beer. Sammie Jo Buenrostro read a brief news release announcing the official resignation of Theo Crixell due, it said, to the offer of a position with a private firm.

" A private firm? Is that true?" she asked.

"It's a partial truth."

"A partial truth? A lie, then." Smiling at her husband.

Sipping his beer from a frozen mug, he explained how Theo had come to his office in a nervous state two days before Lee's escape.

She raised an eyebrow, but he shook his head. A coincidence, he said. He then mentioned the threats to Theo's family and waited for a reaction from his wife. There was none.

The beer finished, he called his cousin, Jehu Malacara, and the date for a weekend of fishing was set. Sammie Jo looked up and smiled as she winked at him. He then called Theo Crixell. "Charley Bones, need some help, and how are you?"

"Hello, Chief Inspector. Look good, feel great, and all's well with my world."

Buenrostro chuckled lightly.

"Boy, I'll tell you, Rafe. I had no idea I had six weeks vacation time coming to me. It shows to go you what can happen when you're having fun. Six weeks coming to me, and Mandie never complained.

"But I'm out of it. Did you get Dugan's letter today? Short and sweet is how I like 'em."

Theo Crixell was certainly talkative, Buenrostro thought. Must be the release of job pressure.

"Need some help."

"Ha! Fire away, son."

"Just how much Gómez property, real and personal, did Treasury collect, Theo?"

"Like I told you a hundred years ago, fifteen million, give or take. I don't know how much the Mexican feds came up with, though. But from our end, there were the condos at Padre, the farm land in Belken County, some of which was used for airstrips from where they smuggled stuff in and out. Let's see, the Arabian horses I mentioned, the fighting roosters, other extensive land-holdings in Dellis County, and then the bulk of it in offshore money that Treasury weaseled out of some Caribbean dictator or other. Why?"

"Who conducted the local bank search?"

"What local search?"

Buenrostro then detailed Felipe Segundo's visit to two of the four banks in Klail, Dorson's phone calls to the other Valley banks, and his own request for subpoenas to the D.A.'s office.

"Probably in the records somewhere, but I don't remember seeing that end of it. You don't think some guys in Treasury omitted those funds on purpose, do you?"

Buenrostro: "Try this. The money was so close to home someone reasoned that Lee would never be so stupid as to leave money in the local banks."

Theo Crixell laughed aloud. He was still laughing when he said, "That's a big, big possibility. Listen, those fed bastards are so conceited, they think we're a buncha suck-egg mules down here. It's part of the old tradition when Bill Bennett was drug chief in Washington and becoming an expert on drugs and morals. In short, knowing everything about everything. Yeah, I can see it now: We'll go after the big money, overseas laundering and so on, yeah. Big amounts of publicity. And of course no one disagrees with a higher-up in D. C. You ever notice that?

"Anyway, whoever comes up with an idea, no matter how sound it is, if it differs from that given by the current chief, the guy becomes a pariah. Now, the investigative branch does its job, no complaints. But there's no focus, and we in the legal end of things have a time of it."

Crixell suddenly sounded tired, as if the subject had drained him. After a pause he said, "I'm okay, really, but I'll never get over it. The phone threats to Mandie and the kids did it for me. Of course, the arrogance, the narrowness of what my former bosses called focused thinking–well, that came a close second."

Buenrostro said, "We always have your current phone number, Theo, but only because you or Mandie gives it to us. How did these people reach you with an unlisted number?"

"Wish I knew, but they sure as hell called. Never took 'em over two days after the number was changed to get to us.

"You know, Rafe, I never could get any commitment from the investigative guys to present a personal view, a personal opinion. The truth is that there's so goddamn much dope and shit coming over, that half the time they just stumble over it accidentally, and then they have the unmitigated gall and nerve to call it a haul."

Buenrostro laughed suddenly. "So, you don't think that someone's in cahoots with Felipe Segundo?"

"Oh, anything's possible, cousin. But my guess is that no one thought the Gómezes would keep money here in Klail."

Buenrostro paused for a moment. The Gómezes would, he thought. It's part of the thrill of getting away with something. And a handy amount of working cash is a nice fallback.

Buenrostro: "One more thing. Do you know MacMichaels, the fed guy who does bank examining and such? He's a friend of Jehu's."

"True blue."

"Well, that's good enough for me. You're a good friend, Charley Bones."

"Thank you, cousin. Still planning to make the St. Joe alumni dinner?"

Buenrostro said he was and then mentioned the planned weekend fishing He got a "no thanks" from Crixell, followed by the soft fiction of "some other time, perhaps," and both rang off.

"How's Theo?"

"Couldn't be happier, but still can't fish worth a dip. What are you reading?"

Fourteen

i

The next Monday morning, a four-year-old boy in Palmer Heights Estates ran after his older brothers to get them to play with him. He ran, shouting at them, and then stumbled in the tall grass surrounding the exclusive neighborhood. His brothers ignored him and went on their way. Getting up, he realized he had tripped over a man lying face up, eyes wide open, mouth agape.

He pounded on the front door of the first house he came to. Crying and screaming, he yelled at a startled neighbor that a dirty old Mexican man in the field had scared him.

The woman and a daughter followed the youngster to the middle of the field. When they arrived and saw the body, they looked at each other. The woman picked up the child and ran home to call the police.

Peter Hauer took the call and rang Dorson at home.

On his way to the office, Buenrostro got a call on his car phone.

The District Attorney: "It's to be a conference call, Chief Inspector. You take it in your office, me in mine, and the section heads in theirs, see? This way none of us have to have to leave our offices."

"What time?"

"Let's make it for nine-thirty this morning, okay?"

"Right."

A conference call, he thought, and with the four section heads in the courthouse not five minutes away from each other. Jesus.

The phone rang a second time.

"Buenrostro."

Ike Cantú: "Chief, a call just came in about a body out at Palmer Heights, and that's where Auto found the Silverado last week. Sam and Pete are going out there right now."

"I'm on my way to the Estates. Call the D.A.'s office. Tell one of his secretaries I'm on a homicide investigation."

Two hours later in the squadroom, Sam Dorson went through Daniel Varela's effects. His wallet had been untouched.

Peter Hauer took out his notepad, flipped to the list of people involved in the case, and drew a cross next to Varela's name.

ii

In Barrones, Lu Cetina waited patiently as she heard the numerous clicks it took to connect with the Klail City telephone system. The telephone company was legally right in designating border calls as international ones; still, she thought it a silly piece of business. After all, Klail City and Barrones were separated by a river that ran half dry for six months of the year.

She half-heard the accustomed whirr followed by the familiar voice of the switchboard operator: "Good afternoon. Belken County Court House. Which division, please?"

The call was put through and Ike Cantú answered the phone.

"Hello? This is Lu Cetina. Is your boss in?"

"He's on the other line with the D.A., *directora*. Can I help?"

She paused briefly and said, "Just tell him this: We've caught the men responsible for the parking-lot murders, and–"

Ike Cantú reacted immediately. "Sorry to interrupt you, ma'am. Hold on, will you?"

He burst in the door and blurted out Lu Cetina's message. Buenrostro raised his hand and said, "I'll have to call you back, Chip."

"Line two."

Buenrostro said, "Lu."

"Yeah, how about that, Rafe? An anonymous tip. Can you guys come over here? I don't want to leave my office. I've been here since we brought 'em in last night."

Buenrostro said, "Be right there," and rang off.

Sam Dorson dialed the Barrones city police and told them of young Daniel Varela's death. When he finished giving them the information, he waited for Peter Hauer to type the brief report on Varela. This done, Dorson faxed the report to the Barrones federal office, and then, he and Hauer called on Henry Dietz at the morgue.

iii

The time was nine forty-five a.m., and Klail City's downtown area would be filled to the choking point by ten o'clock. By that time, the store owners would have finished lining up the help and giving them their daily pep talk; after that, the unlocking of doors from the inside, the employees standing at the ready by their cash registers, the customers streaming across the two bridges by the hundreds and sweltering on the sidewalks ready to spend their money, and the day, on the Texas side.

At the motor pool, Buenrostro said, "You drive, Ike." He buckled up and turned off the radio transmitter. He then picked up the cellular phone and dialed the desk man.

"De la Cruz, Detective Cantú and I are on our way to see Director Cetina. Pass this on to Detectives Dorson and Hauer: Tell them it looks like Brinkman's all over again. Brinkman's, got that? They'll understand."

He hung up and rang Chip Valencia's number.

"Sorry to ring off like that, Chip. It looks like Lu Cetina's men collared the parking lot killers."

Valencia's excited voice came on: "Great, great job. Get 'em over to this side as soon as you can."

"I'll get back to you with the details, how's that?"

"Perfect. I'll hold the press conference as soon as you get back. Keep in touch." Sounding tough.

"You can stop grinning now, Ike."

"He's a lawyer, Chief. Mexico won't extradite."

Cantú was partly right. Extradition would call for bigger fish, not these types. The murders at the cafeteria parking lot had been committed in the States, true. But as citizens of Mexico and arrested there, the killers would be tried in Barrones.

"Maybe he's just excited, Chief."

Buenrostro shrugged.

They rode in silence as Ike Cantú drove into the narrow streets of downtown Klail.

"Get some sun on your nose, Chief?"

"Did a spot of fishing in the bay."

"How'd you do?"

"They were biting, not much sport there."

"You, ah, you went to St. Joseph's, didn't you?"

A nod. "A school where the men who teach dress up as women."

"That's funny. Who said that?"

"My father, years ago."

"Me, I went to Klail High."

Buenrostro looked at Cantú. "I finished at Klail."

"Well, you know, I'd seen the graduating pictures in the school's hallway , and one of the guys in the pictures looked like you. I just wasn't sure."

"Why the interest in St. Joe?"

"This girl I go with now, well, she finished there five years ago when St. Joe's and Villa María merged." Cantú changed the subject abruptly: "Why did you want to be a policeman?"

"I read law up at Austin. After I passed bar, I decided not to practice and became a county patrolman instead. Not much of a story."

"And then you went into plainclothes, right?"

Buenrostro nodded again.

"How about you, Ike, why did you become a policeman?"

"A cop is all I ever wanted to be. Ever since I can remember."

Ike Cantú gave a surprised chuckle. "I can't even remember why I wanted to be one in the first place. Maybe I saw a movie. I don't know."

As they approached Klail's downtown area, Cantú slowed down, and Buenrostro told him to take a left at the next block.

"When we get there, go straight and then hang a right at midblock."

Cantú did so and found himself in another alley.

"Straight again. This'll take us to the bridge." An illegal but efficient move.

"Soon as we cross, stop at Mexican Customs, and I'll call Lu from there."

After a slight delay due to the crowds and the buses packed with tourists and Mexican nationals alike, they reached Customs and surrendered their guns. Buenrostro was issued the usual receipts and pocketed the two forms. He used Customs' phone to call Lu Cetina's office.

A woman's low, sexy voice: *"Buenos días. Se comunica con la oficina de la directora del orden público. ¿En qué se le sirve?"*

Buenrostro identified himself.

"Un momentito, señor jefe inspector, si me hace usted el favor. Gracias." Buenrostro smiled and thought: A conservative macho society that teaches its women to flirt from childhood.

"I'm at Customs, Lu. Where do we meet?"

"The old *municipio* building. I'll meet you over there. My darling husband just dropped off a change of clothes for me there, and I'm having food brought in."

"Oh?"

"Taking no chances. Tip came in yesterday afternoon, and I decided to stash 'em in one of the secured offices over there. Don't worry, I've got my own men on guard."

Buenrostro cradled the phone. He thanked the Customs man and told Ike Cantú to drive to the heart of downtown Barrones. "Anything new?"

"We'll see."

They drove in silence.

A young cop in the familiar blue uniform worn by the Federales was talking to another policeman when he spotted Buenrostro's unmarked car. He went to the street, saluted, and pointed to a special visitor's spot.

A brown-shirted traffic policeman went to Buenrostro's door, opened it, and led him and Cantú to the director's improvised office.

The policeman said, "Looks like rain, *jefe inspector.*"

Buenrostro looked at the ominous clouds scudding in from the Gulf and gave the standard answer: "It's August," he said, smiling.

The federal office building, a mixture of gaudy Mexican colonial architecture set off with an impractical modern glass front, had been built during Mexico's oil-crazy days. Fifteen years later, the structure showed signs of rapid aging. Neither Cantú nor Buenrostro paid much notice to the stress-cracks in the walls or to the grimy windowpanes.

A portrait of the current president graced two of the walls in the bench-lined reception area; they saw his portrait again along the main hall leading toward Lu Cetina's special office. At forty-three, the youngest president in Mexico's interesting history, his face showed a well-formed mustache over a half-smile. There was a hint of irony in those clear eyes; green eyes which marked him as a North Mexican, a *norteño.* Having a Northerner as president was a novelty since *norteños* were seldom trusted in Mexico City. They were too competitive, too hardworking. The fact that Mexico's only well-organized revolutionary movement had been born in the North did little to foster trust in those people coming to Mexico City from the northern cities of Monterrey, Saltillo, and Torreón.

The president came from a small northern town with the challenging name of Libertad. Cynical civil servants and reporters on the government-subsidized newspapers, given to joking about the ruling party, bit their tongue when the economic reforms went into high gear under his administration. For all his power, however, the president knew and accepted that political reform had to follow economic reform. Economic reform, unfortunately, had been going since the Glorious Revolution of 1910.

The brown-shirted cop stood by the door to the director's reception room and asked the secretary to announce the chief inspector's arrival. All very formal, something which the Valley-born Buenrostro and Cantú took in stride.

Fifteen

Between hurried bites of a sandwich lunch, Lu Cetina took less than five minutes to summarize the arrest. An anonymous tipster had called her office at six o'clock the previous afternoon. He'd given them the names, the room number at the flashy Flamingo Hotel on the Barrones airport road, and said that the men were heavily armed.

"That," said Lu Cetina, "was a given."

With fifteen federal policemen in plainclothes, she and her men waited from seven in the evening until one in the morning, and then they broke the doors down.

The hit men, she went on, shared a large room. Aside from empty fast-food cartons, liquor, and clothing strewn around the room, each man had a woman in bed with him.

The arrest went off quickly and rather quietly. The women were sent off to the bathroom; the *federales* pointed their guns at the two men who were told to stand facing the wall. The other cops tossed the room.

Among the effects, they turned up two cellular phones, two bags of cocaine, some marijuana baggies, several empty bottles of Old Parr, a bundle of Mexican pesos and American dollars, three Uzis, and two recently oiled U.S. Army .45s. While the men dressed, an officer took the women's clothing to the bathroom. The entire operation–and here Lu Cetina shook her head at the highblown phrase–had taken less than ten minutes.

"Coffee?"

Ike Cantú asked for a soft drink and Buenrostro ordered mineral water.

"Any ideas on this?"

Cantú first looked at her and then at his boss. There was a rap at the door, and a janitor knocked and walked in with the drinks.

Buenrostro spoke first. "You were still assigned to Mexico City when we captured Dutch Elder's killers, weren't you? Ike here was a car patrolman at the time. Joe Molden, Dorson and Hauer and I were in on the collar.

"We'd done our homework, and we were also getting close to discovering your predecessor, Lee Gómez, although at that time we didn't know he was involved. We thought he was cooperating with us. At any rate, based on an anonymous tip, we went to Brinkman's Hotel and made the arrest."

He paused. "We waited, much like you did. And then we beat the door down, and brought them in. Nothing to it. Sound familiar?"

She looked puzzled but said nothing.

"Later Pete Hauer checked on the phone calls to the motel and to Homicide. The anonymous tip calls had come from Lee's phone at the ranch. Here's something else, though. The guys we collared hadn't been paid for the job. They'd been in the hotel about a week, waiting for the payoff."

Lu Cetina placed the coffee cup on her desk. Looking straight at Buenrostro, she said: "These two claim they weren't paid either. Not in full anyway. They got a down payment and the rest promised when the job was done."

Buenrostro: "Did they know who contracted them for the job?"

"No. According to them, everything was arranged by phone. A medical doctor, they said. They couldn't come up with the name, though. Only weak point in their story."

Buenrostro: "They didn't say Olivares, by any chance?"

"No, they blanked out on the name. Anyway, they were told to wait by their contractor, and that they could order food, liquor, women, whatever. All they had to do was to stick around and wait for the money to be delivered."

Ike Cantú broke in: "They could charge for the women? I can understand food, lodging, liquor . . ."

Buenrostro said, "The Gómezes probably own the Flamingo and the whorehouse."

Lu Cetina shook her head and then nodded in agreement.

"Let's go see them, Lu."

SIXTEEN

i

"I will again introduce myself to you. My name is María Luisa Cetina de Gutiérrez. I am the Director of Public Order for the northern and coastal regions. We met early this morning. Have you been treated well?"

The two men nodded.

"These two gentlemen to my right are members of the Belken County Homicide squad. This is Detective Isaac Cantú, and the other gentleman is Chief Inspector Buenrostro.

"Identify yourselves. You first."

"My name is Ramón Quevedo. I am fifty-three years old, I was born and I live in Control, Tamaulipas."

"My name is Gabriel Quevedo. I am fifty years old, and I was born and live in Control, Tamaulipas."

"These are the ground rules: You have to speak louder. I will ask questions and you can answer, individually or together. If either of you is in disagreement with the other, you may interrupt and give your view or assessment. Is this understood?"

The men nodded that they understood.

Yes, they remembered the name Olivares now that Director Cetina mentioned it. The amount for the job? Three thousand, American, with five hundred up front, each. Hotel expenses included.

"We'd crossed the bridge at Control and then drove to Klail City."

Lu Cetina told them to back up.

"You." Pointing to Ramón Quevedo.

"Can I say we or I?"

"Whatever is convenient. Please listen, this is a cassette recorder, and there is a secretary next door taking down what we say. I ask you to speak clearly." She moved the recorder toward them.

"A kid picked us up in Control which is where we live. He then took us to the Flamingo Hotel here in Barrones, where we stayed overnight. The same kid showed up the next day and drove us back to Control early in the morning, and that's where we crossed the river."

"What was the youngster driving?"

"A Silverado, almost new. Wine-colored with gray stripes."

"And then?"

"We crossed and went downriver to Klail City."

"What is the youngster's name?"

"No idea."

"What time did you arrive in Klail?"

The men looked at each other.

"Sometime in the morning."

"All right, you're in Klail City. Now what happens?"

"The kid drives around Klail and says he's to take us to a cafeteria for the job. We say he's crazy and then he explains we're to do the job in a parking lot near the cafeteria."

"Who do you know you are to kill?"

"The kid says we're to look for a black Lincoln. Two types in dark jumpsuits will be waiting around."

"Who were the men? Who did they work for?"

"No idea."

"And you drove there?"

"The kid took us there."

"Okay, the kid took you there. And then what happens?"

At this point Ramón Quevedo looked up and asked for a cigarette. He was handed one and waited for a light.

"Well, the *chamaco,* he takes us to the parking lot. We see the Lincoln, and I say: 'Get closer.' I make him drive by the Lincoln car two times and then we park right behind it."

Gabriel Quevedo raised his hand.

"No, we parallel-park behind the car, and then we get out and walk to the front of the Lincoln."

"True. And then we turn around, and that's when we open fire."

"Where's the Silverado at this time?"

The men looked at each other.

"No idea."

"How long did you fire at the men?"

"How long? Ten seconds, fifteen maybe. A long time."

"And then?"

"And then the driver comes up again, stops, I get in first and then him, Gabriel."

"And how did you get out of the parking lot?"

"Slow, is that what you mean?"

"Yes."

"Yes, slow. We tell the kid to take us to Palmer Heights Estates, but he doesn't know where that is. We tell him to drive to a gasoline station, and we buy a map of Klail City in one of the machines. The kid he drove us there, and that's it."

"What about the youngster, the driver?"

"Oh, we kill him too. Those were the orders."

"How did you kill him?"

"Gabriel did that."

"Yes. I broke his neck."

"What did you do with the body?"

The men looked at each other.

"Ah, yes, we threw it out in a field, near that place."

"Palmer Heights Estates?"

"Yes."

What did you do with the Silverado?"

"We were told to park it in a driveway."

"A particular driveway?"

"No, just any driveway. Just not to leave it in the street."

"Who said that?"

"Dr. Olivares."

"Now you have to get out of there. How'd you do that?"

"I used my cellular. I call a taxi, he crossed the bridge at Klail, and he takes us to the Flamingo."

"Just like that?"

"Just like that."

"Do you remember the taxi company?"

The men talked to each other.

"Yes, a red and green. Four door. Mexican cabdriver with Texas plates."

"So you're at the Flamingo."

"Yes, the clerk, she recognizes us and says we have the same room from the day before."

"Did you make a reservation for the same room?"

"No. She said it was available for us."

"And then?"

"And then we wait. Gabriel here, he calls the Gold Palace, and we have two women delivered to us."

"No other phone calls?"

"To us?"

"Yes."

"Dr. Olivares, he called three days ago last Friday. Once in the morning and once in the evening. He called yesterday also. He says we did a good job. He asks about the kid, and we tell him not to worry about him anymore."

"When were you to be paid the rest of the money?"

"Last night, but he called and said he was running late. That he would pay us today."

"And then what happened?"

The men laughed.

"You arrested us, that's what happened."

"Have either of you seen Dr. Olivares? Heard his voice before?"

They talked to each other again.

"No."

"How sure are you?"

"Positive."

"You hungry?"

They looked at each other again.

"Yes."

"Elizondo!"

An old veteran's face appeared through the mottled glass partition.

"Sí, señora Directora?"

"Take them to lunch."

The old cop cuffed them and rattled the glass.

The door opened and an army sergeant ordered a twelve-man squad to escort the two men to their private dining area.

ii

"After lunch, we'll go after them again. These are the type of guys who call themselves *gente dura*."

Buenrostro said, "The hard guys. Well, it's a cinch we won't break them by force. We'll just probe here and there, they're bound to say something we can use."

Back at the office, Buenrostro asked for another bottle of mineral water. "For an imaginative guy, I'm surprised Lee used the same name again. Not surprised he stiffed them, though."

"What do you mean?"

"It's part of the little boy in Lee Gómez and in Felipe Segundo, too, I guess. Lee likes to take small, safe risks, and he enjoys rooking somebody, but somebody small usually. As for the killings, he's like a kid in some ways. As long as he doesn't have to see the blood, those people can disappear like leaves off a tree.

"But there's a danger in that character flaw, as well. If cornered, Lee–and perhaps Felipe Segundo too . . . If cornered, Lee will turn on anybody. Family, if it comes to that."

"That's pretty strong," she objected.

"I'm just talking here, but I bet I'm not too far off the track. Lee enjoys fooling people, a sign of immaturity, of arrested development. Has to do with childish competition."

"From Felipe Segundo?"

"Maybe. But I also think they're a team, and that makes them tough. Lee's the type of coward who isn't a complete coward."

Ike Cantú reacted to this. "How do you mean?"

"He's afraid of the dark, say, of monsters, anything, but not if there's someone there with him. Even if that person does nothing but stand there, Lee will not act like a coward then."

"I've heard of that type," said Lu Cetina.

There was a rap at the door and Buenrostro took the offered mineral water from the old cop. *"¿Un vaso, señor jefe inspector?"*

Buenrostro thanked him and said no, he'd drink it straight out of the bottle, American style. The old cop smiled and saluted as he left.

"That's Rosendo Elizondo. Up for retirement and poor as a church mouse. Good thing he had the foresight to marry a woman who owns a coffee shop."

"No raises, Lu?"

"Some, and these recent, but not enough to help out old vets like Rosendo there. Poor, low, and infrequent pay accounted for much of the bribery here and all over *mi México lindo y querido.*" She said this deprecatingly.

Talking seriously, she said, "Elizondo's my right hand man."

"Anything on our Canadian friends," asked Buenrostro.

"Only that no one's seen them in Montreal or Marseilles, their usual hangouts. Of course, if they didn't get stiffed like these two, our Québecois could be having themselves a time God knows where. They didn't come cheap, I'll bet."

"They're unaccounted for, along with the pilot Grayson," said Buenrostro, evenly. "I'd like to get Felipe Segundo to cross the river."

She looked up and said, "With that fresh body in your morgue, I'll tell him you need his help, that we hope it's not Lisandro, but the identification could give him peace of mind."

Ike Cantú: "To change the subject on you, *directora.* District Attorney Valencia wants to know when he can start extradition proceedings."

"Oh," blithely, "just as soon as the sun sets in the east, I imagine," and then she laughed heartily. "By the way, I can have food brought in. Hungry?"

Both said no, and Buenrostro asked: "When do we go around with the Quevedo brothers again?"

She glanced at her watch. "We'll give them fifteen more minutes to freshen up. We're not inhuman." Smiling.

Buenrostro. "A youngster found Daniel Varela's body in Palmer Heights this morning. I imagine the prints you sent us will match the ones on the body and prints we got from the Silverado. The faxes should be here by now."

She dialed her main office and asked for recent faxes from Belken County Homicide.

"What?" She cupped the phone: "Reporters. Tell them I'm busy. Get rid of them and check on some faxes I'm expecting from across the river. Bring them over to this office when they come in."

"Where's your bathroom, Lu?"

She motioned to a side door, and Buenrostro entered the private toilet.

Ike Cantú: "Good interrogation, *directora.*"

"You'll get there, we all do," she said kindly.

The phone rang, and she said, "Yes. I see. Thank you."

Cantú asked, "Daniel Varela's prints?"

She nodded slowly. "Well, one less to worry about."

"Can't you just go to the ranch and arrest the Gómezes?"

"Could you, if they were on your side?"

Ike hesitated and then said, "We need probable cause."

"As do we," she said, smiling.

Ike went on: "Are the Quevedos under an obligation to answer questions the chief puts to them?"

"Yes. We'll call him a special deputy. That's not a legal fiction, by the way. I question the way I do because whatever judge of instruction I get, he'll ask me even more rigorous questions. Your boss's questions will be part of the charge I'm building."

She paused, briefly. "The Quevedos don't know how much they *do* know."

A policeman brought her the faxes; she checked her own file on Daniel Varela's fingerprints and then compared them with the faxes sent by Hauer.

Just then, Buenrostro re-entered the main room, and Lu Cetina said, "The prints on the Silverado belong both to Daniel Varela and to the Quevedo brothers. Are we ready?"

Seventeen

The brothers were again escorted under military guard to the mottled glass room and told to sit down.

"Remove the handcuffs," said Lu Cetina, gravely.

"You did very well. Chief Inspector Buenrostro has some questions too. He speaks Spanish. You will pay close attention and answer truthfully. If you do not answer truthfully, both of us will find out immediately.

"Remember, speak clearly."

Rafe Buenrostro sat in a straightbacked chair directly in front of the brothers.

"Are you familiar with the Gómez Solís family?"

Both said yes.

"Do either of you know any of them personally?"

"No."

"How do you know of them?"

"They belong to the old families."

"Have you ever visited their home or homes?"

"No."

"Do you know where the Gómez Solíses live?"

Gabriel: "Soliseño Ranch."

"Been there?"

"No."

"You?"

"Me neither."

"But you know of the ranch and of the family?"

"Everybody knows about them."

"I don't. Tell me something."

"They're rich."

"Land rich?"

"Yes, farming and ranching."

"Anything else?"

The men talked to each other.

"We hear *cocaína, heroína, mota. Drogas.*"

"You hear. Do you know for a fact?"

"For a fact? No."

"A rumor, then?"

"Yes, but one hears this all the time."

"So, by hearing the rumor often, it becomes a truth?"

Gabriel: "I know a workman there."

"Farmer?"

Ramón: "Yes, a workhand."

"Go on."

"His name is something Morales. Seldom leaves Soliseño, but when he does, he comes to Control, not Barrones."

"Not Barrones."

"He says it's orders. He says he owes a death on the ranch."

"Owes. He killed someone inside the ranch?"

"Yes, he says he owes a death there."

"Is he drinking when he says this?"

"Yes, but he's not drunk. He just says it."

"To make himself *interesante*?"

Ramón: "I would say so, yes. He's not *gente dura*. Hard people do not need to feel important."

"And why is that?"

"Because when you're hard, that makes you important, and people know it."

"People in the town of Control?"

"Yes."

"And away from Control?"

"I don't know. Perhaps."

"So, because you are *gente dura*, you received the phone call from Dr. Olivares to kill someone?"

"Yes."

"Did you talk to the man Morales on any of this?"

The brothers talked among themselves again.

"No. Our work was in confidence."

"And you've met Dr. Olivares?"

"Unknown to us. He called."

"But you received five hundred dollars."

"The post office at Control."

"So, he knows who you are, but you do not know who he is?"

"Yes."

"You have a question, Ramón Quevedo?"

"For the *directora*."

"Go ahead."

"Who did we kill in the parking lot?"

"Locals. They used to work for the Gómez family."

"Locals, like us?"

"Yes."

Buenrostro came back on: "Back to this Morales person."

"Yes."

"Is it talk or truth that he has killed someone in the ranch?"

"He talks and swears us to secrecy."

"But you're telling his secret to us."

"We know we are not the only ones he talks to."

"But this something Morales is not a hard guy."

"He is not. He's a farmer, that's all."

Gabriel Quevedo: "Yes, I've never heard he's done piece work, like my brother and me."

"Piece work?"

"Yes, like you say, *un contrato*."

"So he's not *gente dura?*"

Ramón Quevedo: "He's hard at Soliseño Ranch."

"Meaning?"

"You go there, without authority or invitation, you do not come out."

"Morales says this to you and you believe him?"

"Yes. What is there not to believe?"

"Proof."

"Yes, I see. One moment."

A few seconds later, Ramón Quevedo said: "We have no proof, you are correct."

Gabriel Quevedo: "Who is that crazy kid we killed?"

"A youngster. He stole the Silverado."

"The Silverado had Texas plates, originally. We changed them."

"Thank you. Did Dr. Olivares give you a reason why you had to kill the youngster?"

"No. He gave us money."

"What if I were to tell you Dr. Olivares told *Directora* Cetina you were at the Flamingo?"

"We thought this was a serious conversation."

"And what if I were to tell you, that a few years ago, he had two hard men killed on the Military Highway. At a *cantinita* called the Kum Bak Inn."

"That's unknown to us."

"I'll tell you. He hired four other hard men, and after the piece work, as you call it, a man calling himself Dr. Olivares turned them in to us in Klail City. He said the men were in a hotel. The same way he turned you over to *Directora* Cetina."

"Why are we being told this?"

"Because one of the men he turned in to us is out of the Texas prison."

"A man from Control?"

"No, a man from Barrones. He is known as a skilled driver. An albino."

Gabriel Quevedo nodded. "El Camarón Salinas, the man who looks like a pink shrimp. We know of him. He was an associate of the man called El Barco Zaragoza. Those are old timers, but they're hard. Honorable in their way."

Buenrostro cut in: "Not just an associate of El Barco, a childhood friend. Dr. Olivares meant to kill a competitor, and he hired El Barco Zaragoza and Salinas to do the job. And then he betrayed them. Accidentally, one of our friends was killed there by mistake."

"A policeman was killed? In Texas?"

"*Un abogado del distrito*. Amounts to the same thing in importance to us."

"And Dr. Olivares is responsible?"

"Yes. How often does the workman Morales come to Control?"

"No schedule."

"Could we have some help from you?"

The brothers looked at each other and Ramón Quevedo said, "We don't see how."

"Think about it."

"We're thinking."

"Do you read English?"

"No."

"Do you read *El Heraldo* from Jonesville?"

"Not usually."

"A few days ago, a man named Lisandro Gómez Solís escaped from the Belken County jail."

"We know who he is."

"Since the escape, the youngster has been killed, the two men in the parking lot are dead, the two men who helped Gómez escape have disappeared, and an airplane pilot is missing."

"You are saying those other three men are also dead?"

"We have proof as to the first three, the ones you killed. We have no proof of the last three, but it's very possible."

"You are driving to a point here?"

"Yes. You're the point. Dr. Olivares turned you in. He wanted you dead, and that's why he telephoned the *directora*. But she is an intelligent person. She and her men waited until you fell asleep. That's why you are alive."

"And that's why the *directora* is alive. We would not have gone alone."

"That's what Dr. Olivares was counting on."

"We will think on this."

"Think hard."

"You want Morales, it's that simple."

"Is it simple?"

"A manner of speaking, I apologize."

Ramón Quevedo: "May I address the *directora*?"

"Go ahead."

"On the matter of privileges. We will pay for our food. We have wives, too."

"Your privileges will depend on your cooperation."

"Is it not a matter of federal law to be allowed visitations?"

"Absolutely, but I am under no obligation to keep you in Barrones. My jurisdiction extends from here down to Tampico and from here, upriver to Laredo."

"A sizeable responsibility and territory."

"One last question."

The men looked at Buenrostro.

"In Control, does Morales talk to anyone else?"

"We will think on this too."

"Elizondo!"

The veteran cop opened the door, and the soldiers led the Quevedo brothers away again.

iii

Lu Cetina said, "I hadn't given much thought to the pattern of the missing men. There's something in that."

She walked with Cantú and Buenrostro to the parking lot.

"You'll have copies of both interrogations in your office by tomorrow morning. I'll call Felipe Segundo in a little while. You think he'll cross the river to identify the body?" Doubtfully.

"I think he will and more so as soon as he and Lee know these two are alive. The Quevedo brothers don't know what Lee looks like, but he's not the type to take chances on slip ups of any kind. He's got to get the heat off him and get back to doing business. Now, Felipe Segundo will set a date and break it at last moment. He'll do this a few times, but he'll come. They're cute, that way."

"Why are you so certain?"

"Lee's a ruthless man of weak character, and that's what makes him dangerous and predictable in some ways. He's clever all right, but he's not *gente dura.* That means he has no loyalty for anyone. A fundamental weakness, Lu."

"And you think this man Morales may be the key?"

"If Lee hasn't had him killed already." Levelly.

"Good God, Rafe."

"I think Lee means to start a new gang from scratch. He probably thinks he was betrayed from within."

They shook hands and Buenrostro thanked her again; they agreed to meet whenever Felipe Segundo confirmed he was crossing the river to identify the body.

In the car, Buenrostro said, "That removes the two killers and young Varela from the list. We're down to Grayson and the Canadians. Lee Solís has been a busy man."

Ike Cantú thought on the Varela women. "Chief, I'll call Mrs. Varela at Theo Crixell's, and tell her we found Daniel's body. You think there'll be a need for an autopsy? To cut him all up?"

"Henry Dietz will find the broken neck soon enough. Why'd you ask?"

"Well, the women still have to identify him, and an autopsy . . ." His voice died out.

Rafe Buenrostro fell silent for a minute.

"You say Mrs. Varela works at Theo's?"

"Yeah. He got her a Social Security card, too. She can retire pretty soon if she wants to."

"Well, hell, Ike, that's how the Gómezes got Theo's new phone number whenever he changed it."

"You saying those women are in this?"

"No, not necessarily. The kid asks for the phone to reach his mother whenever it's changed, see? He's the one who passed it on to Lee or to the twins, his new friends."

The irony of that last remark was not lost on Ike Cantú.

Ike Cantú: "And that Morales man the Quevedos spoke about?"

Buenrostro: "He may or may not exist. It's a common name, after all. Still, we planted a seed."

Ike Cantú asked: "Amity or the old bridge, Chief?"

"Let's take the El Jardín district. "

"Old bridge it is."

Eighteen

By eight o'clock the next morning, Ike Cantú had finished his second reading of the parking-lot folder. He initialed the last page and returned the folder to Buenrostro's in-basket. As he came out, Sam Dorson handed Cantú a cup of coffee and the two went over the two interrogations faxed to them from Lu Cetina's office.

"Pete read this yet?" asked Cantú.

"Not yet. He just left for the dentist's."

Dorson took a sip of coffee. "Well, what do you think?"

"The brothers think they can cut a deal with Lu Cetina, but I don't see her giving anything away."

They were on this when Buenrostro came in.

"Coffee?" offered Dorson.

"No, thanks. I have a note here from Henry Dietz saying the families took the bodies back to Barrones early this morning."

"That include the Varela family?" said Dorson.

Buenrostro looked at the medical examiner's release forms and nodded.

"The folder ready?"

Ike Cantú: "On your desk."

"I got three calls at home, last night. The first was from Chip Valencia, who called to congratulate all of us on a job well done."

Dorson and Cantú snickered.

"The second came from Hackett, the new FBI supervisor here. He asked me why we requested the Canadians' fingerprints from Washington and why our interest in Lee Gómez's escape.

"I told him. As he sees it, Lee's a federal fugitive and that makes him none of our business. He also said that we'd already had our day in court. In brief, Lee Gómez is not our responsibility."

"Did he want our help in any way? Some cooperation?" said Dorson.

"No. We're to stay out of it."

Cantú: "And what authority does he have to order us around like that?"

"None," said Buenrostro, smiling.

Dorson: "Lee's still wanted for the Dutch Elder murder, period. Hackett, you say? Where does the Bureau come up with these guys?"

Buenrostro: "The third call came from Art Styles. Art said Hackett leaned on him for giving us information."

Cantú: "How did Hackett's office know about our request on the Canadians?"

"According to Art, the local bureau office receives copies of any field request made to Washington."

"They must be choking on paper, those people," scoffed Cantú.

Dorson: "Well then, Mr. Hackett can just go jump in and out of the Rio Grande."

"Anyway, Styles was boiling mad."

"At us?" Cantú surprised.

"No. Art said he'd do whatever it took to help us out. Told me that as of now, DEA has its finger in the pie since Lee's federal indictment also mentions drugs."

Dorson laughed.

Cantú: "Oh, great. Now we have DEA and the FBI fighting among themselves."

Buenrostro: "It's not Immigration's fight, I don't think. Anyway, Art Styles wants no part of the other two."

He went into his office.

ii

By midmorning, Buenrostro initialed the final report on the three murders and rang for a secretary from the steno pool. He then called his wife, checked on the next weekend's early drive to the bay and made a date for lunch. He was about to phone Art Styles when Dorson walked in.

"Chip's secretary just called. He's on his way down. Get this, he wants you to convince Lu to extradite the Quevedos."

"If that's what he wants, I'll make the call."

Dorson's eyes revealed a mixture of surprise at Buenrostro's remark and then anger at Valencia for suggesting such a thing.

"Lu will think you've lost your mind. Tell her it's the D.A.'s idea, which it is."

"I think she's intelligent enough to know where the idea comes from."

"I hear Himself out there."

"Show him in."

After the usual greetings and new congratulations, the district attorney made his pitch for extradition.

"Chief Inspector, do you mind–I say, do you mind if I listen in? I promise I won't interfere." Smiling.

Buenrostro turned on the amplifier and Valencia sat himself down to wait on one of the uncomfortable straightbacked rattan chairs.

After the usual international clicks and whirrs, Buenrostro introduced himself and asked to speak with the *directora*.

Lu Cetina came on the line. Without a word of greeting, Buenrostro immediately went into his formal request for the extradition of Ramón and Gabriel Quevedo, who had been charged with putting to death Julio Salas, Gustavo Rocha, and Daniel Varela in Belken County.

The line seemed to have gone dead.

Buenrostro waited, and Valencia rose from his chair and looked in rapt attention at the amplifier.

They heard Lu Cetina clear her throat after which the voice came on evenly. She explained, as if to a child, that the Republic of Mexico, under its established constitution, does not extradite its citizens for crimes committed outside its national boundaries.

Had there ever been exceptions, Buenrostro asked in a flat voice.

The answer was absolutely not. That agencies of the American government have, on occasion, kidnapped Mexican citizens and tried them through its court system is one thing. For the Mexican government to surrender a citizen to a foreign power, aside from being a direct deprivation of the citizen's civil rights under existing Mexican laws, was also tantamount to a surrendering of the nation's sovereignty.

Valencia stared at the amplifier in anger and surprise.

Her voice rising, Lu Cetina also said that under no circumstances would she, as an agent of the Mexican federal government, recommend such an impertinence to her superiors.

Heating up, she then expressed disappointment on a most personal basis. And most particularly, she added, in view of her unstinting cooperation with the chief inspector and his personnel in the last eighteen months, in spite of the, ah, the, ah, unfortunate circumstances and events caused by her predecessor. She, María Luisa Cetina de Gutiérrez, was dismayed, and, yes, frankly disappointed by such a request. Aggrieved even.

"I take this very personally, Chief Inspector."

Buenrostro thanked her for her time.

"Well!" said Chip Valencia. "I've never heard such high-falutin' Spanish in all my life. And where does she get off climbing on that high horse of hers, anyway?

"My mistake, Chief Inspector. I should have gone straight to the mayor of Barrones on this one, and, failing that, right to the state capital in Victoria, no question.

"I promise you, it's not over yet.

"I, ah, I only hope you weren't too embarrassed by that woman's overbearing attitude. No one speaks to one of my men in that manner, no one." He walked out the door without saying goodbye.

iii

Dorson and Cantú went into the chief inspector's office and sat down.

Buenrostro dialed the Barrones number, identified himself to the secretary and waited.

Lu Cetina, laughing: "How was that, Chief Inspector."

"Pretty impressive," he said, laughing as well. "I've got Dorson and Ike Cantú in here."

"They hear it?"

She then heard the laughter of the two detectives.

"Anything new on your side, Lu?"

"Not much, only that the owner of the VW Kombi showed up. We talked to him and let him go."

"Who is he?"

"A motivational speaker, of all things. Yah. He was in Tampico on business. The Kombi's his hunting wagon. Not a plant, like I thought it was. But I'm going to keep an eye out for a couple of days anyway."

"Lu, did the Varela women speak to you? They gave us some pictures of Daniel posing with some new friends. It turns out that the new friends are the Gómez Solís twins."

"You've got the pictures there?"

"These are copies. The family's got the originals."

"I'll send old man Elizondo to talk to the Varelas. Did you know Felipe Segundo has a couple of sons in their twenties?"

Buenrostro: "Lu, I think those are Lee's kids, aren't they?"

"Not the way I hear it. Anyway, fax me the pictures, and I'll pass 'em around. Anything new over there?"

Buenrostro sighed audibly. "Only that new FBI chief of station you mentioned. Hackett."

"Good luck, my friend." she rang off, laughing.

Nineteen

The reception for Boyd Hackett took place in the federal side of the courthouse. Buenrostro spoke mostly with his section heads and took his leave with them at the end of the affair. He then rode the elevator to Chip Valencia's office. There he shook hands with one of the young aides, greeted the chief administrative assistant, and walked into the main office.

"Ah, Chief Inspector, take a seat, won't you?"

Buenrostro took in the spacious room. Something new: a second parson's table with a light-green portable telephone resting on it. The crimson British campaign chest now held a color TV set; a VCR, numbers flashing, was hooked up to the set.

Behind Valencia's desk, the usual: a photo of a smiling Chip Valencia shaking hands with Ronald Reagan, another of Valencia with George Bush. The present incumbent was missing. The usual plaque awards from the service clubs covered most of the same wall.

The desk showed two small photographs: Valencia's wife and two children. It was a neat desk with no paperclips lying around, no papers of any sort to ruin the studied decor, and no in- or out-baskets either. Official but friendly, or was it the other way around? Buenrostro could not remember how Valencia had once described his office.

The new parson's table also held a cut-glass bowl filled with chocolates, and Sheriff Norm Andrews grabbed a handful. Buenrostro sat on one of the armchairs.

"Great job on the double homicide, Chief. Oh, and the car thief, the one found in Palmer Heights. Kenny Breen is writing up a release for the papers, and Homicide is being cited for a fine job."

After a slight pause, Valencia went on, "I guess we're going to have to forget the Gómez Solís extradition business for a while, although I've asked Boyd Hackett to look into it. Possibly Washington, even."

Norm Andrews, mouth full of chocolate, nodded in agreement.

Buenrostro waited. First, a preliminary cough by the D.A., followed by, "At the reception, I took Hackett aside for a bit. The FBI has promised to cooperate and to help us in anyway it can in this affair."

Buenrostro, evenly, said, "It would be a good idea to remind them of our jurisdiction. Lee Gómez is still wanted by the state for murder and now for unlawful flight . . ."

"Right, right," said Valencia, frowning.

"And, we're working closely with the Barrones police and with the *federales.* We may need money for the uniforms' overtime."

"No problem," both men replied at once.

Buenrostro rose slowly and stood behind the armchair.

"A press conference any time soon, Chief Inspector?" This from Norm Andrews.

"Tomorrow morning at nine. Sam Dorson's in charge, and Kenny Breen will be on hand for the news releases."

Valencia beamed. "Splendid, yes, splendid. And don't forget, you need anything–anything, mind you–we're here to help."

Buenrostro nodded and left the room.

Outside, he shook his head slightly and glanced at his watch: three-fifteen. In the hallway he met Ben Lyons, the county clerk.

"Been in to see Chip, I see?"

Buenrostro smiled as they entered the elevator. "Lucky you," said the old county veteran as he and Buenrostro shook hands. They rode the elevator to the basement in complete understanding.

Peter Hauer was going over the Quevedo brothers' faxed interview when Buenrostro came into the squadroom.

"Here's a note from Gwen Phillips. Ike took the call about an hour ago."

Buenrostro said, "Anything from Sam yet?"

A shake of the head from Peter Hauer.

Buenrostro went to his office and called Gwen Phillips, Valencia's executive assistant prosecutor.

She came on the line. "Another lovely reception, Rafe."

Buenrostro laughed lightly. "What have you got for me?"

"We served the last warrant last night. Disrupted a fancy dinner party, too. Anyway, my three junior D.A.s went to work on the books early this morning, and before banking hours, too. How's that?"

"Probably scared those bankers to death."

"We did that. A powerful instrument, the subpoena."

Rafe Buenrostro gave another light laugh.

"We came up with seven active accounts for Lee Gómez, but no sequestration of funds orders issued by the feds."

"I thought as much. I talked to Theo about that."

"How do you mean?"

"He said the feds had cleaned out Lee's money in the other Valley banks. But he wasn't surprised when Sam found the ones the feds missed here in Klail. That's why we called you."

"I guess the Klail stash was too obvious for the publicity hounds," said Gwen Phillips.

"Yeah, that's what Theo said. How much?"

Gwen Phillips let out a soft sigh. "Our accountants came up with thirteen million and some odd cents here and there. Enough to jog on, I'd say."

"Can we sequester the accounts?"

"Done. He's a fugitive from justice, and he's wanted by the state."

"Thank you. I've just reminded Chip and Norm Andrews that we've got jurisdiction. I'll get back to you, Gwen."

"Always here, Chief."

He thanked her and rang off. He poured himself a glass of ice water and glanced at his watch: three thirty-five. He went into the squad room where Hauer was scouring the coffee pot.

"Thirteen million at Klail State and Bishop's S&L."

Hauer looked up and said, "Arrogant bastards probably used their own names, right?"

Buenrostro nodded. "Lee and Felipe Segundo are going to have to get going with that new gang of theirs. To do that, though, they probably have another bunch of money hidden someplace."

Hauer agreed. "Yeah, that's a cash-only business, all right."

Buenrostro said the important thing was to get Felipe Segundo across the river to view the body the lab had rigged up for identification. For a few minutes they talked on the possibility of paper companies the Gómezes might have set up. From this they talked about the upcoming St. Joe's reunion.

Hauer: "Since you missed the last one, some of the out-of-towners are bound to ask about the arm." Buenrostro nodded at this.

Buenrostro said, "I need to meet with Lu Cetina early tomorrow morning. Eat breakfast across the river."

Raincoat over his shoulder, he turned at the door and said, "Call Art Styles at Immigration. See if he can make it for breakfast. If he can, I'll pick him up around seven o'clock."

While Buenrostro waited for Peter Hauer to set up the meeting with Lu Cetina, there was a knock at the door and desk sergeant de la Cruz ushered in the county jailer.

"Chief, this here is Officer Henry Saldaña, and he's got a present for you."

The jailer said, "I've got a man named Morales in a holding cell downstairs. Says he's a farmhand at the Gómezes' Soliseño ranch and that he wanted to talk to the head man, *el jefe*. Calls himself Tibu Morales.

"He'd heard about two brothers named Quevedo that had been arrested in a Barrones motel. Well, in he walks into the courthouse, reports to a policeman, hands him five marijuana cigarettes and turns himself in. Stripped, fingerprinted and Mirandized, Chief."

"Good man. Bring him to my office. Pete, set up the cassette recorder."

Five minutes later, de la Cruz and four uniforms brought in a squat, black-haired, dark-eyed man. Not a drop of Spanish blood there, thought Buenrostro.

"Your name is Tiburcio, is it?"

Morales smiled. "A natural mistake, *señor jefe.* My name is Víctor Morales. I'm called Tibu, short for Tiburón."

Hauer: "Shark, eh?"

Morales smiled again and nodded. At this point, desk sergeant de la Cruz produced a heavy-duty baggie with Morales's effects. "I checked all his ID, Chief. He's who he says he is."

While the two uniforms stood at the door, Peter Hauer rose from his chair, opened the door to Buenrostro's office and waited as de la Cruz led the prisoner to a chair facing Buenrostro's desk.

Dark-skinned all right, but also reddish from the sun, noted Buenrostro.

"You're here on a misdemeanor."

"I thought I had enough marijuana for a felony in Texas."

"Not anymore."

Hauer placed the microrecorder and several minicassettes on top of the table. Morales then raised his hand and said, as if in a courtroom:

"I promise to tell the truth at all times, *señor jefe.*"

Twenty

Buenrostro and Morales looked at each other for a second or two.

"¿Y qué, hablas inglés?"

"No, señor, muy poco."

"Nos iremos en español, entonces."

"Cuando usted guste."

Buenrostro pointed to the recorder and the cassettes. Morales nodded in agreement.

He had escaped from the ranch, he said, in fear of his life. Buenrostro thought this a novel approach but said nothing. He'd left because last night when he'd returned from Control, don Felipe Segundo told him, "Deaf-mute Farías has been killed in a tractor accident."

That, Chief Inspector, is a lie. Deaf he was and mute, too, but my cousin wasn't stupid enough to fall off a tractor and under the cultivator discs. Not him. No, never.

Why, it was like saying that he had fallen off his wife during the act. That's when I, Tibu Morales, knew my days on the Gómez ranch were numbered, and the numbers were neither very big nor very many.

Buenrostro waited.

And what was worse, Morales went on, was just last week; a week ago today, he repeated, pounding both fists on Buenrostro's desk. Yes, just last week ago today, don Felipe Segundo had killed his own brother, don Lisandro. And what did the chief inspector think of that?

Peter Hauer stared hard at Morales.

Buenrostro: "So don Felipe Segundo murdered his own brother?"

When Morales heard the chief inspector quote him word for word, he began to look around the room. His eyes widened, his breathing quickened and came in short gasps.

"Water? Is there any water here?" Hauer walked to the fridge and poured him a glass. Morales took it in both hands, took a long draught and this appeared to settle him down.

He then took a deep breath. Yes, the Chief Inspector doesn't want to believe this, does he? I, Tibu Morales, can read faces, and the Chief

Inspector's reveals incredulity. Well, the Chief Inspector is wrong. Don Lisandro Gómez Solís is dead. By the hand of his brother and his own sons.

At this point, Buenrostro raised his hand. Didn't Morales mean Felipe Segundo's sons?

A harsh scoff from the prisoner. Don Felipe is a butterfly, you understand? He prefers young boys, like a butterfly that settles on beautiful flowers. The boys, Juan Carlos and José Antonio, are not don Felipe Segundo's boys; they belong to don Lisandro.

Buenrostro shook his head slightly.

What the chief inspector is hearing is the truth. And here is a bigger truth: The twins don't know who their father is. They think it's don Felipe Segundo. Well, I, Tiburón Morales, am here to say that the twins are wrong; that the world is wrong.

Buenrostro glanced at the recording machine and toyed with a microcassette while he waited for Morales to catch his breath.

The boys were born here in Klail City, with the nuns at Mercy Hospital, and I know this because my younger sister, Tecla, was their nursemaid. She was a big, healthy farmgirl and she had milk enough for five babies, if it came to that. That's it; the truth. The boys are the sons of don Lisandro.

That's a surprise to the chief inspector, isn't it? Ha! And here's another. The boys put the, the, the *tiro de gracia*, the shot to the head, to their own father. Except they didn't know it was their own father. They still don't know it.

I think they're crazy too.

Morales finished for the moment. Could he have some more water and a cigarette, please.

Buenrostro rose and knocked on the door. "I need a pack of cigarettes and some matches."

One of the patrolmen handed him a half pack of Delicados and a cigarette lighter. Peter Hauer refilled the water glass and placed it on the table.

Morales nodded his thanks.

The Chief Inspector wants to know about last week? Simple. My cousin Farías was operating a backhoe; a dangerous machine, right?

Well, he was good at anything like that. It was around mid-morning. Yes. About that time.

Don Felipe Segundo and the boys were inside the house and when Mr. Grayson's little plane flew over, out the three of them came. Don Felipe Segundo told me to get in the backseat of the jeep, and away we went to where the planes land. The strip runs east and west of the big house and the barns where we keep the equipment, the trailers, the *cocaína*, the *heroína*, the marijuana. Everything.

Did Morales know Mr. Grayson?

Oh, sure. A Spanish-speaking gringo, with a pretty wife.

Buenrostro waited.

The twins, they take the other jeep and all of us go to where the plane is going to land. Everyone was excited, laughing, happy, and waving at the plane. We're going sixty kilometers an hour on hard dirt, and I'm holding on to my hat. Don Felipe Segundo, he takes his eyes off the road and yells to me, "Don Lisandro is coming home, Tibu. He's in that plane."

That was a surprise to me. Anyway, the plane lands and that's when the world goes crazy. There's don Lisandro smiling and waving at the boys and at his brother. My cousin keeps working on the backhoe. The plane leaves again. It goes up straight, begins to rise, it tries to turn, and then, just like that, the engine fails. The plane has no power and it crashes.

But that's not all. Don Lisandro is still waving and laughing and this is when don Felipe Segundo gets off the jeep and shoots his brother. Don Lisandro is hit in the arm and the bullet knocks him on his knees. Don Felipe Segundo shoots a second time while don Lisandro is trying to get up. The second shot knocks him on his back. Don Felipe Segundo shoots him a third time and then one of the boys walk up and shoots his own father, Chief Inspector, his own father.

Right away, don Felipe Segundo tells José Antonio to help me roll don Lisandro in a tarp and to tie the bundle on the hood of the jeep. Then Juan Carlos is told to shoot the men in the plane, just in case.

Don Felipe Segundo laughs when he removes the gun from don Lisandro and tosses it to me. After this, young Juan Carlos goes to tell my cousin to bury the plane. That job takes two hours or more because my cousin has to recover some of the big parts of the plane and buries everything in a big, big, deep hole between the tall sorghum rows.

"So don Lisandro is dead." A statement, not a question.

"Like the song says."

"And don Felipe Segundo wants to kill you."

"He wants to kill everybody."

"Are you hungry, Morales?"

Surprised, Morales said, "Why, yes, I believe I am."

"What would you like?"

"First, a beer, a Miller Lite, my favorite."

"Do you know of an eating place called Lucio's?"

"Best *norteño* food on your side of the river."

"I'll have some brought over. How does rice, beans, guacamole, chalupas, an order of white cheese green enchiladas, and flour tortillas sound to you?"

"The president of the United States does not eat any better than I do." The four policemen escorted Morales to his private cell.

"Pete, call Lu and tell her about Morales. We'll have copies of the cassettes made by the time her messenger gets here."

Hauer fiddled with a letter opener. "What do you think?"

"I'll talk to Morales again right after he eats. Lee Gómez dead. That's a hell of a note."

Hauer: "I'll say."

He picked up the phone and dialed Lu Cetina's number.

Twenty-one

i

While the four uniformed policemen escorted Morales to his cell, Peter Hauer called for an order to go from Lucio's Cafe.

Buenrostro called the lab for copies of the cassettes. He labelled them and put them in his shirt pocket. Hauer cradled the phone and looked at Rafe Buenrostro.

"That closes the case on Lee Gómez Solís."

Buenrostro looked at the recorder. "Most likely, but I'm crossing the river tomorrow as planned. When Felipe Segundo comes over to identify the body, Lu'll have somebody at one of the bridges to tail him when he returns to Barrones."

"You think he'll cross to this side?"

Buenrostro mentioned the thirteen million in the local banks. He added that Felipe Segundo didn't know of the sequestration orders, and that was covered since Gwen Phillips had instructed the bankers not to breathe a word about it. Felipe Segundo needed working capital. That would bring him over. He'd use the body at the morgue as an excuse to cross the river.

"But which bridge, Rafe?"

"Art Styles will cover the four area bridges, no worry on that account. What Lu needs is reliable people on her side of the river."

Hauer pursed his lips for a moment. "I thought she'd cleaned those stables months ago. Not so?"

Buenrostro replied that money was still the biggest player across the river, and that Lu Cetina could still have a devil of a time. Still, the Belken County police would help. They'd keep her informed.

"What can they charge Felipe Segundo with across the river?"

Buenrostro said, "We can't hold him, either, but he's got to cross over to check on the money. The question is when."

Hauer said, "Well, posting men at the bridges and at the banks is going to take manpower. That calls for a lot of overtime."

"Chip wants the tank and all that firepower, Pete. He'll do anything to impress Boyd Hackett." He then explained Valencia's and Norm Andrews' promises about money for overtime.

"That's judo, Rafe."

Puzzled, Buenrostro asked, "How's that?"

"Using the opponent's strength and power to your advantage."

Buenrostro smiled. "I thought I was using psychology."

"No," laughed Peter Hauer, "it's judo, all right. Come on, Rafe, it's going on seven. I'll give you a ride to the parking lot."

ii

Buenrostro pulled into his driveway fifteen minutes later. The time was thirteen after seven. His wife, reading a book, looked up and helped him get out his jacket slowly.

"Tough day, Chief?"

A kiss before answering. "Long. What'd you have for supper?"

"Cold roast beef, fresh radishes, onions, garden tomatoes."

"I'll have some of that tomorrow. I have any beer left?"

"Yes, you do. I'll put one in the freezer."

"I'll just run up for a quick shower." Midway to the second floor, Buenrostro stopped and said, "Lee Gómez is dead."

Sammie Jo said, "Is he?"

Buenrostro told her of Morales's interview. The disarray at the Gómez Ranch, Morales's fear, and of the deaths of the pilot and the pair that got Lee out of the courthouse jail.

She asked if that were the end of the case, and Buenrostro said no. They'd be helping Lu Cetina, but he didn't know what evidence or charges she could bring up against Felipe Segundo. Sammie Jo Buenrostro argued that there had to be something. He shrugged and said, "I'm not up on the Napoleonic Code. Lu's case has to be made through a judge of instruction, but in any case, Lee's dead according to Morales.

"I'll be going back to the courthouse in a bit to check on him."

"Any chance of excavation, exhumation, out there?"

Buenrostro thought for a moment. Standing at the top of the stairs, he said, "Don't think so. Lu has to have a reason to get into the ranch.

Call Aunt Aggie for me. Ask her if she supervised Pediatrics at Mercy when the twin boys were born to the Gómez Solises."

She checked her watch. "It's going on eight o'clock, Rafe. The old dear goes to bed about now, but I'll try."

Dialing from the hall phone she said, "What's this about?"

"A bit of trolling, but it's also a check on Morales's accuracy. Keep that Beck's Dark chilled."

Sammie Jo Buenrostro laughed and dialed the Diocesan home for aged nuns. The home was a red-brick, seven-story high rise which had fallen into default by the builder who went bankrupt halfway through the job. Her father wrote off the loan as a loss and used part of the escrow money and part of the bank's to finish the building. Once completed, he donated it to the Sisters of Mercy.

Sammie Jo Buenrostro talked to the receptionist briefly.

She was right, the Sister was in bed.

Twenty-two

Thirty minutes later, Buenrostro was back in his office. The copies of the cassettes were on his desk; he placed them in the safe and checked the recorder for sound.

He handed a near-freezing can of Miller Lite to Morales. Buenrostro then called the desk sergeant and said, "I'm available only to my wife and to the squad, de la Cruz."

"Don't bother with the cuffs," he told one of the patrolmen.

"The chief inspector should know that I have not slept in thirty hours, but I am awake. The food reconstituted me.

"Anyway, *jefe*, I drove to Control yesterday. I went to a grocery store to place the monthly order, drank one beer at Chinese Fong's place, and then parked the pickup in front of Arturo's Restaurant. I took a room at the Escorial whorehouse.

"Early this morning, I returned to the grocery store, and I told the owner I would be back in a couple of hours. I then went to Arturo's Restaurant again, and half an hour later, at the appointed time, a taxi drove me to the bridge. I approached a county policeman, showed him my marijuana cigarettes, and here I am. The taxi driver sold me the marijuana."

"So don Felipe Segundo knows you are gone?"

"Perhaps not. Maybe he thinks I'm staying at the Escorial or at the Gold Palace whorehouse."

"There's a Gold Palace in Control as well?"

"Yessir, they're both owned by the Gómez family."

"Morales, I'm now going to talk about the Quevedo brothers. They hold you in respect as a reliable person. I talked to them a few days ago after Director Cetina captured them at the Flamingo."

"The Quevedos, of course. Ah, I know the Flamingo."

"How?"

"From don Lisandro, He used to send us there when we wanted company. But now don Felipe Segundo, he does not want us to go to Barrones."

"He give a reason?"

"He does not have to give or have a reason. Besides, he starts yelling whenever one of us asks a question. That's the way he is."

"The Quevedo brothers also say you are reliable."

"The Quevedos speak that way of me?"

There was admiration in the voice; wonderment too.

"The chief inspector is a serious man. I have heard this many times. You heard them say this?"

"Your name came up, and I asked if you were considered a reliable man."

There was a moment of silence as Morales stared at the floor.

"Let me say something to the chief inspector. I am a farmer and once I killed one man, and one man only. He was on ranch property."

"The Quevedos know of this and said so."

"Yes, and it is true, but that is not very much. Anyone can kill an enemy, someone like that. But to kill like Ramón or Gabriel Quevedo, that's different. I like to think I am hard, but . . ."

Buenrostro waited a second or two before repeating that the two Quevedos considered him, Morales, a reliable person.

"I am that. I do not lie. I have seen many, many, many terrible things at that ranch. I draw the line on the use of children, but then don Felipe Segundo is a sick man, and so I understand. I do not approve, no, but I recognize that that is a sickness with him."

"You told Ramón and Gabriel Quevedo of the man, then?"

"I brag to them."

"In the matter of the twins, what about them?"

"They're no good, neither one of them. I raised them, Chief Inspector, but I think they were born under an evil eye."

"You believe in the evil eye, Morales?"

The man nodded rapidly. His dark features took on the rigidity of a death mask before he spoke again.

"My mother knew the prayers. Years ago, when I first went to work for old man Gómez himself, don Inocencio, my mother took me aside. She said: 'Work hard, do not open your mouth, eat their food, but do not trust the young masters.' She meant don Lisandro and don Felipe Segundo.

"My mother died at age one hundred and three, Chief Inspector, and she also saw the twins grow up. They are worse, she advised. Seeds of a bad tree.

"For once in her life I thought she was wrong. I raised the twins, and, and, and loved them as a father loves his own sons.

"Too late I admitted I was wrong. So, I worked for them, ate their food, remained loyal, but would not play the fool."

There was a knock at the door. Peter Hauer and Ike Cantú.

"Called you at home, and Sammie Jo said we'd find you here. I thought Ike needed to be brought up to speed on this."

Hauer and Ike Cantú sat down by the door and looked at Morales.

"Last week, last Tuesday, the day of the killing, I made my plans to leave."

"Lee Gómez's killing," Hauer whispered, turning to Ike Cantú.

Morales turned away briefly and then spoke into the recorder.

"New people were coming to the ranch. Juan Carlos said they were South Americans. After my cousin was supposed to have died on that tractor accident of theirs, I was the only one left of the old crowd. Antonio Zavala? Dead. Aniceto and Cosme Guzmán? Both dead. Salas and Rocha, the barn burners? Murdered on this side of the river last week. In broad daylight, too.

"This I got from a woman at the Escorial. The whores, they know everything."

Buenrostro spoke: "The Quevedos killed those two. Go on."

"Well, after my cousin died three days ago, I feared I would not be allowed to go to Control for the monthly groceries. When young José Antonio gave me the keys to the pickup, I went to the kitchen and asked the cook what was needed. I wrote everything down, slept in the shed, skipped breakfast, and drove to Control early the next day.

"The only preparation was the taxi cab. I called from the grocery for a cab to pick me up the next day at Arturo's Restaurant. One cannot be too careful with people who have the evil eye, because, sometimes, they can read people's minds."

"But you got away?"

"Luck, *jefe*, and perhaps my mother's prayers from heaven."

"Now, Morales, do you know of a man called El Camarón Salinas? He's known as an expert driver and as a good man with a machine gun called the Thompson. An albino, and he's *gente dura*."

"I don't know such a man."

"He worked with, not for, a man named El Barco Zaragoza."

"Well, everybody knows of him, sure."

"But you yourself do not know Salinas?"

"As I said."

"He too was betrayed as the Quevedo brothers were betrayed."

"But this Salinas is alive?"

"By luck. I was a lieutenant at the time, and Salinas was saved from death only because my chief inspector was a wise man."

"No, I do not know the man Salinas."

"What can you tell me of the new men?"

"The South Americans? Young, secretive, and sometimes they use words I don't understand. They say 'ya, ya' a lot. Most of them look like you: clear-eyed, fair skin. Spanish. Like I said, they keep to themselves. I told myself that don Felipe Segundo did not buy himself a bargain."

"Sorry?"

"Those people are *gente dura.* Young, yes, but already tough. They also brought their own money."

"Are you saying it's a partnership? *¿Son socios?*"

"*Socios*, yes."

"We're almost through here. I'll tell you a story, Morales."

Morales nodded and looked Buenrostro in the eye.

"A few years ago, don Lisandro ordered the killing of some men in a country road cantina. El Camarón Salinas was the driver, but this is the point: One of our men was killed by mistake. He was an important man, and he was a friend of mine."

Morales leaned forward and said he understood. Buenrostro gauged the time on the microcassette.

"All right. Don Felipe Segundo bought a brand new white truck a few days ago."

"Yes, a General Motors product."

"A personal set of questions, Morales. Do you have a wife, and if so, is she in trouble?"

"I am widowed. I have no sons, and the only skin I guard is this one that holds my skeleton."

"You will be moved from place to place, from time to time. This is the way we do things in this country sometimes. If you left no trail, you have little to worry about."

"A personal question, Chief Inspector. You are a married man?"

"Yes."

"Do you worry about your wife, the children?"

"We have no children, but yes, I worry about my wife."

"A wise thing to do. You are facing madmen. My fear is that those South Americans are worse."

"One last thing, and you can rest. You are sure you saw Mr. Grayson in the plane?"

"No question."

"He is dead. You know this?"

"For a fact."

"And the other passengers?"

"Dead, too."

Buenrostro phoned the motor pool and asked to be driven home. While he waited for the car, Hauer and Ike Cantú labelled the new cassettes and took them upstairs for extra copies.

At five minutes to midnight, Buenrostro clicked on the lights to the rear screened porch and entered through the kitchen. There was a note on the breakfast table: *Hungry? The roast beef is delicious, and I saved some of the vegetables for you. S. J.*

He drank a glass of cold water and went upstairs.

The phone rang at exactly five twenty-one a.m. Buenrostro lifted the mouthpiece, put it on hold, and tiptoed to the kitchen.

"Yes."

There was a brief silence before Sam Dorson came on the line.

"Sorry, Rafe, but I've got bad news. Theo Crixell is dead. Murdered."

"Where are you?"

"In my car, on my way to the yacht basin. Pete's already on his way, and so's Dietz with the technical squad. Look, I've told Ike to come by and pick you up."

"Who got the call, and when did it come in?"

Dorson gave him the background information, and Buenrostro said he'd be ready in ten minutes.

Sammie Jo came down to the foot of the stairs. She looked at her husband as he put the phone down slowly. Looking up, he said, "Theo's been murdered. They found his body at the yacht basin."

"Oh, Rafe, I'm so sorry." She began to sob and stopped suddenly. "Rafe! Mandie and the girls, where are they?"

A grim Rafe Buenrostro said he didn't know. "I've got to get dressed. The warm-ups clean?"

Sammie Jo ran to the bedroom closet and brought underwear and the warm-up suit as Buenrostro got out of his pajamas.

"Ike'll be here in a few minutes. Call Theo's brother out at the ranch. I think that's where Mandie and the girls are. And call Sam's car phone as soon as you reach Mandie."

Sammie Jo Buenrostro put her arms around her husband. "Be careful," she whispered.

He kissed her on the cheek and walked to the driveway as the front lights of Ike Cantú's car threw a glow onto the front porch.

Twenty-three

Dorson, arms crossed, stood on the concrete sidewalk at the entrance of the marina. The weather was clear, the water calm, and the boats rocked gently in their slips. The technical squad's lights had turned early dawn into midmorning. Dorson's eyes took in the masts covered with blue sails which contrasted with the gleaming white of the thirty and fifty-five footers, the catamarans, as well as the occasional dory standing by for duty.

A tow truck operator puffing away on his pipe leaned against a lamppost and waited.

The trunk of the white 929 four-door Mazda revealed the bloodied body of Theo Crixell. Meanwhile, the technical squad was going about its business of dusting, taking photographs in and around the car.

Dorson had seen his share of blood during his sixteen years on the force, but this, he thought, this ranked among the worst: slashed chest, throat, hands and arms. Tortured. But how did they get hold of him? A phone call, perhaps, and if so, how did they come up with the unlisted number? He stopped for a moment, swore, and said, "Daniel Varela." So, reasoned Dorson, it wouldn't have mattered how often Theo changed his number; the kid would get it from his mother.

He looked up and saw Hauer and a man in white ducks heading in his direction.

"This is Harry Atkins, he's the night manager."

"My name's Dorson. You place the call?"

Atkins said he did and explained how he saw the car blocking part of the sidewalk. There'd been a party at the fifty-footer on slip H A the night before. The party broke up around four; when he had gone on his usual round at four-thirty, he found the car blocking the sidewalk. Soon after, one of the early tarpon fishermen complained about the car blocking the way. He'd checked the license plate and found it did not belong to a club member, and that's when he called the towing company. The tow truck driver started to hook up the car and it was he who noticed the blood on the sidewalk.

"Who gave the party?"

"The Gilberts. Two women, Rhonda and Winona. They have a party every week."

"On weekdays?"

"Whenever, officer. They got money."

"Where are the Gilberts now?"

"They don't sleep in. The yacht's a party boat. They raise it up every six months or so, scrape its bottom, and set it down again. Like I said, a party boat. I got the address in this here book."

"Who cleans up?"

"We got high school kids who do that. They'll be in this afternoon."

Dorson said, "Not today." He then told two policemen to place yellow tape around the yacht.

"Who's the manager and when does he come in?"

"She, detective. Her name's Merle Blankenship, and she comes around seven, about the time I go off. She's down in Cancún, though."

Dorson looked up and saw Ike Cantú and Buenrostro get out of their car and walk immediately to the white Mazda.

Dorson said, "Take over, Pete."

Hauer: "I need those phone numbers, Mr. Atkins. Let's go to the office."

Buenrostro stared hard at Theo Crixell's car. "Get it to the motor pool as soon as you can, and don't wait for the county tow truck. We'll use this one here."

Buenrostro stopped suddenly and looked at Sam Dorson who was swearing softly. "What did they do to him, Rafe? He was covered in blood."

Buenrostro said, "Henry Dietz will tell us that end of it."

Dorson swore again. "And there was a wild party going, not fifty feet away."

"Get on that guest list right away. We'll roust those partygoers out of bed. I'll be at the courthouse. Ike'll join you inside the yacht as soon as they're through in there." He and Dorson parted in silence.

Buenrostro called his wife on the car phone and learned that Mandie Crixell and the girls were indeed staying at the ranch.

Sammie Jo broke the news to Mandie and said she'd be driving out to Relámpago to be with her. Buenrostro then called the lab and was told Dr. Dietz was still somewhere out at the yacht basin. He replaced the car phone in its case and drove to the courthouse.

He immediately thought of Daniel Varela and Theo's unlisted numbers.

With the Varela kid in the picture, the trail of thought led straight to the Gómez family. Buenrostro walked into his office, checked his messages, and found two from Chip Valencia. He glanced at his watch. Five to seven, too early for the D.A. to be in his office. He dialed anyway.

"Belken County District Attorney's office. This is Adam Jurado."

"Rafe Buenrostro, Adam. I've got two calls from Chip. What's up?" He noticed that his voice had a tone of irritability to it.

"It's about Theo, Chief. Chip got a call at home this morning, and he called all of us to the courthouse."

Buenrostro turned the phone away for a moment, breathed deeply and said, as evenly as he could, "We're on the case, tell him that." He hung up without a further word.

The phone rang again and he answered it. It was Dorson. He would take the Gilbert women and after that, Peter Hauer and Ike Cantú would see to the guest list. Fourteen in all including the Gilberts, and one surprise, he said: The pilot's wife–widow–Laura Grayson was one of the party guests. Peter Hauer was on his way to see her now.

Dorson described the mess in the yacht. Cocaine dust in the main room, and the smell of marijuana remained as strong as ever in the enclosed quarters. It had taken the lab crew the better part of an hour to crate, box, and bag the bottles, glasses, dishes, cigarettes, napkins, and anything else they could find. Part of the technical squad worked on the sofas and carpets, the bathrooms and the bedrooms. With the yellow tape in place, Dorson ordered two policemen to stand guard. Buenrostro brought Sam Dorson up to date on the Morales interviews.

"Lee's dead?" repeated Dorson, dully. Buenrostro said he'd call Lu Cetina to see how she was doing on getting Felipe Segundo to cross the river to identify the body.

After the call to Lu, he called Henry Dietz and asked for a preliminary autopsy. Irene Paredes, Dietz's top assistant, said her boss was working on Theo now.

He thanked her and rang off.

Two hours later, a sleepy-eyed Henry Dietz walked into the empty squadroom. He knocked on Buenrostro's door, served himself some freshly made coffee and sat down.

"Theo was shot twice. A Glock. This was followed by a beating and then came the mutilation. And semen, Rafe. No penetration. Someone masturbated and wiped the semen over Theo's body."

Dietz shook his head. Buenrostro listened carefully and tried to show no emotion. Finally, he sighed and walked around the room to relax.

Henry Dietz went on. "He'd been turned over, the blood emptied into the trunk, and that's how some of it dripped onto the sidewalk. He'd first been wrapped in heavy-duty laundry bags, though. We found them out in the parking lot. A trail of blood led us to them. I'm just giving you the bare bones here. I'm having the full report typed upstairs. You got anything?"

"No, but Mandie and the kids are safe."

"Thank the Lord for that. The work of a sadist, Rafe."

"You said that. One person, you think?"

"No, I'm just talking. It could've been more. Had to be, to carry the body to and from."

Buenrostro said, "For Mandie's sake, we're saying he was shot and killed and that's it. Chip hears about the mutilation, and he'll call the papers in a second."

He stood in the middle of his office and looked at his desk. It held a picture of a St. Joseph's class reunion taken a few years back.

"Thanks, Henry."

Dietz nodded, deep in thought.

"A bit of news for you. Lee Gómez was killed the day he was sprung out of here."

"Good," Henry Dietz said, and left the room.

Buenrostro took the interview tapes out of the safe. An hour later, he returned them to the safe. He then opened his office closet, drew a pair of slacks and a shirt, and rode the elevator to one of the basement showers.

Morales thinks the Gómezes are mad. A possibility. It could be the twins are dipping into their own dope. What's the Gilbert connection? Is there a connection? These and other questions occupied his mind while he showered. A few minutes later, he rubbed himself briskly and set his mind on the case again.

The Varela kid, befriended by the Gómez twins, gave them Theo's number. That's easy. Young Varela's murder? Get rid of everyone connected with Lee Gómez's escape, including Lee himself.

But Lu Cetina had foiled the killing of the Quevedos, and Felipe Segundo had to be wondering where the brothers were. And now Morales. No reason for Felipe Segundo to think that Morales had turned himself in. As for the Quevedo brothers, there was the matter of payment, and Felipe Segundo would have to think on this.

Buenrostro returned to his office. No new messages. It was now nine o'clock. He made himself a second pot of coffee.

It's usually the other way around, isn't it? he thought. First a beating, then maybe a slash or two for pain and suffering, and then the shooting. But Dietz said Theo'd been shot first. Did Theo put up a fight? And what got him out to the yacht basin in the first place? Probably a simple explanation to that, too.

But the question is, what did Theo Crixell have? Nothing new, he decided. The day Lee escaped, Judge Ochoa was set to rule against him and his lawyers. The trial was to start in a week's time. Building on the information the county handed to the feds, the government would tack its sentence to the state's, which would come to fifty years for Lee. No parole there.

Theo resigns because of the threats to his family, but that doesn't help Lee's situation since Theo had already nailed an airtight box around him. It didn't matter who tried Lee. Theo hadn't resigned until he had brought the best case forward.

Trust Theo Crixell to hang in there.

Buenrostro picked up the phone, dialed home and left a message for his wife. After this, he put on a tie and took the elevator to the District Attorney's office. In the hallway he ran into four secretaries who were sopping wet.

"Morning, Chief," one of them said, laughing. "Aren't we a mess? Raining like it won't quit." He looked at them and before he spoke, one of them said, "Yes, I know. It's August."

The secretaries took off their shoes and rode in the elevator with him.

TWENTY-FOUR

Two days later, Cantú and Hauer sat at their desks after having turned in their reports on the partygoers. They listened to the Morales tapes one more time before Hauer returned them to Buenrostro's safe. He drew a Sprite from the fridge.

Just then, Dorson entered the squadroom and sneezed.

"What a day. After yesterday's downpour, I got an allergy attack coming in from the motor pool. I must've sneezed a hundred times between here and there. Will you look at this shirt? Anybody got a spare?"

Dorson blew his nose into an already damp handkerchief. He looked at it and threw it into a wastebasket.

Cantú went to the closet and handed Dorson a shirt. Dorson's eyes were already bloodshot from his sneezing.

Hauer to Dorson: "Seen Rafe?"

"Just saw him in the hallway. Talking to the desk sergeant. You guys come up with anything?"

Cantú answered for him and Hauer. "Finished the yacht interviews, and then Pete and I listened to the tapes again. A country churchyard, Sam. Lee's dead. The French-Canadian guys are dead. Grayson. And there we were, chasing the wrong guy for a week."

"An uncomplicated man, Morales. Things got too crazy for him out at the ranch." Dorson reached for a Kleenex and suppressed a sneeze. "Yeah, those cassettes were something. They killed Lee, just like that. Some family."

Rafe Buenrostro entered the room and leaned on a filing cabinet. "Sam, you go first. And what happened to your shirt?"

"Allergies." He sat down, blew his nose, and took out his pad.

"Struck oil in Flora. A middle-aged Lothario named John Blasig admitted he saw a white Jimmy in the lot. Had a hell of a time getting it out of him, though. Seems he was in a Mazda with a woman other than his wife. The car belongs to a Jay Taylor. Mr. Taylor was the widow Laura Grayson's escort that evening, and Blasig bought the dope."

"Talk about a merry widow," said Hauer.

Dorson blew his nose again. "Called Taylor from Blasig's house and asked him what kind of car he had. A 626 Mazda, smaller than Theo's and cream, not white.

"Anyway, I wormed out Blasig's dalliance just in time. His wife drove up, blocked my car at the driveway, and came storming up the porch wanting to know just who the hell I was. She said her husband knew 'nothing about no Mazda car.' I said this was a murder investigation, and I also wanted to know where they got the dope for the party. That rattled her, and she blurted out Blasig had bought it off two young Mexican hunks who looked like brothers. The partygoers all pitched in to pay for a thousand bucks worth of crap, she said.

"Blasig's relieved as hell, of course. Said he'd seen the white Jimmy the young guys drove. and they headed toward Jonesville. 'Round midnight. No 929 Mazda, though."

Hauer cut in. "The 929 was there later. Laura Grayson saw it. So did Taylor. Around three or so. I called Taylor from the widow's house, and he confirmed the 929 and the time, give or take half an hour."

Rafe waited for Cantú, who was filling a large tea glass with ice cubes and water.

"My six," Cantú said, "were either drunk or coked out, and that included an old couple in their seventies, the Stevensons, from Edgerton. They left around four, at least that's what they think they did. Checked with Marina Cabs and got the time: three forty-five. A multiple fare shared with a lovely couple, the Almanzas. Last thing these two remembered before the ride home was going to one of the cabins in the yacht for a roll. They found the bed occupied, so they just went at each other on the floor. They too saw the 929."

Hauer laughed and asked, "They told you about the lovemaking?"

Cantú shrugged. "Anyway, they gave the Stevensons a ride to the Bliss Hotel, the one here in Klail. The other two, Howard Politz and his secretary-girlfriend, Wanda Baum, left earlier, around two. They didn't see the 929. I took a statement from the Almanzas that they saw the 929, and they signed what I read to them."

Cantú took a sip of ice water.

Hauer walked to a corner wastebasket and got rid of his empty Sprite can. He leaned against the nearest wall, and read his notes.

"The widow. She saw the 929 and the white Jimmy both. The Jimmy around midnight, the 929 around four a.m. Claims she doesn't do dope and didn't see who bought it or from whom."

Dorson said, "Bull."

"That's her story. But Taylor came through, as said. Now, I called a friend at Southwestern Bell and he's sending us a record of calls to Theo's house from two months back. About the time the harassment began. It'll be faxed today."

The interoffice phone buzzed as Hauer was finishing his report.

Cantú picked up the phone: "Yes, what? What? Yeah, got it. Thanks." Cantú looked around and smiled before he said, "Art Styles. Felipe Segundo just crossed at Los Indios Bridge. Driving a white Jimmy, and he's got one of the twins with him."

Dorson: "Los Indios? That gives us an hour."

Buenrostro: "The locksmith'll be waiting in the parking lot. We'll drown Felipe Segundo with paperwork, that'll give Dietz's people enough time to go over the vehicle."

Turning to Ike Cantú, he said: "Go up and get the locksmith. Sam, call Lu–she's waiting for our call. We're going to settle the twins' birthright, and we'll find out if Morales knows what he's talking about."

Smiling at Hauer, he said, "Pete, who do you know at the phone company?"

TWENTY-FIVE

As Buenrostro dialed, Hauer asked, "What was your aunt's name when she was at Villa María and Mercy?"

Buenrostro flicked on the amplifier. "Sister John Birkman. Eighty-five, if she's a day."

The operator came on the line in time to hear Buenrostro say his aunt's name.

"Yes, she's here, and who shall I say is calling, please?"

"Her nephew. My name's Rafe Buenrostro."

"Oh, yes, of course, the policeman. I'll put her through."

Agnes Rincón-Buenrostro came on the line.

"Hello, Aunt Aggie. It's Rafe, how are you?"

"I'm fine, dear. How is your lovely wife?"

"She's doing well, thanks."

The formalities over, he said, "I need a favor. I need for you to go back some twenty years, Aunt Aggie. About the time you ran Pediatrics at Mercy."

"Yes?" The voice was slightly hesitant.

"It's about the Gómez Solís family. From Soliseño Ranch. I'm asking about twins born some twenty years ago. Do you remember the mother's name? And do you recall who the father was?"

The other three detectives kept their eyes on the amplifier.

"Of course, I do, you silly boy. Her name was Blanca Gallardo, of the upriver Gallardos. They're not related to us, you understand. She married . . . oh, that husband of hers. That young pup I never cared for, God forgive me. Didn't he become a policeman, too?"

Buenrostro waited.

After a few seconds she came on again. "Yes, I remember now. His name was Lisandro, and he was a policeman, one of their *federales* over there. Wasn't there a scandal? Give me a second now, okay?"

Buenrostro massaged his shoulder, which had stiffened from the damp weather.

"He's the Gómez Solís, Rafe, not the woman. She's a Gallardo, like I said."

"Now, did the couple raise the children?"

"What was that?"

"Did they–Blanca and Lisandro, did they raise the twins?"

She scoffed at that and said, "Well, I don't see why not? They were both young, in good health, and they had property. What a question."

Dorson, Cantú, and Hauer broke out in grins.

Crotchety, but on target, thought Buenrostro.

"Think back, old girl. Was there anything? A death, a divorce."

She interrupted. "Divorce? In those families? Where's your common sense, boy?"

Buenrostro refused to let go of the bone.

"I heard Lisandro's older brother had raised the boys as his own. Is that news to you?"

"Oh, I didn't care for the older brother, either. He was too good-looking and bound to get into trouble, I'm telling you."

Buenrostro laughed. "Is it coming back, Auntie?"

"Yes, and I apologize for calling you silly. I'll be forgetting my manners next. The girl Blanca went mad, didn't she? Anyway, it was said she went mad when the twins–they were boys–when the twin boys were not two years old. There was an annulment. The Mexican bishop stepped in. Who did you say raised them?"

"I didn't. But I heard it was the older brother."

She laughed this time.

"Yes, the pretty boy I just mentioned. The one your father called Charles the Fifth, although his real name was Philip the Second. A king's name. *Felipe Segundo.* Wasn't that pretentious of them? And why do you want to know? Probably some nosy police matter, isn't it?"

"Yes, it is. When are you retiring anyway?"

Her clear laughter came over the amplifier again.

"I'll remind you I retired from Mercy ten years ago, and Sammie Jo gave me a television set at my retirement party. I'm now taking care of the older nuns here." She giggled this time. "I'm only eighty-five, Rafe-Boy."

He thanked her, said goodbye, and replaced the phone gently on its cradle.

Hauer: "She's some girl, that aunt of yours."

Buenrostro smiled and said, "Corroborates what Morales said. Pete, go upstairs and make two more copies of the cassettes. When you get back, give one to Sam, place one in our files, and the originals go into the wall safe. Stay at the lab until they hand them to you."

Dorson asked, "Any beer left?"

Buenrostro pointed to the small fridge. He called the desk sergeant.

"De la Cruz, has Mrs. Buenrostro called?"

"No, sir. No calls."

Dorson opened the beers and handed them out.

Ike Cantú: "Will Lu have trouble convincing that judge of instruction?"

"Not if we keep Morales alive. The cassettes should help her."

Cantú again: "So who else knows he's here?"

"Phil Moody at Vice, and that's it. Haven't told Chip yet."

After a long pull at his beer, Dorson said, "You know, Lu may just want us to keep Morales on this side of the river until she's assigned a judge of instruction."

A short while later, Hauer came back armed with the tapes, and Dorson opened a beer for him.

Cantú: "Isn't some judge on this side going to ask about a court-appointed attorney for Morales?"

Dorson: "He's not under arrest. He's under protective custody."

Hauer to Buenrostro: "What's the plan?"

"No plan. A grieving brother is coming over to identify a body that washed up on our side of the Rio Grande."

He laughed, and both Cantú and Hauer, puzzled, looked at him.

Buenrostro said, "I'm sure they washed the Jimmy and scrubbed it clean. It doesn't matter. The lab people will find something. They always do. Let's go upstairs and talk to Phil Moody at Vice about Morales. We need to move him to the Flads jail."

Twenty-six

"Now, we're not to give any importance to Felipe Segundo's presence. Ike, he doesn't know you. Put on a lab coat and lead him to the morgue. We'll see what happens after that. After I see Phil Moody, at Vice, I'll pick up Morales downstairs."

While they waited, Dorson worked on his notes as he listened to the Morales tape one more time while Hauer moved paper around as he arranged the Theo Crixell file. Hauer inserted the Morales cassettes into a brown, letter-sized envelope, identified it, and locked the tapes in his top desk drawer.

A few minutes later, he dialed the front desk and asked for a clerk to run off a copy of the Crixell paper file.

For his part, Cantú called Henry Dietz. "I'm bringing in Felipe Segundo as soon as he comes in."

Dietz gave a nasty laugh. "I always enjoy a good performance." He hung up.

An outside call came in and Hauer picked up the phone. It was Buenrostro: "On my way to Flads. See you."

Cantú poured himself another glass of water as Al Contreras, the morning desk sergeant, entered the squadroom.

"Visitors from across. Here's his card. He's a got a young guy with him."

Dorson read the card. "Felipe Segundo Gómez Solís. Ingeniero Agrónomo."

He said, "Your show, Ike," and handed him the card.

Ike Cantú put on a lab coat and said to Contreras. "Tell them I'll be there in a few minutes." He went out the side door.

After this, Hauer and Dorson signed for a county car and drove to Bishop's Savings and Loan. From there, Dorson walked to the Klail State Bank, two blocks away. They were to wait at each institution to see if Felipe Segundo attempted to withdraw the family money.

Vice President Billy Ed Perry was grace itself when Dorson asked for a phone. He called Lu Cetina and said he'd be delayed.

After a brief introduction, Ike Cantú led the Gómezes to the elevator. Cantú took stock: Felipe Segundo in a fancy white guayabera shirt with red piping on the front; embroidered initials on the top right-hand pocket. Sunglassses. Tailored denims. Light-tan suede cowboy boots. A five-star Stetson in his right hand. No jewelry except for a Rolex.

The young man had introduced himself as José Antonio Gómez. As tall as Cantú at five-ten, but stocky, not trim. Mustached as was his father, he wore his white silk shirt with the first three buttons undone to show an ample supply of chest hair and gold chains. The shirt was cut jacket-fashion, and Cantú guessed it too was tailor-made. Washed-out Levi's covered his hand-tooled black half-boots. He wore neither hat nor sunglasses, and his tanned skin contrasted with the deep set green eyes.

Two secretaries entered the elevator with them. The women took stock too, but father and son looked straight ahead. Leaving the elevator, Cantú pointed to a gleaming white door. He knocked before entering and held the door for them.

An attendant greeted Ike Cantú, who asked for locker number seven. He initialed a standard form and then joined the pair, who stood under a bright light some fifteen feet away.

At this point, white-coated Henry Dietz walked into the refrigerated room and nodded to the group. He checked his watch and scribbled briefly on a notebook lying on top of a small steel desk. After this, he went through several keys, found the one he was looking for, and locked the notebook in the top drawer.

Situation normal; a typical day at the office.

As Dietz left, Cantú said, "That's Dr. Henry Dietz, the medical examiner. You wish to talk to him?" Felipe Segundo shook his head.

Presently, the attendant wheeled in the body for identification. Neither man reacted at the sight of the mangled body. Felipe Segundo looked at it briefly, said it was brother's and requested removal of the body for burial at the family cemetery in the Soliseño Ranch. And when could this be arranged?

At this point, Cantú led them to the morgue's main office and had them fill out an international transfer request. A bothersome but necessary formality, he explained.

A few minutes later, Cantú showed them a death certificate which also took time to fill out. When the Gómezes asked about arrangements, Cantú said the county would make them, and that he'd call the family at the ranch later that afternoon. This was agreed to. It took another twenty minutes to sign, notarize, and have seven copies run off. When these were distributed, Ike Cantú once again led the way to the elevator. When they reached the lobby, Ike Cantú offered to accompany them to the parking lot. They thanked him after a polite refusal, and thanked him again for his time.

On his way back to the squad room, Ike Cantú checked the elapsed time: forty-five minutes. Ample time, he said to himself.

Sitting at his desk, Cantú typed a brief note giving the time of the visit to the lab by the Gómezes. He reread a copy of the Crixell file placed on his desk by the desk sergeant.

Half an hour later, Cantú finished reading the file and locked it in Sam Dorson's desk. He was rinsing the glass when the phone rang. It was Buenrostro. "Just crossed the Dellis County line. Anything new?"

Cantú told him about the visit to the lab and their request for removal of the body. Buenrostro said, "Have the desk sergeant call Felipe Segundo later this afternoon. He's to tell them everything's been arranged. Sam there?"

"No, he and Pete went to the S&L and the bank. They haven't called yet."

Buenrostro rang off and drove Morales to the Flads jail.

TWENTY-SEVEN

i

Sam Dorson and Peter Hauer were back at the office by one o'clock; the Gómezes had not checked on their bank accounts. Dorson then called Art Styles, who told him the Gómezes had returned by way of Control. After this, Dorson called the lab and asked for Henry Dietz, who answered the phone on the first ring.

"Sam, I'm finishing the DNA right now. I'll call you back in an hour or so." Dorson said he'd be at the office waiting for the call.

He checked his watch; time to call Lu Cetina.

After half a dozen tries to connect with the Barrones central operator, he heard a faint whirr come over the line.

"¡Bueno! Diga. ¿Qué número, por favor? Repita, por favor. Ocho, nueve, cero, tres, cuatro, dos. El ocho, nueve, cero, tres, cuatro, dos. Entendido. Un momentito, por favor. Ya."

"Lu?"

"Hi, Sam. Sorry about the delay. Same old thing, last night's rain storm fouled up the phone system. How're the allergies?"

"Oh, they're doing fine." Static came on the line, and he waited.

"Can you hear me all right, Lu?"

"Yes. How about you?"

"Fine, fine. Let me bring you up to date."

Dorson told her of Morales's transfer to Dellis County, of the upcoming transfer of the anonymous body to the Gómez Ranch, and the connection between the white Jimmy and Theo Crixell's murder.

For her part, she said the new people at Soliseño Ranch were South Americans, as Morales had indicated. As for the photos, she went on, smudges and all, they were clear enough for three different student groups at the dancing clubs to identify Daniel Varela and the Solís twins. Four of the youngsters had gone to school with them as kids at Don Bosco school.

And now, she added, with luck running her way, she had drawn Manuel de Jesús Avila as her judge of instruction.

"Things are looking up, Lu."

"Sorry? Can't hear you."

"I said things are going your way, finally."

"Yes, and about time." Static crackled along the line for a few seconds and stopped as quickly as it started.

"Lu?"

"Yes, I can hear you okay now. Look, I've assigned two full-time men to Control to watch the Soliseño Ranch. But here's the best part, a group of businessmen from Tampico donated two Pipers to us. We'll use one of them to fly over the ranch as soon as they've overhauled. That'll be some two, three weeks from now. How's that?"

"Congratulations. Anything else?"

Lu Cetina said it was a personal favor, and it concerned the Quevedo brothers. Since the murders took place outside of Mexico, the judge of instruction would most likely request a primary investigating officer from Texas to corroborate the evidence.

Sam Dorson replied that he had done this on another occasion, and he couldn't foresee any problem in anyone of them presenting evidence. With this settled, they both rang off.

ii

Enrique Salinas, the albino, was back home from his visit to the doctor. There was nothing to be done, he was told; the cancer was inoperable. As he was helped out of the car by his son Eduardo, he asked to be seated in the garden; they would drink their limeade there. The weather remained stiflingly hot and humid, and he preferred to sit on the patio, instead of in the house that was cool only because it was kept shuttered and in partial darkness. Eduardo moved his father's cushioned chair under the cool shadow of a chinaberry tree and went to the kitchen for some fresh limes.

Sitting as comfortably as his pain would let him, El Camarón thought of his old friend, El Barco Zaragoza, a victim of diabetes and now suffering the loss of an unhealing leg. His mind went back to the obligation, the favor, he had promised the chief inspector. True, the chief inspector would never approve of what Salinas wanted to do for him, but that didn't bother Enrique Salinas. A favor was a favor.

Studying his son as the young man poured the limeade, the elder Salinas said to himself: "He will carry out our plan, our revenge."

Enrique Salinas coughed violently and brought his handkerchief to his mouth. No, no sign of blood. Not yet, he thought, but it'll come.

"What's the date, Eduardo?"

"The twelfth of August, the day of San Fortino."

Eduardo smiled at his father and lifted his glass to him as if making a toast. Enrique Salinas smiled at his son and then shaded his eyes. Even in the dark shade of the chinaberry tree, the sun was far too bright for his albino eyes; he adjusted his sunglasses.

The two sat in silence for over a quarter of an hour. Eduardo served his father the remaining half glass, cleaned up the serving table and went into the kitchen.

El Camarón had made up his mind: "I'll ask him to carry out his father's last favor."

iii

"Want to stop for a beer, Morales?"

"Yes, thank you, Chief Inspector. You know, I've never been to Dellis County before today. What accounts for the absence of palm trees, the *huisache*, the *retamas*, and the scrub oaks in this part of the Valley?"

"It's the beginning of the upper Valley's dry area. Haven't you ever been upriver from Barrones, on the way to Laredo?"

A shake of the head. "This looks like another country. And poor, too. The people are the same, yes, but I don't see much green grass. What grows here?"

"Sandy enough for cantaloupes and watermelons, I imagine. I understand you are a good farmer, Morales. The Quevedos laughed when we asked them if you worked as a farmhand."

"They do not know everything. I was raised on a farm, Chief Inspector. But this land here, full of limestone, alkaline and gravel and caliche pits, is not inviting. Not like the lower Valley."

Buenrostro: "There's a restaurant."

"You are hiding me from don Felipe Segundo, aren't you? Well, I am not afraid to die, but one must not look at death in the eye prematurely. Do you agree?"

Buenrostro smiled. "You've committed no major crime we can charge you with. You're with me as a special guest."

"And you tell me this because . . . ?"

"Because you can leave whenever you want to."

"I choose to stay, Chief Inspector. To return to Control, to the ranch, is to seek one's death before its appointed time.

"One question, Chief Inspector: When I order from the menu, what can I order?"

Twenty-eight

i

At six o'clock the morning following Theo Crixell's funeral, Rafe Buenrostro, cup of coffee in hand, went to the east porch of his house and looked for the morning paper. He had been at this for a minute or two when he finally spotted the plastic-wrapped edition resting in the middle of a particularly thick bougainvillea bush.

The *Klail City Enterprise* carried a brief story on Theo's funeral in the City-State section. He folded that section and placed it in the magazine rack; a call to the crime lab brought him up on the latest reports.

Thirty minutes later he took a shower and dressed for work. Sammie Jo joined him for his second cup and asked about work.

"Sam called late last night on a DNA report. We're sure now that the Gómez twins murdered Theo out of vengeance. For now, it's a Mexican affair, but if we catch them on this side of the river . . ." He left the sentence hanging.

He took a sip and went on: "We've faxed Lu Theo's fingerprints, the pictures at the yacht basin, some shots of the Jimmy taken at the courthouse parking lot, the DNA material, and so on." He checked his watch. "The reports from the technical staff as well as statements by two witnesses are being faxed now."

Sammie Jo said, "All you can do is wait for the twins to cross, isn't it? Otherwise, it remains a Mexican case."

"That's about it. If we nabbed them, we'd indict them here, fight the extradition, and try them here, of course."

Sammie Jo poured herself a cup of coffee and passed the toast to Buenrostro.

"Is this is a foolish question, Rafe? Why doesn't Lu barge in with federal troops and arrest that Felipe Segundo person and those two budding monsters of his?"

"She could, but it could mean a lot of bloodshed. She's in a bind, Lu is. What she'll do—and this is a supposition—is that she'll build a case, present it to the judge of instruction, and try to convince him. This is a sort of cart-before-the-horse type of thing."

"How do you mean?"

"Lu usually arrests someone on suspicion and rounds out the case after talking to the person charged, and then she presents her case to that judge I mentioned." He took a deep breath and exhaled slowly. "They just may have themselves a bloodbath over there. Gotta go."

He bent down for a kiss, winced a bit and Sammie Jo said, "I'll make an appointment and have the doctor look at that shoulder again."

Buenrostro pulled a face. "It'll hurt for a while, he told me so."

"Men," she said, as she walked to the driveway. She blew him a kiss as he drove away.

Buenrostro called his office. De la Cruz, that morning's desk sergeant, answered.

"It's me, I'm driving in. Can we get through to Barrones yet?"

"Earlier we could. Not now. Last night's sudden rain came on top of the other one on the previous night. But we got the faxes through early this morning. You never know with Teléfonos de México, Chief."

"Well, on the chance they reach us, keep the director on the line until I get there."

"Yessir."

The all-night guard said good morning and held the door for him. Buenrostro entered through the side door into an empty squad room. He jiggled the coffee pot. Empty. He prepared a pot before going to his office.

"How's our Barrones connection, de la Cruz?"

"No luck, Chief. Shall I make us some coffee?"

"It'll start to perk in a minute."

He sat down and wrote down the names now connected to the case. After this, he wrote the word *motive*. A takeover. After a while, he walked to the coffee pot and served himself a cup. He sat at his desk again. As simple as that, and as brutal. Felipe Segundo takes over from his brother, and he also took over Lee's sons. Why keep the adoption a secret?

Probably not relevant, he said to himself. His mind wandered. The Varela family? Victims. And there was Mrs. Grayson, newly widowed but partying at the yacht basin where the twins showed up. As for her husband, all he had was Morales's testimony. As convincing as it sounded, it remained testimony until the bodies were dug up.

When Lu brings Felipe Segundo's file to the judge of instruction, Laura Grayson will learn she's been a widow for over two weeks. Some news, he thought.

The French-Canadians. They knew the risks; bet they never figured on a double cross, though. Wonder how much they were offered?

The beginnings of a cemetery. The two at the parking lot, young Daniel Varela, Grayson, the Canadians, and Lee.

He thought on the Quevedo brothers momentarily. Lucky.

Buenrostro went back mentally to Morales's statement. Ah, yes. His cousin, the deaf-mute, had been murdered. *Mr. Grayson? Oh, sure. A Spanish-speaking gringo, with a pretty wife.* And other workers, whose names Morales had mentioned and Buenrostro had already forgotten. *I was the only one left of the old crowd . . .*

So Felipe Segundo was re-forming the gang and the operation. No one across the river except for Morales knew anything. Felipe Segundo could begin with a clean slate. What was it Lu Cetina told Sam Dorson? That she feared Barrones would wind up looking like Chicago during Prohibition. Too late, Lu, the surviving Gómez brother beat you to it.

He thought on yesterday's services for Theo at the cemetery. And where was Chip Valencia? And Norm Andrews, for that matter? Out politicking with the local God-fearing, tax-paying citizens who had a finger in every city and county commission hearing and decision. Then it struck him: If the services had been by invitation only, that must've been Mandie's decision. He'd have to ask Sammie Jo.

He laughed softly and remembered somewhat vaguely not having had much to laugh about lately. How like Theo Crixell to have the last word, he thought. He walked into the squad room for a second cup of coffee.

ii

Three miles west of Klail City on the way to Flora, a late-model gray Dodge minivan parallel-parked a block away from the Flora Pawn Shop. Three men crouched in the back, waiting for orders. The man in the front passenger's seat talked to the driver.

"Remember, Del, you wait until Tomás back there stands by the front window of the pawn shop. As soon as he starts the first swing of the sledgehammer, you gun this thing. He gets out of the way, and then you crash right smack into that front glass window. It don't matter who comes rushing to the plate glass after Tom breaks the damn thing. Run 'em down if they're standing there. That'll add to the confusion, anyway. You should be doing forty to fifty after a block or so, right?"

The man called Del nodded absently.

"Remember, don't stop. You barge right in halfway to the store, if you have to. We'll be outta there in less than ten minutes."

The leader then turned to the man he called Tomás. "Start walking."

The leader moved to the back of the minivan. *Mexicans,* he thought. He spoke to them in fluent Spanish. "All right, you know exactly where the guns are stacked. Don't stop for anything else. We don't want money. We want guns and ammo, stick to that. I'll shoot through the roof, that'll panic whoever's left standing.

"I'll help relay the boxes and Tomás will push 'em into the van. Questions?"

He looked across the way; the man with the sledgehammer was ready.

He then leaned over and said, "Go, Del. Kick this thing in the ass. Move it!"

The minivan shot out toward the pawnshop and crashed through the front window. The driver revved the motor and put the engine on neutral. The falling glass was followed by the crashing of the van into the middle of the store amid the cries of frightened customers. Some of them hit the floor. As they did so, the driver ran over them at full force. He then put the van in reverse and ran over the bodies again.

The van's windshield was partially covered with blood, as was the hood. The driver again ran over the dead and injured as the crew began loading the minivan.

The operation took twelve minutes. The men piled in the back of the minivan and waited.

"Go." That was the only word said, but no one heard it save the driver, who U-turned onto the country highway and drove westward. He drove a quarter of a mile and turned sharply onto the first dirt road on the left, toward the river. When the minivan came to a halt, the men in the back, still puffing from the exertion, dashed out of the backdoor on signal.

They began unloading and stacking the weapons and the ammunition into two waiting 210 Cessnas. That took twenty minutes.

The leader said to the Mexicans: "Here's fifteen-hundred dollars, men. Until you're better paid." The three placed their weapons under the seat of one of the Cessnas and shook hands all around.

The driver of the minivan mounted one of the planes and waved at the man called Tomás.

The Mexican nationals pocketed the money and walked across a sugarcane field; from there, they made for the levee facing a farm across the river and sat down. The man called Tomás offered his friends a cigarette; they sat down and watched the Cessnas fly across the river into Mexico. Within a few minutes, the planes disappeared into a cloudbank.

The men then removed their shoes, tied them together, and clamped their teeth on the shoelaces. Without a word, they dove in and swam across the Rio Grande.

Twenty-nine

Sam Dorson took his coffee cup with him when he answered the telephone. The words came in a rush: "Help! Stop! Thief! You bastards!" Dorson told the caller to cup the mouthpiece and to speak directly into it.

"Listen! We got five, maybe six, dead and wounded people here. Jesus."

"What's your name, and where are you calling from?"

"My name's Dan Ríos, and I'm calling you from the Flora Pawn Shop, we're on the west side highway. Got that?"

"Got it."

"No, don't hang up. Call an ambulance, a bunch of 'em, and doctors, and all the cops you got. This place is a madhouse, and now I got looters here. It's a pawn shop, for Christ's sakes."

"What's going on?"

"A big robbery here. People killed, blood all over, looks like a butcher shop . I'd say six dead, maybe . . . Hey, you! Drop that goddamn box! Ain't you got no respe–" The line went dead.

Hauer followed Dorson to Rafe Buenrostro's office.

"Sounds like a bad one on the Flora highway pawn shop. Six people may be dead."

"Call Bob Vela at Robbery, tell him we'll help out."

"Ike, you go with Sam. Let's go, Pete."

On his way out, Buenrostro said to de la Cruz: "Send a couple of ambulances and the EMS wagons to the Flora Pawn Shop, on the west side of Flora."

"West. Got it."

De la Cruz called out: "You want Dr. Dietz and the staff out there?"

Peter Hauer shot an impatient frown at de la Cruz and ran toward the motor pool with Buenrostro trailing.

"Be there in twenty minutes, tops."

"Use the bubble machine, Pete."

In the first car, after Ike drove through the last traffic light on the highway toward Flora, a shaken Sam Dorson turned off the siren. "I hate fast driving, you know that."

"Sounds like a bad one."

"We'll see when we get there."

Ike Cantú looked in his rear view mirror and said, "Man, Pete's about to catch up with us."

"Seventy-five's enough for me, Ike, and for God's sake watch it when we get to Flora. No idea what's going on in town."

They made it to the pawnshop in eighteen minutes.

The local police were having a time controlling the crowd. Some fifty yards away a small liquor store was being ransacked. As a bonus, somebody had set it on fire.

Four roving country patrol cars drove up behind Cantú and Dorson and the patrolmen began pushing the crowd away as the four members of the Homicide Section pushed and shoved to get inside the pawn shop. The people from Robbery pulled up and fought their way to the pawn shop.

Presently, a firetruck stopped by the burning liquor store and two more Flora patrolmen drove there to prevent further thievery and possible injury to the thieves stupid enough to brave the fire.

Five minutes later, the Klail City EMS vans and ambulances pulled in, sirens going. The patrolmen again cleared the way for them.

Six Flora policemen drove up to the pawn shop and Buenrostro said to the sergeant: "Do something about the crowd."

The patrolmen lined up, extended their arms, grabbed each other's forearms and began walking forward. Most in the crowd cooperated, although the usual grouches yelled about their civil rights.

Peter Hauer went over and stood between the perspiring patrolmen and the crowd.

"We need your help, so back off. Anyone impeding this investigation will be arrested immediately and taken to the county jail. Any takers?"

The grumbling subsided somewhat and Hauer said, "All right."

Sam Dorson yelled out, "Who called County Homicide?"

A tall, gray-haired man standing away from the crowd stepped up. He wore a neat, light-blue jumpsuit and white Adidas.

"Are you Mr. Dan Ríos?"

"Right."

"Ike, take him to the car."

Rafe Buenrostro, hands in pocket and looking as if he were uninterested in the goings on, cleared the way for the technical staff. One of the women from the EMS truck said, "No survivors here. Looks like they were run over, Chief."

Henry Dietz stood next to Buenrostro.

"What a mess. Glass punched in, looks like. From the tire tracks, I'd say the bodies were driven over a couple of times."

Peter Hauer gritted his teeth. The first body he saw had been cut in half. The second one, slumped over a cash register, had no head. Hauer didn't move, but it wasn't nerves. There was evidence to think of, and he left that to the technical squad.

The only thing Homicide could do at this point was wait. The photographer kept popping away and asked Buenrostro, "May I, Chief?"

"Sorry." Buenrostro stepped out of the way, and walked to the edge of the highway.

Henry Dietz called out: "Sharp. Sharply, now. You, officer, get over to a grocery store, will you? We need a dozen trash bags."

An hour later, eight bodies had been removed and a lab technician made thin plastic paper imprints of the minivan's tires. As Hauer walked by some empty shelves, he heard a moan. He looked around, then at the floor.

"Hey," he called out. "Need some help here."

The photographer came over and took some more pictures. Two local policemen lifted large display cases and discovered a body. The man moaned again.

Hauer yelled out, "EMS!"

Two young men came over and looked at the wounded man.

The photographer came up. "I need another set of pictures."

"You got it."

Within minutes, the EMS personnel set up a plasma transfer and placed the man in a rollbed stretcher. The man winced in pain and moved his head. Hauer bent over.

"A minivan. Gray. Son-of-a-bitch crashed into the plate glass. He did it on purpose. Tell the cops."

Hauer turned to a county patrolman and read his badge number.

"Tell your partner you're going to Klail with EMS. Find out who this man is, and see if he says anything else. Let him do the talking."

The patrolman and Hauer then looked at each other. Both were covered in blood. Hauer shook his head and went to see Buenrostro. "Found a survivor, bloodied but unbowed. Angry as hell. Kept his head, though. Says a gray minivan crashed into the place on purpose. Can swear to three guys."

"Counting the driver?"

"Didn't say. He's got a couple of bad gashes on his arm and neck. Bleeding stopped for now, and they're pumping blood back into him. They're taking him to Klail General."

Buenrostro looked around and said, "Pete, go west, take the first left you come to and drive toward the river. See what you can find out there."

Hauer drove for a few minutes, took the first left turn, and parked the car. He spotted the tire tracks and followed them. Crouching but walking at a steady clip, he pulled out his .38 and released the safety.

He looked around and noticed the trampled sorghum and sugar-cane fields. He cut through the fields and sneezed as soon as he walked in. He looked around and saw some wider tracks.

A plane, he thought. He looked at the smooth landing strips and at the tire tracks. Two planes. Gutsy *cabrones*. He walked back through the sorghum and pulled out a handkerchief to cover his nose. His eyes began to water, and he sneezed again.

He followed the footsteps toward the levee. Two, no, three men. Sat down here. He took out his handkerchief and wrapped the cigarettes butts. He walked to the water's edge. Barefooted and swam across, he said to himself. Shoebiters. He shouldered his gun and headed toward his car.

Back at the pawn shop, Ike Cantú told him, "Two witnesses. The manager, his name's Dan Ríos, and an old guy on his way to Klail General. Ríos had his back to the plate glass window. He was way in the rear of the store setting up a VCR display when he heard the crash.

"Says some guy first shattered the plate glass with some sort of hammer, and then, not one second later, he said, a minivan came crashing inside the store. People started screaming. Then some guys came out and headed straight for the automatic weapons. No hesitation.

"He himself stayed right where he fell to the floor. And then he heard the van go out and come right back. A moment later, here it comes again. Glass flying all over the place. One guy fired at the roof the couple of times, but that was it."

Hauer shook his head. "Scare tactic. What did you say about automatics?"

"Yeah, crated up."

Hauer asked: "What the hell is a pawn shop doing with crated automatic weapons?"

Ike looked at his notes again. "The manager says the crooks loaded the van with gun crates and ammo, nothing else."

Hauer interrupted him, and asked: "How did he see all this, Ike?"

Cantú said, "Well, he just got up, he says, but the guys didn't see him, maybe they didn't care if he did see them. Ríos says it was all business, no talk."

"Where's Rafe?"

Dorson said, "With the FBI. They came in while you were away."

Peter Hauer stopped to look around and a man from the technical squad came up to him.

"Henry says Rafe sent you to look for some evidence. Got it with you?"

Hauer explained where he'd been and said, "You'll need two or three of your people out there." He pointed to westward and said, "Take the first left, it's an all-weather road. Here, I picked up these cigarette butts out there."

Hauer looked around. Broken glass, a thousand shards of it were being gathered by the busy technical staff. There was blood on the two cash registers, on three grocery pushcarts with boxes of merchandise on them, and on the floor he was standing on. He looked at his shoes and winced. Blood-soaked on top of the mud.

The familiar tape was lined around the crash site and then along the empty shelves which held the merchandise. He looked at Ike Cantú: "Automatics in crates."

Cantú said, "Yeah, I thought about that too. Everything else here is on display. Stolen or pawned, but it's out for the world to see. And now this, wholesale automatic weapons inside the crates."

Dorson said, "Probably with the cosmoline still on them."

Hauer asked Dorson, "What's that firetruck doing over there?"

"Oh, that. A fire at what used to be a liquor store. The Flora citizenry made off with what the fire didn't."

Hauer asked, "The thieves did that, you think?"

"It'll get sorted out." Dorson, resigned.

Dorson again: "I'm getting that district manager in here." He picked the telephone directory and turned quickly to the Yellow Pages.

Dorson looked at Peter Hauer's bloodied clothes. He handed him the phone. "Here," he said. "Call Myrna to bring you a change of clothing."

Just then a patrolman came over to Dorson. "Detective, the chief inspector gave the FBI guy a ride to the courthouse. Said he'd see you at the office."

"Ike, have a patrolman pick up the district manager at the chain's office in Klail. I want to know what the hell a pawn shop's doing wholesaling automatic rifles. Take him to the courthouse. He gives you any trouble, charge him with obstruction."

On his way out the door, Dorson said, "I'll check with Henry Dietz. See you in a minute, Pete."

A short while later they drove back in silence. Upon arrival, Hauer checked the squadroom closet and found his wife had delivered the change of clothes and a pair of loafers. From this he went to the basement showers.

Dorson rang for the desk sergeant. "Any calls?"

"Just one. Mrs. Buenrostro says she's staying another night with the Crixells at the ranch."

He hung up the phone and examined his suit. Ruined.

Fifteen minutes later, Ike Cantú brought in the pawn shop's district manager. Dorson looked at Cantú's clothes and thought: We're a bloody mess, all of us.

Thirty

When the district manager for the pawn shop chain walked into Homicide, Bob Vela from Robbery was there waiting for him. Cantú took a statement from the manager, who showed them his wholesale license. The rifles had been ordered from across the river, he said. Wholesale? He shrugged his shoulders, signed the deposition, and was taken upstairs to talk to two detectives from Robbery.

Later that afternoon, Henry Dietz signed off on the lab report on the murder/robbery at the pawn shop and had it hand delivered to Buenrostro's office.

TO: HOMICIDE SECTION.
ATTENTION: R. BUENROSTRO, CHIEF INSPECTOR.
FROM: HENRY DIETZ, M.D., MEDICAL EXAMINER

The plane strip is ample for two planes. The tires are the usual ones used by small aircraft. Shoe prints around the tire tracks indicate where the loading took place as do the indentations on the grounds made by gun crates.

Footprints near the banks of the river indicate three individuals walked to river's edge, sat down, smoked a cigarette apiece, and removed their shoes. Conclusion: The individuals swam across the river.

Seven separate complete pairs of adult fingerprints found inside and outside vehicle; a 1983 Dodge Minivan. Grand Theft Auto identified vehicle as stolen; claimant identified property at motor pool. Photographs taken and vehicle to be released pending authorization by Robbery Section.

Two fingerprints identified as those of owner and a friend, Harry Nebenzahl (share same address, 617 Ohio Street, Klail City). No criminal records. Additional fingerprints tests identified two individuals as James Atteberry and Willis Allen. Prior records for pair: armed robbery and smuggling.

Three unidentified prints faxed to Director Cetina. These are her findings: Fingerprints belong to following small time gangsters: Andújar, Pedro; McIntyre, Benito H.; and Marroquín, Ernesto.

Relatives of dead at murder/robbery scene have claimed bodies to be released pending authorization by Homicide Section.

Witness Dan Ríos released from Klail General Hospital; injuries not serious. Surviving victim, Flavio Ignacio Castro, remains at Klail General. Condition: fair to good.

Copies of this report also forwarded to District Attorney Florencio Valencia; Sheriff Norman Andrews; and to Lts. Bob Vela, Robbery, and J. Molden, Auto.

Henry Dietz, M.D.
Medical Examiner for Belken and Dellis Counties

Ike Cantú finished reading the report, made a copy for the squad and placed the original in Buenrostro's office. As he handed Dorson a copy, Dorson handed him Dietz's report on the white Jimmy.

Blood found on GMC truck is that of former Federal Assistant District Attorney Theodore Crixell. Fingerprints belong to Juan Carlos and José Antonio Gómez, as per records furnished this office by M. L. Cetina de Gutiérrez, Director, Barrones Federal Police.

Cantú served himself some iced tea and read the extensive report. Reading it a second time, he marked off what he considered the salient points:

Victim's car, 929 Mazda, washed on day of homicide; receipt from A-One Carwash found under front seat. Fingerprints on door of driver's seat belong to Juan Carlos Gómez. His fingerprints also found on trunk latch and upper part of trunk door. José Antonio Gómez's prints found on dashboard and on the inside of the window on the passenger's seat. Director Cetina's faxes of the brothers' fingerprints match those found in the vehicle. In all: six good matches.

Weapons: Two Glocks. Wounds: two; one to the head, one to the back. Victim Crixell dead after first shot.

Other weapons used: Two knives; one serrated, one smooth-edged. Multiple stabbings and slashings on arms, shoulders, legs, scrotum, thighs, feet; two fingers and one thumb severed. Body neither tied nor gagged.

```
Fabric of pima cotton found on victim's clothing
and inside trunk. Pima cotton usually found on expen-
sive guayabera shirts. Colors: navy blue; white.
Similar fabric found on GMC truck; not necessarily
same shirts but of high-quality pima cotton.
```

Cantú stopped reading and placed the report in a manila folder. Two men did the job, he thought. He placed Theo Crixell in the driver's seat. One or both of the twins approach him, guns drawn. Taken out of car, told to open trunk, and shot in the back of the head, then in the back.

Why were the shots not heard at yacht basin? Because of the wild party at the Gilbert's yacht. He gritted his teeth.

The stabbing begins soon after. Clothes as bloody as mine and Pete's at the pawn shop.

Cantú made a note on his pad: *Call on partygoers: ask how dope sellers were dressed.*

He went back to the mental images. Blood found on scene led to parking lot. Several witnesses saw the Jimmy in parking lot.

When? During dope buy? Partygoers return to the yacht, the twins wait around for Crixell, who's been called on some excuse or other.

At this point, Cantú gripped the ballpoint and unknowingly broke it in half. He glanced at his hand briefly and let the two pieces fall on the floor.

Back to Theo.

His family? Safe, at his brother's ranch. Question: What was Theo doing at the yacht basin? A woman? He decided he didn't know Crixell that well.

Supposition: Did the twins use a woman to call Crixell? If so, was it Laura Grayson? He wrote another note to himself.

How did the twins get him out of the house? Daniel Varela?

But he's dead, thought Cantú. But did Theo know? One of the twins says he's Varela. He's in trouble. Will lawyer Crixell vouch for him and go to the yacht basin where he's being held by the police.

Ike Cantú rose from his desk and muttered: "Oh, I'm a great detective. Making up stories like that."

Dorson looked up and said, "What's up, Ike?"

Cantú: "How did the twins get Theo to go out there? To the yacht basin?"

"Maybe they didn't, Ike."

Cantú thought on this for a short while. He walked around the squad room, head down, thinking hard.

"I give up."

"He could've been kidnapped."

Cantú rolled his eyes. "Come on, Sam."

Dorson told him to reread Henry Dietz's report; the part about the fingerprints. "The twins drive out to Theo's, they ring the doorbell, he answers, they push him in, they check around the house and then one of the twins makes him drive to the yacht basin. The other one follows."

Dorson stopped and looked at Ike Cantú.

No? The twin in the passenger car holds a gun on Theo and leaves his prints on the dashboard, the glove compartment, the inside of the window, the armrest. Wherever. The other one yanks the door open. Theo opens the trunk, they push him in and each one fires a shot.

"Think on it, Ike. Sometimes it's simpler than we realize."

"As simple as all that, Sam. You think?"

Dorson shrugged and went back to reading the file.

The phone rang in Buenrostro's office; after three rings, the call transferred to the squad room. Ike Cantú reached across the files and answered it.

Henry Dietz. There were two pages missing from the report. An inadvertent mistake, but it happens, he said rather philosophically. He was sending them the omissions.

A few minutes later, a lab assistant handed the missing pages to Ike Cantú who then made a copy of them and attached the original pages to Buenrostro's file. Cantú read the copy and stopped by Sam Dorson's desk.

"Tires, Sam."

Dorson looked up in amazement. "What was that?"

"The missing pages. The lab people scraped the white Jimmy's tires when it stood in the courthouse parking lot and found some gravel and caliche evidently missed by the carwash. Anyway, the stuff matches that found in Theo's Mazda. You were right."

Dorson: "The Crixells live in Green Acres, and there's nothing but all-weather roads out there. Dietz was bound to find something. He's nothing if not thorough."

The phone rang again and Dorson answered it this time. Buenrostro said, “I’m still here at the Commissioners’ Court. They’re on break now.” Chip Valencia had brought Boyd Hackett and some other FBI expert to testify, with statistics to back them up, of the need for increased armament for the Belken County police force.

Dorson let out a soft groan. “My sentiments,” said Buenrostro. After a slight pause, he added, “If Lu calls, I want to talk to her. Here’s what we’ve got: Say the judge of instruction allows her to charge the Quevedo brothers, this means she can move against Felipe Segundo. She wants to dig up the bodies that Morales says are there.”

Dorson said, “If they’ve gone crazy out at the ranch . . .” and then stopped in midsentence. Whatever Sam Dorson had been about to say, he’d changed his mind.

Buenrostro came back on. “Break’s over. Chip’s about to trot out his two experts. See you.”

Thirty-one

The phone rang in Lu Cetina's private office.

"Yes?"

"Good morning, *directora*. This is Judge Avila, how are you?"

Her judge of instruction. Doing well, she replied; at the same time, she drew the Quevedo brothers' file from the top desk drawer.

The judge's well-known modulated voice betrayed no Mexico City singsong; he'd spent the last twenty years of his judicial life in northern Mexico, and the slightly nasal pronunciation had replaced the pronunciation peculiar to the capital city.

"To business. What do you have for me?"

"Evidence of three homicides in Klail City, Texas, ten days ago. The presumed murderers are the brothers Ramón and Gabriel Quevedo, residents of Control, Tamaulipas. They have confessed and admitted their responsibility as well as their guilt in the commission of the crime.

"We have been assisted in this regard by the cooperation of the chief inspector of Belken County's Homicide Section."

"His name?"

"Rafael Buenrostro."

Lu Cetina could hear the scratching of Judge Avila's pen.

The justice's voice purred. "Son of a *norteño* father, perhaps?"

"A great-great-grandson, I believe."

"Ah yes, one of our Illustrious Santa Anna's lost children."

She made a face, but said nothing.

"A small joke, *directora*." She heard the faint flick of a lighter. Probably lighting himself a big, fat, thick Upmann cigar from Havana via Veracruz, thought Lu Cetina.

"You have explained to the chief inspector the necessity of a primary investigator's attendance during your presentation to me? Speaking of which, will you be ready anytime soon?"

Was a delicate answer called for? She decided it wasn't and said to herself: Oh, the hell with it.

"Would two days from now suit Your Honor?"

No hesitation on the other end. "Eight o'clock."

In the morning was understood. She glanced at her watch; would Dorson or any of the others be available, she wondered?

"*Directora*, as a matter of judicial curiosity, not inquiry–to make that fine distinction–were the homicides acts of revenge for a third party? In brief, a conspiracy."

Had the man heard something? She decided to take Judge Avila at his word regarding judicial curiosity.

"The Quevedo brothers were assigned what the Americans call a 'contract' to murder two men at a parking lot in Klail City and then their driver after the fact."

"Your sister city," the judge said needlessly.

She plowed on. "The brothers murdered three Mexican nationals at the behest of a party known to them as Dr. Olivares."

"From?"

"No known address, Your Honor. From our evidence, the name is an alias. The Belken detectives are familiar with the same name since it was used in other homicides committed in their county some time back.

"Interesting. Is it both relevant and provable?"

"Yes."

"Will the *directora*'s presentation of the facts lead, and this is a hypothetical consideration, will the presentation lead to a charge of conspiracy at a later date involving the man of mystery?"

"Without surrendering any national sovereignty to the State of Texas, we expect continued cooperation with the chief inspector and his superiors."

"Very good."

She took the phrase not as approbation but as a way of bringing the conversation to a close.

"It is now ten-thirty, *directora*. I'm at a Border Judges' Conference meeting at the Klail City Holiday Inn. I would appreciate it if one of your men would deliver the material within the next hour. One of my clerks will be at the front desk waiting for it."

No flies on him, thought Lu Cetina. "I should like to request that my man present the papers to His Honor in person."

"As always, *directora*, a pleasure to talk with the daughter of an old friend of mine."

"Goodbye, sir."

Lu Cetina told herself she was not one of those to misjudge Manuel de Jesús Avila's manner. The manner was, as her father had once told her, meant to disarm the unwary. Those who mistook His Honor's ways for pomposity or vanity would soon be disabused; the judge was an astute close reader and questioner ready to pounce on any mistake made by the presenting officer regarding civil procedure against the alleged criminal. The judge's decision to go forward with the charge and trial assured a fair trial based solely and strictly on the merits. He was also incorruptible. He'd served through four presidents and could rise no higher than his present position. The cost of probity, she reminded herself. She stopped thinking on Judge Avila and once again began to read her reports page by page, slowly and deliberately.

A stray thought came to her. A matter of very recent historical fact. The governor, no less, of an important state, Nuevo León, had been forced to resign six weeks ago; he was not alone. Four federal judges followed him along with forty district judges. She read the clipping again. Sighing softly, she asked herself: "Yes, but who will replace them?"

She and her men had used no violence during the arrest or during the incarceration. The Quevedos had requested no legal counsel to represent them. No offer for leniency had been offered; she had asked for information, received some that would not violate the men's rights under the Napoleonic Code, and Chief Inspector Buenrostro had then questioned them closely as well. She went over the Buenrostro sessions one more time. No civil procedure violation there, she concluded.

There was, however, the matter of conjugal visitations; had she threatened to withhold them? Well, that was a vague point; she decided there was not enough meat there for the judge of instruction or, if it came to that, for the opposing counsel, to gnaw on.

Lu Cetina knew Judge Avila was famous for sinking fishing expeditions from both sides of the bar.

The Quevedos had been kept in a clean, private cell; fed adequately, they were also free to buy supplemental food within reason. They had been asked a second time if they wished legal representation at the last session two days ago, and they had again refused any. Conjugal visits? Yes, and those too within reason.

She turned the last page; her signature and full title were on the left side of the page, the Mexican eagle-and-serpent seal in the middle, and the Quevedos' signatures on the right. A red, white, and green ribbon affixed by ocher sealing-wax attested to the official notarization of the statements.

Satisfied, she surmised the brothers would seek legal counsel once Judge Avila cleared the way for the formal charge and trial.

She rang for her second in command.

"Put on your civilian clothes, Elizondo, and take this to the Holiday Inn in Klail City. A federal judicial officer at the front desk will take you to Judge Avila's quarters. The judge won't say anything, but he expects you to ask for a receipt. Do so. Call me from his room when he dismisses you."

The veteran police officer took the leather handbag given him and saluted.

Lu Cetina then called Belken Homicide.

Thirty-two

Young Eduardo Salinas woke with a start. He had dreamed he had attended his father's funeral. He nodded and thought, Yes . . . the old man was fading fast. He flicked on the bed lamp and checked his watch as he reached for his light cotton bathrobe. Five o'clock. Daylight was an hour and five minutes away.

Mustn't wake the old folks, he said to himself. He used shaving soap instead of the electric razor.

He closed the door to his private toilet quietly and turned on the shower, where he began to think on what lay ahead. After drying himself, he picked up at his watch and saw he'd been up for twenty minutes. White denims, a starched white shirt, and a wide-brimmed straw hat. He pulled on his walking boots, opened the walk-in closet, and then holstered a Rossi M-68 to the small of his back. He lay the Browning, a Hi-Power MKIII Matte 9mm, on top of the bed. From the closet's top shelf he gathered ammunition boxes for both handguns. He folded the Browning, the ammunition, and a pair of dark sneakers inside a long-sleeved navy-blue jumpsuit and stuffed the gear in a small leather briefcase.

He tiptoed out of his room through the narrow hallway leading into the patio. Standing by his parents' bedroom window, he crossed himself, and then walked to the high gate that opened to the street. Once outside, he breathed in the morning clean cool air. Rounding a corner, he walked briskly to the garage stalls a block and a half away from the house he shared with his parents.

He unlocked the garage and drove his dark green Chevy utility wagon into the street. He let the engine idle while he stepped out to lock the garage. A milk truck passed by and the driver waved and smiled at him. Eduardo Salinas nodded and drove west toward Control.

He drove carefully, stopping at every intersection. He checked his watch again: five forty-five. An hour's drive to Control.

He turned on the air conditioning and immediately stopped thinking about his plans for that night.

An hour later, he checked in at a one-story pink stuccoed motel on the outskirts of the small border town of Control and asked for a corner room. After this, he pulled out of the motel's gravel driveway and headed for the nearest cafe.

After a light breakfast, he ordered another a pot of coffee. While he waited, he smoothed out a detailed sketch of the Gómez ranch property. It had been provided by his father's old partner, El Barco Zaragoza.

Eduardo Salinas studied the sketch one more time: A red X marked the selected entry point in the eight-foot electric fence; thirty yards beyond that, a quarter-mile long mesquite grove would provide ample cover. After that, the sorghum and the sugarcane crops would cover him the rest of the way to the three main barns, and from there to the various sheds housing the cars, Jeeps, semis, tractors and the farming equipment. After that, he had a clear shot to the main house, which was surrounded by thick hedges of pink and white oleander bushes.

That evening at eight-thirty, one of Zaragoza's men would pick him up at the motel and drive him to the ranch property. He would climb onto the roof of the man's Bronco, jump over the electric fence and make his way into the woods. After seeing to the Gómezes, he would retrace his steps to where Zaragoza's man would have dug a passageway under the fence, and from there head back to Control.

He turned to the other side of the sketch and studied the diagram of the house. Using his index finger, he moved from the formal living room, complete with piano, to the large television-play room, and on to the screened porch; he noted the position of the four bedrooms, each with a private bath; then on to a half-bath in the hallway; from there to the kitchen and finally to the laundry room.

The coffee was served and young Salinas closed his eyes: the fence, the grove, the sorghum and cane fields, the barns, the sheds, the main house. He checked the map sketch: Perfect score.

El Barco Zaragoza had told Eduardo Salinas's father that the Gómez family had recently hired some South Americans; however, they'd not been seen around the property or in Control for over a week. Zaragoza said they were most likely transporting the product across the Rio Grande. And there'd be no dogs to worry about.

Eduardo Salinas took a sip of coffee and studied the diagram of the long ranch-style house one last time.

Fifteen minutes later he returned to the motel, placed a call to El Barco Zaragoza and left a message. He set the alarm clock and dropped off to sleep almost immediately. At six he awoke and ate a light snack. At seven forty-five there was a soft rap at the door and Eduardo Salinas looked through the venetian blinds: Zaragoza's man.

Salinas opened the door to a squat, red-headed, green-eyed man in his fifties.

"Ambrosio Luna," the man said. His hands were as hard as boards. He wore a loose, short-sleeved light-green guayabera shirt.

"Hungry?" Luna asked. Eduardo Salinas shook his head.

Luna took an easy chair and lit a cigarette as Salinas washed up and put on his navy blue jumpsuit and the dark sneakers. Luna offered him a Walther PPK-S .380 stainless with silencer attached, but Salinas said he would use his own.

They drove off without a word. Some twenty miles away from the spot picked out by Luna, he said: "The South Americans have not been seen the last three days. One of the workers is a deaf-mute, and he and the woman cook sleep in the smaller of the sheds. Another hand, a man named Morales, has also been gone for a few days. As you know, the main house is surrounded by oleanders, so you should have no trouble picking off whoever comes out of the house when they start running toward the big barn.

"I'll pass you the gadget under the fence. It's timed for nine thirty-five, and I'll be waiting for you at the other spot when you get back."

"How old is this information?"

"Three days."

Eduardo Salinas nodded.

Ten minutes later, Salinas sat in the mesquite grove. He crossed himself and headed toward the crop fields. Five minutes later he came to a clearing from where he could see the lights in the Gómez house.

I'll see them but they won't be able to see me, he said to himself, as he moved closer to the house. There's the kitchen. The living room and the television-play room are next. He then saw a handsome middle-aged man watching television. That must be either Felipe Segundo or don Lisandro. Where are the twins?

He looked at the luminous dial on his watch. Eight minutes to go. Ah, here's one of the twins coming out of the kitchen. Where's the other one? Not important. They'll all come running out of the house as soon as the barns go up.

A minute later he stood by the barns. He checked the biggest one for a possible alarm system. Finding none, he closed his eyes for a few moments to adjust to the darkness. He slid the barn door open and held onto the cigar-box container as he walked between two Cessnas, one parked right behind the other. He then uncapped one of the diesel tanks of a Peterbilt tractor and wedged the detonating device between the gas tank and the cab. After he pressed the timing button, he walked out the door and then crouched as he ran toward the oleander hedges surrounding the house. The time was nine forty-three, and he waited.

The force of the explosion blew part of the barn roof, along with the semi, on top of the barn nearest to it. Flaming pieces of the Cessnas flew through the air, spewing gasoline, and caused the third barn to catch fire as well. The flames from the second barn engulfed two of the three sheds as Eduardo Salinas, holding his Rossi M-.68 in his left hand, waited behind the hedges facing the front door. Soon after, the third shed began to catch fire.

Immediately after the second explosion, Eduardo Salinas saw two figures running out of the house. He waited for the third man, and when no one else appeared, he ran toward the two figures in front of him.

Another loud explosion erupted from the third barn as Salinas approached the men, who screamed and cursed as they stood by helplessly. One turned toward the approaching Salinas and waved his hands, as if to say, "Look at this."

Eduardo Salinas took careful aim and shot him in the chest. The second man did not hear the shot as he concentrated on the raging, crackling fire. Salinas walked up to him and fired two shots in quick succession into the back of his head. He then walked back to the first man and fired a shot in the man's temple. He felt some blood splatter on his jumpsuit. He reloaded the Rossi and walked to the main house. The time was now nine fifty-five.

Gun in hand, he stood behind the hedges and looked into the living room. His eyes went from there to the television room, which led to the screened porch. In a crouch, he walked around the house and entered through the kitchen. Once in the hallway, he opened an adjacent door. He checked the laundry room: nothing. Back to the empty living room. Gun cocked, he then kicked in each of the doors to the four bedrooms: again nothing.

When he heard a fourth explosion, Salinas walked out through the back way only to be bowled over by a man whose hair was on fire. The man, naked and screaming, dashed into the living room. Salinas got back on his feet, ran after him, and shot him in the back at point-blank range.

The man, thrown forward, arms flailing by the force of the .68 millimeter gun, fell face down against an oversized sofa. Salinas walked to him. The fire had spread to his back and arms. An older man; must be the deaf man, he thought. He shot him a second time.

Eduardo Salinas then looked through a window. The fire was now spreading in the direction of the vehicles in the storage area. One of the Jeeps, tires ablaze, blew up as parts of it fell on one of the burning sheds. After this, he ran at a trot toward the sorghum fields and did not look back again.

He stumbled as he ran toward the clearing in the middle of the field. Recovering his balance, he stopped to get his breath. He counted to thirty and then sprinted toward the mesquite grove and from there to the electric fence.

Ambrosio Luna was wiping his hands when Salinas came up to the fence. He holstered his gun and crawled through the hole dug by Luna.

"Two, that's all," he said, panting.

"Two? Gómezes?"

"Right. I went through the house twice. Nothing."

"I heard two more shots." Luna said.

"Yeah, I think it was the deaf-mute you told me about. He was on fire."

Ambrosio Luna nodded and said, "It's a good night's work, son. We'll get the other two soon enough. You hungry?"

Eduardo Salinas shook his head, grinned, and began getting out of his jumpsuit.

Thirty-three

The phone in Buenrostro's house rang at exactly two-thirteen a.m.

"Rafe, Lu. Sorry to get you up, but I just got the call myself. The Gómez ranch caught fire."

A sleepy Buenrostro said, "Say again?"

"The Gómez Solís ranch, Rafe. It caught fire. I'm on my way to Control right now. I'll be at Customs."

He reached out for his wife until he remembered she was staying with Mandie Crixell and the girls at the ranch.

He dialed Homicide and relayed Lu Cetina's message to the desk sergeant. He dressed hurriedly. At two forty-five, Dorson, Hauer, and Cantú met him at the courthouse motor pool. The plan called for Cantú and Dorson to bring Morales from the Flads jail to Control, and from there to the Gómez ranch.

The desk sergeant handed them some coffee in styrofoam cups. Once in the motor pool, Hauer and Buenrostro took an unmarked car while Dorson and Cantú headed toward Flads.

When Hauer and Buenrostro arrived on the Mexican side of the bridge, Lu Cetina came out and waved them over to the Custom shed. The streets were deserted save for a lone garbage truck rumbling through the quiet streets of the sleeping border town. The usual Gulf mist hung in the air, but it would soon dry up when the sun came out.

"Jeeps, soldiers, and dogs," said Hauer as he watched four motorcycle cops and eight army Jeeps heading toward the Gómez ranch. Hauer then said, "Lions and tigers and bears. Oh, my." Buenrostro looked at his partner, shook his head, but grinned all the same.

Over coffee, Lu Cetina thanked them for coming over.

"I don't want the state or the city police working on this. I've got Elizondo, and he's a help, but anything you can do . . ." That understood, she then explained that a neighbor, some four kilometers from the Gómez ranch, had heard a series of explosions and had then driven to the Control police station.

"That's him, over there," she said, pointing to a middle-aged farmer wearing a summer Stetson. The uniformed man sitting next to him was a night watchman. When asked, the man repeated what he'd seen.

Fire and explosions followed by more explosions. Flashes of fire. The time? Oh, early, nine something, before ten o'clock. His wife woke him at the first explosion, he said. He then looked outside and that's when he saw the fires. But his truck wouldn't start, and then he'd had a terrible time getting the tractor going. When he did start it, he drove into town.

He'd gotten to Control a little after eleven and went looking for the night watchman. Fifteen minutes later, he pulled in to Customs, and that's where he found the night watchman. It was he who had called the Barrones police.

"And what time was that?"

The night watchman looked at Lu Cetina's badge and said gravely, "Before midnight."

"At what time is daybreak this morning?"

The watchman looked at his old pocket Hamilton. "Six oh two, *señora Directora*." The time was now three-thirty a.m.

At this point, the head of Customs came out with a huge pot of beef stew and corn tortillas.

"We got workman's breakfast for everybody."

As he said this, Dorson and Cantú walked in, with Morales in tow. They sat down to breakfast as a group from Barrones reported in. The crime lab people, she explained, and they too sat down for breakfast.

Two hours later, at five-thirty, Lu Cetina rode out with Buenrostro and his men to the ranch, where they were met by the eight-Jeep caravan. The crime lab technicians in their white-and-green ambulances and VW vans drove through the open iron gates. It was now daybreak and bright enough to go to work.

She posted two *federales* by the gate and said, "Six oh two. That old man was right."

While the ten crime technicians set about doing their work around the area, she ordered the soldiers and the policemen to stand by as needed.

The cumulus clouds coming in from the Gulf ran from pink to orange to pale yellow, with an occasional break of blue sky, which presented a vivid contrast with the pitch black of the still-smoking, burned-out hundred-yard swath where the barns and sheds had once stood. Lu Cetina called for two Jeeps and she, Elizondo, and Morales, and the men from Belken Homicide headed for the main house.

From the outside, the house looked peaceful, in order. The pink and white oleander bushes were undisturbed, as was the porch and, seemingly, the rest of the house.

Buenrostro, Lu Cetina and Morales waited on the porch as Peter Hauer sprayed insect repellent on and around the screen door. Dorson and Cantú took their cue and sprayed the back of the house before they entered through the kitchen.

Dorson pointed to some sooty tracks on the floor.

Turning his head, he said, "The footprints lead to that big room there."

At that moment, Hauer yelled: "I've got a man here. Bad burns, and two mean looking holes in the back of the head." Looking back, Hauer yelled out, "Keep the doors closed before the flies take over." He used his ballpoint to pick up the shell casings and put them in a small baggie.

The burned man's head was a mess. Parts of his arms and back were badly charred, and flies feasted on the dried blood until Cantú sprayed them away.

Dorson bent over and said, "Not Felipe Segundo nor one of the twins, that's for sure."

Ike Cantú said, "Must've come in the back way and was then shot here. Why naked, though?"

Dorson stepped back and said, "Let's say he's one of the hands. He's sleeping, gets burned somewhat–wherever he is–sees the rest of the place in flames, and heads for the main house, where somebody pops him."

They were at this when Buenrostro and Lu Cetina walked in with Tibu Morales.

"Sam, stay with the technical squad. When that's done, go to the barns, the sheds. You know what to do."

Suddenly, a soldier ran inside the house. Two more bodies had been found just twenty meters from the house, he reported to Lu Cetina. She detailed two of the lab men to go to the scene, and Dorson went with them. At this point, Hauer handed the baggies to a lab man.

Lu Cetina ordered a five-soldier detail to come with her; with Morales leading the way, Buenrostro, Cantú, and Hauer followed. Morales told the soldiers where to dig, and within five to ten minutes they came across part of a broken wing of a white-colored aircraft.

"Where else, Morales?"

The man pointed to another spot and the soldiers began to dig once again. Four bodies this time.

Morales then pointed with his chin and said, "Over there, that's where Deaf-mute Farías buried *Señor* Gómez, the pilot, and the others."

Buenrostro said, "One set of fresh tracks over here."

Morales raised his hands and said, "I don't know anything about those tracks, *señora Directora.*"

Hauer followed the footprints which cut across the fields and pointed toward the barns. As usual, once in the sorghum, Hauer began to sneeze.

Two more soldiers came running up until Lu Cetina raised her hand. "Be careful, there."

Suddenly, at a spot twenty yards away, a lab technician yelled out: "I've got a woman here; head's bashed in. Looks fresh. Hold it, one, no, two, maybe more. All men."

Morales then spoke: "The South Americans, maybe. I can get the backhoe to run, if it's not ruined." Ike Cantú walked with Morales to the partially burned shed.

For his part, Hauer walked out of the second clearing and headed for a mesquite grove. The tracks were easy to follow on the plowed soil, and when he got to the grove, he yelled out: "Rafe! Lu! Over here!"

They drove toward Hauer.

"The tracks come from the road over there. Only the one set. He must've taken a different route going out."

From another part of the fence, some fifty yards away, two soldiers began signaling to them. When they got to the soldiers, she said, "Fresh digging. Another dead one, you think?"

Buenrostro shook his head. "Too shallow to bury anyone, but deep enough for someone to crawl under. Best way to avoid the electric fence. And it's been dug from the other side."

Hauer nodded at this. He took off his poplin jacket, crawled under and said, "Some wide tire tracks; riding high. Empty pickup, or a good-sized van, is my guess."

Lu Cetina turned to the driver. "Shove your rifle under the hole and escort Detective Hauer. Those tracks should take you to the starting point."

She drove Buenrostro back to the house. The tech squad was going about its business. The time was now seven-twenty, and the heat was becoming oppressive. Buenrostro glanced at the palm trees; the leaves were barely moving.

On the porch, Dorson shared a cigarette with Antero Rivas, the head of the Barrones crime lab. Lu Cetina and Buenrostro joined them outside.

Rivas blew out a long cloud of blue smoke. "Two bodies by the big barn, plus the one inside the house. All three shot twice *and* in the back. But here's what did the damage to the place."

He pointed to a laundry bag on the ground; in five separate clumps, burnt wire and pieces of metal had been fused together by the heat. "Plastique. One massive charge. Someone took no chances, María Luisa. The other parts belong to a semi's gas tank. Good job."

Rivas went on. "We've also come up with foot tracks going from barn to barn. They lead to the house and then around it. Our man wore sneakers of some sort. I've got photos for the lab."

Dorson said, "Can I borrow the Polaroid?"

Rivas handed it to him.

Lu Cetina said to Rivas: "We've counted nine bodies so far. It looks as if five of them were killed no more than two, three days ago." Pointing, she went on. "They're over by the cleared ground between the sorghum and the cane fields."

After this, she and Buenrostro walked around the house with Dorson snapping away. A few minutes later, Rivas walked to the two clearings, where one of his men reloaded another Polaroid. When the pictures had developed, Rivas returned to the house.

At this point, Ike Cantú walked in with Morales. Dorson told him of the South Americans and the woman.

"The cook," said Morales, simply.

Dorson: "Plus three here, with one twin missing."

Meanwhile, Hauer had found the place used by the shooter to get on the property, and he and the soldier drove back to the house.

Perspiration ran down the front and back of the shirts of everyone present. The soldiers, in their heavy fatigue clothing, were wet through.

Hauer pointed to the mesquite grove and then said the tracks led around the farm road paralleling the fence.

Lu Cetina: "My men will be here all day today and tomorrow. Longer if you need them."

Buenrostro nodded. "A two-man job. The shooter plus a driver."

Hauer: "For what it's worth, it didn't take him much time to do the deed. Ten, twelve minutes, I'd say. A pro, but not quite, somehow. I mean, why would he burn the dope?"

Rafe Buenrostro said, "Ike? Sam?"

Cantú spoke first. "Must've used a map or a sketch to move around. He knew where he was all the time. Had to. The fires were a diversion. That's why we found the bodies in front of the house. Good planning. Nerves, too."

Dorson said. "Luck helps."

Lu Cetina , matter-of-factly: "We've got a missing twin. First thing I'll do when I get back is to make phone calls to the *casas de cita,* the fancy whorehouses in Barrones. Maybe we'll hear something. Anybody here think the remaining twin's responsible for this?"

After a while Dorson said, "No. This looks like revenge. A payback of some sort. To quote Pete, who ruins a couple of tons of product?"

Lu looked at Rafe Buenrostro. "Well, Rafe, what do you think?"

"Let's go under those trees there. The heat's getting to me."

Half an hour later, Buenrostro and Hauer drove Lu Cetina to her office in Barrones while Dorson and Cantú went home to shave and shower. The four Belken County detectives agreed to meet in the squad room at four o'clock.

Thirty-four

The time was four p.m., and Dorson, Hauer and Cantú were back at the office. Fed and showered, they sat at their desks comparing and collating notes on the events of the last fourteen hours when Buenrostro walked in. He stopped at a filing cabinet and leaned against it.

Buenrostro said Henry Dietz would be down shortly. With that, he began the briefing, the usual procedure the squad used to bring itself up to date.

"This is what I've come up with. A shooter who leaves tracks and doesn't care to hide them. He also had a good-sized area to cover in a short time. This points to a younger man. He acted alone but was driven there.

"First he blows up the buildings, waits for someone to run out of the house, and shoots them during the confusion.

"Now, unless he's also a demolition man, the timer was preset for him. This takes a cool head, since he worked on a tight schedule. He's part of a gang; not a loner."

He looked at Hauer.

Peter Hauer set down his coffee: "Since he didn't know Lee was dead, he thought he was going after the four Gómezes. He got two, and he may think he got three. That part I don't know. He may or may not know about the missing twin. Job's unfinished."

Ike Cantú: "Say he mistook the burning man for one of the twins. I don't think he went around checking on who he killed. So, as far as he's concerned, he's still got Lee on the list."

Dorson: "He'll go on the hunt."

Hauer: "Question: Who are the strongest families in the four-state area, in northern Mexico?"

Cantú checked a folder from Vice.

"The Góngora and the Espinel families. The Góngoras are the smaller bunch; they cover the cities of Monterrey, China, and Cadereyta Jiménez in Nuevo León. No direct border contact, it says here."

Dorson: "We know about the Espinels. Older, more established. They handle the states of San Luis Potosí, Tamaulipas and Coahuila, with the Texas side of the Valley as a bonus."

Buenrostro said: "And we know how Lee started his operation as middleman for transport. The Valley was his payoff when he was director of public order in Barrones."

Dorson coughed slightly and said, "Try this: Both families are strong, and they don't want trouble, since there's enough money for everybody. They keep a low profile too. Not the showing-off stuff that the smaller organizations engage in: big cars, gold chains, houses on both sides of the river and at Padre Island, and so on."

Ike broke in: "I don't think we're talking about new blood here, either. Anybody new comes into the Valley, the word goes out immediately. Where does this put us, then?"

Buenrostro: "Let's move on. Sam mentioned revenge as a motive."

Cantú answered for him and Dorson: "Someone was after the Gómezes and not their territory. Dope smuggling is a cash business, and you don't waste the product."

"A settling of unpaid accounts, but not necessarily money," said Dorson.

Buenrostro: "El Barco Zaragoza's men, you think? One last hit for the old guys?"

Hauer: "I say this goes back to the Kum Bak Inn when Lee Gómez stiffed Zaragoza and his gang for the job there, and then betrayed them to us at Brinkman's Motel. Felipe Segundo followed the same pattern when he turned in the Quevedos at the Flamingo. If so, then revenge makes sense."

The room was silent for a few seconds.

Buenrostro: "Try this: the Gómezes lived on old money from the time we arrested Lee in Padre Island. Eighteen months pass, and Felipe Segundo decides it's time to get back into the business. Say they signal the two families that they're ready to go into their middlemen operation, and they're given the go ahead. Felipe Segundo says Lee will be gotten out of the way, and the families say, 'That's your affair, we're out of it.'"

Sam Dorson suppressed another cough before speaking. "So, Felipe Segundo and the twins do their part. Fine. But Pete's saying whoever ordered their killing didn't care about the product or anything else except the killing of the Gómez family."

After a pause, Dorson said, "I don't want to sell revenge, but so far, it's our best bet."

Hauer walked to the office sink, rinsed his coffee cup and there served himself some cold water. He took out his note pad.

"What about the gang that held up the Flora pawn shop? We saw two burned Cessnas in the barns plus the burned automatic rifles in their crates. Those guys are unaccounted for."

Ike Cantú broke the brief silence.

"And we still have the other twin out there someplace. The papers have been told not to say anything."

Hauer asked: "How will he know about the killings?"

Dorson rose from his desk and coughed lightly. "That's covered; cops talk. The word always gets out." The squad agreed on this point.

At that moment, Henry Dietz walked in without knocking, an established pattern with him. He carried two file folders and got down to business immediately.

"It's Theo's blood in the white Jimmy all right. No question." He plopped a folder on Dorson's desk. He then opened the second folder. "Here're the results from the fingerprints at the pawn shop. Three small-timers from Flads over in Dellis County. From your records on the computer, this is their biggest haul yet. The pawn shop regional manager puts the haul at over one hundred thousand, not counting the ammo." He plopped that folder on the table also and walked out without a word.

At this point Ike Cantú said, "The pawn shop guys. We found two Cessnas but where are the thieves? Did the Gómezes stiff them too? If so, those guys had a hell of a motive for revenge. Plus . . ."

A soft knock at the door, and Desk Sergeant Contreras poked his head in the doorway.

"Sorry, Chief. Doctor Dietz just barged in; no way I could stop him."

Buenrostro told him not to worry, and Contreras handed him a fax from Lu Cetina.

After a glance, Buenrostro handed Ike Cantú the message:

```
The soldiers and the technicians found four more bod-
ies when they moved the wreckage from the torn
Cessnas in the barn. I'm on my way back to the ranch.
```

"My guess," said Hauer, "is that those are the pawn shop guys and the pilots who brought over the rifles and ammo."

Desk Sergeant Art Contreras said, "Excuse me, Chief. It's the D.A. He's been calling all morning and half the afternoon. Urgent, he said."

Buenrostro nodded. "Time to knock off anyway. Ike and I will drive out to the Gómez ranch tomorrow morning. Six-thirty, Ike." He picked some of the Polaroids taken at the Gómez ranch that morning, and stuffed them in an envelope as Chip Valencia's voice came over the loudspeaker: "Sorry to bother you, Chief, but I need an update. Can you fill me in?" The detectives looked at the amplifier and headed for home.

Buenrostro said he'd be right up.

Half an hour later, a satisfied Valencia escorted Buenrostro to the hallway. The man seemed gleeful to hear of the multiple murders at the Gómez ranch; Buenrostro said nothing of the four additional bodies reported by Lu Cetina. No need to, he reasoned. Valencia was looking for all the violence he could get on either side of the river to push his request for an increase in firepower.

"By the way, Chief, no need to worry about extraditing the parking lot killers. You did a fine job, but they're small potatoes. They're just part of the package of the systematic violence that some of the undesirable element from across the river has been visiting upon us. We'll come out all right. Don't you worry."

Another prepared speech, thought Buenrostro. Something given by the D. A. to the downtown service clubs, groups of men and women who liked to hear about law and order, as long as they didn't have to see the violence involved. On his way to the office, Buenrostro reached into his coat pocket, pulled out his cellular phone, and dialed Lu Cetina. The connection was a poor one, and he pressed the off button. He then called his home number to leave a message for his wife, and was surprised to have her come on the line. Sammie Jo said Mandie and the girls were fine, and she was no longer needed at the ranch.

"This thing's about wrapped up. I'll take Ike with me to Lee's ranch early tomorrow morning."

Sammie Jo said, "Lu called here a few minutes ago."

"Thanks, I'll call her when I get home. What's the weather up to out in the Gulf? How about that new hurricane?"

"Tragedy was averted," replied Sammie Jo, laughing. "It's moved up the coast toward Galveston, which means good fishing for us. The boat engine needs a minor tune up, and I'll start working on it right now. It'll be ready by Friday. See you."

He dialed Lu Cetina's number again and got through this time.

"Five more bodies, Rafe. No need for you to come out here, just thought you'd like to know. Rivas and his tech squad are out there. I'll call you tomorrow."

Buenrostro thanked her, said good night, and drove home.

Thirty-five

At five-thirty the next morning, Rafe Buenrostro called the Barrones Federal Police. The connection took over a minute to complete, and when the phone rang in Lu Cetina's office, he was told that the director's father had died unexpectedly. She was not expected in her office until the beginning of the following week. Buenrostro left his number with the operator and drove to the courthouse. As he was driving into the parking lot, a call came through.

It was the veteran Elizondo from the Barrones office. Yes, a sad thing about the director's father, but here, said Elizondo, we have an update for *el jefe inspector del condado de* Belken: The old Zaragoza gang was no more. Both El Barco and El Camarón, the albino Enrique Salinas, had passed away the previous night to a better world. Salinas, the albino, died of cancer, Chief Inspector. I think that's why the Texas prison authorities released him. As for Zaragoza, well, he'd lived with his diabetes for many years, but then had come infection, then gangrene, then amputation of his leg, and finally death.

"One man in Control, the other in Barrones," said Elizondo. "And the Director's own father, *jefe inspector.* Death comes in threes, they say." Elizondo then said, "We have faxed possible IDs to your Dr. Dietz–I mean of the five new bodies, *jefe inspector.*"

Buenrostro thanked him, decided not to mention his planned trip to the Gómez ranch, and hung up.

Buenrostro was convinced that Sam Dorson had been right all along: revenge, and he thought he knew who the avenger was. He walked to the window, looking southward toward the river, in the direction of the Gómez ranch. A few minutes later, he took the elevator to check on the new IDs faxed by Elizondo.

The rains had stopped for now and the Gulf breezes began to blow the clouds away. The leaves of the mesquite and *huisache* trees, sopped with water from the previous night, had now turned to a darker green, seemingly overnight.

He thought on Zaragoza and Salinas.

So the old men were dead. Of natural causes, after everything. No embalming in Mexico, he remembered, and so they'd be buried on this hot, cloudless day.

He left a note for Sam Dorson:

> *Crossing at Control. Lu in Mexico City, attending her father's funeral. El Barco and Enrique Salinas dead. Have Pete call on the widow Grayson.*

At the parking lot, Ike Cantú waited for him under the shade of a leafy papaya tree. The traffic was sparse at that early hour, and twenty minutes later Buenrostro greeted the duty sergeant at Mexican Customs in Control and registered their guns. While Buenrostro waited for the receipts, an old veteran came up to him.

Indio puro, Buenrostro thought.

"My name is Silvestre Palacios, Chief Inspector. My father worked for your uncle Julian many years ago." They shook hands and chatted briefly as a clerk made out the receipts.

Back in the car, he turned on the air conditioning again and turned toward the dusty all-weather road leading to the Gómez ranch; fifteen minutes later he began looking out for the landmark: two crossed palms surrounded by mesquite and *huisache* trees.

He drove into the shaded clearing and drove toward a light-blue, four-door '64 Falcon parked on the edge of the fence; the '88 Texas plates were three years old. The car stood under the *huisache* trees, the shadiest spot. Suddenly he heard voices across the woods fronting the Rio Grande. He followed the bent grass to a set of chaparral bushes, where he came across some clothing and various pairs of shoes.

Four naked youngsters swimming in the river. Early birds.

One of the boys saw him and yelled out, "We're just swimming, sir."

"Whose Falcon?" he yelled.

The tallest youngster waved back. Buenrostro walked back to the clearing. From there, he and Cantú walked to the crawl space where the killer entered the Gómez ranch undetected. Cantú looked for new tracks leading to the mesquite grove and found them almost parallel to the original ones along with prints made by the bloodhounds and the Mexican federal police.

They slowed down and walked cautiously out of the mesquite grove and into the sorghum field. Within moments, they cut across the recently plowed ground where Lu Cetina's men had found the multiple burial sites.

They made their way slowly across the sorghum field until he and Cantú stood some fifty paces from the house. Cantú pointed to a shady spot where they could sit unobserved and watch the ranch house at the same time. Every now and then, a faint, cool breeze would cut through the sorghum stalks and offer some relief from the ninety-degree heat.

"You afraid of snakes, Chief?"

"No. You?"

"Yeah, somewhat. What we looking for anyway?"

"Enrique Salinas's son. Eduardo."

"But why him?"

"His father died last night. I think he's come here every day, waiting for another shot at the Gómezes."

Ike Cantú didn't speak.

After a while, Buenrostro said, "A process of elimination, Ike. El Barco Zaragoza died last night and that leaves Eduardo to do the job."

"He was part of the gang?"

"Most likely not, but revenge is a driving force, Ike."

Buenrostro glanced at his watch: eight-fifteen; they'd been there half an hour and still no movement in or around the area. Another half hour passed. At exactly nine-fifteen, a man stepped out of the ranch house, walked to the backyard, and lit a cigarette. Eduardo Salinas, the son of El Camarón.

Buenrostro waited.

Salinas seemed to have made up his mind about something, and walked along the oleander hedges and toward the sorghum and cane fields, where Buenrostro and Cantú waited. As the younger man unknowingly walked toward them, Buenrostro raised his voice.

"I mean you no harm, Eduardo Salinas. This is Chief Inspector Buenrostro."

Surprised, Salinas dropped to the ground and unholstered the silver-plated Rossi.

"We're coming out," Buenrostro warned. "Detective Cantú and I will be some fifteen paces to your left. You don't need the gun."

Salinas got on his feet, brushed the dirt off his clothes and watched the swaying of the sorghum stalks as the two detectives made their way out of the field.

Once in the clearing, Buenrostro and Cantú clapped their hands and waggled them to show they were unarmed. Eduardo Salinas kept the Rossi in his hand.

Buenrostro asked, "Is that your Falcon in the clearing?"

Surprised at the question, Salinas said, "No." Motioning with the Rossi, he said, "Let's get back in the field, where it's cooler."

Before they sat down, Salinas said, "*Buenas tardes, jefe inspector,*" and then clipped the gun to the small of his back.

"What brings you here," Buenrostro asked.

"I think you know, sir. I am looking for don Lisandro Gómez Solís."

Buenrostro looked at Eduardo Salinas. "He's been dead for close to a month now." Buenrostro explained that Director Cetina had decided to say nothing about Gómez's death for the time being.

"You say that don Lisandro Gómez is dead?"

Buenrostro nodded. He then mentioned Tibu Morales and his story.

"Who did I kill then, innocents?"

"No, no innocents."

"Who, then?"

"Don Felipe Segundo, one of the twins, and a worker. Who helped you with the bombing and the fires?"

"No one," he said proudly.

"You're a dynamiter?"

Eduardo Salinas said, "In that regard, I had help from my late father's friends, but as for entering this place, no. I, alone."

"Revenge."

Salinas asked, "What else? What would you have done?"

Buenrostro said nothing for a few seconds.

"Tell me, Eduardo, have you seen a Jimmy? That's a GMC truck, it's white, new, and in good condition?"

"Why?"

"Have you?"

"No."

"It belongs to the Gómez family."

Salinas smiled and gave a mocking laugh. "What's left of it, *jefe inspector.*"

The three men looked at each other in silence.

"You came back for don Lisandro." A statement, not a question.

Salinas said, "You did not tell us don Lisandro was dead when my father and I visited you at the courthouse."

"We learned of this later on from the man Morales."

"This Morales is a gunman?"

Buenrostro: "No. A farmer. Look around. This is his work."

"He does not need killing."

"That's right."

Eduardo Salinas offered them a cigarette before lighting one for himself.

"What now, *jefe inspector?*"

A good question, thought Rafe Buenrostro. "Your job here isn't finished, is that it?"

Salinas nodded slowly. "My father died last night. We're to bury him this afternoon."

"Have you been coming here every day?"

"Since the soldiers left, yes. And what about you, sir? Will you tell Director Cetina about me?"

"No."

This caught Eduardo Salinas by surprise. "Oh?"

"She will soon figure it out for herself."

"With your help?" Salinas's voice tensed up.

"The director is an intelligent person."

"And honest, from what I hear."

"And honest, yes." Buenrostro looked at Salinas, who had relaxed somewhat.

"You are deciding what to do about me?"

"You helped my father, I could never harm you. Is your father alive, *jefe inspector?*"

Buenrostro said nothing. His father had been murdered when Rafe Buenrostro was seven years old, and was a memory kept alive only by a series of photographs.

"No, he's dead."

"As mine."

"Do you plan to kill José Antonio, the remaining twin?"

"Do I have a choice?"

"I have another question. Do you know something, anything, about a recent robbery at a pawn shop on the Texas side of the river? We think it was a guns-for-drugs arrangement with the Gómez family."

"No."

"Did you see the five men asleep under the Cessnas there, in the first barn?"

"No. I know of no five men. I planted the French plastique in the middle barn. Very effective."

"Do you plan to come back here?"

"Until the last Gómez is dead. Did the *jefe inspector* know these deaths were what my father meant at the courthouse when he said he would do you a favor?"

"Had I known, I would have tried to convince him otherwise."

They looked at each for a few seconds until some early morning heat lightning broke their silence. After this, Ike Cantú led the way through the fields until they came to the clearing. In a few minutes they stood by the crawl space; Salinas went first. When they arrived near the shaded spot, Buenrostro noted that the Falcon remained in place. He heard the youngsters again.

"Swimmers," he said, unnecessarily. "We could drive you to Control or to Barrones, if you wish."

"Control, sir, I have my car there." He then said, "I was driven out here."

Cantú: "How do you reach your contact in Control?"

Eduardo Salinas looked at Ike Cantú: "The phone at the ranch house has not been cut off." He opened his eyes and smiled. "They'd trace the call to my friend, but it's a public phone." He smiled again.

He turned to Buenrostro: "You are not wearing a gun? Obeying the law, as usual?"

Buenrostro looked at young Salinas for a moment before saying, "A calculated risk."

Puzzled by this answer, Salinas said, "You expected to find me there? Not the twin, but me?"

"I had an idea."

They drove in silence until they came to the outskirts of the town of Control and its dusty streets. "Which hotel?"

"That one, the pink one. I recommend it, *jefe inspector*. A clean, well-lighted place."

Buenrostro smiled. "Did you read that in the original or in the Spanish translation?"

"Like you, I too went to St. Joseph's. You haven't changed much from the pictures in the Refectory, sir."

Buenrostro pulled into the gravel driveway and stopped by the main entrance.

With his hand on the door handle, Salinas said, "The last twin belongs to me. He is hiding somewhere in the area. Maybe even across the river. If you knew where, you wouldn't tell me, would you?"

"No, but we'd arrest him."

"*Directora* Cetina will never find me."

Buenrostro said nothing for a moment, and Eduardo Salinas got out of the car.

"Buenrostro said, "Is the gun you now carry the one you used that night?"

"Yes, a Rossi. Most dependable. Want to see it?"

Buenrostro shook his head.

Before Buenrostro drove off, Salinas said, "Goodbye, sir. I will give my mother your condolences and your regards."

Thirty-six

i

Ten days later, Lu Cetina sent a two-page fax to Buenrostro.

The time was ten-fifteen and the outside heat forced the groaning air conditioning to work at full capacity; as a result, the window panes had clouded over. Hauer rang the morning desk sergeant and asked for a gallon of iced limeade.

He sat at his desk to read the fax when the interoffice light came on his phone.

"Homicide, Hauer."

"Good morning, Pete. This is Norm Andrews, how's it going?"

Hauer temporized.

"Your boss in?"

"He's upstairs, sheriff, at the Commissioners' meeting."

"What's that? What meeting?"

Hauer looked at the phone and then said, "An emergency meeting. All the section heads are there with the chief inspector. Let's see, it started about twenty minutes ago, and–"

Sheriff Andrews banged the phone down.

Peter Hauer laughed and turned his attention to the fax.

PARA: R. Buenrostro, Jefe Inspector, Condado de Belken. Departamento de homicidios.

DE PARTE DE: María Luisa Cetina de Gutiérrez, Directora de la Sección del Orden Público, Municipio de Barrones, Tamaulipas, México.

PAGINA UNA DE DOS PAGINAS:

Morales a big help, and thanks. He won't be charged. The man is a fantasist, but no killer.

Dead woman identified as Natalia Dávila, cook & housemaid. Fortyish; cause of death: A wound to the chest and a fractured skull with a sharp instrument. Latter possibly an ax. Weapon used: a .38 Taurus. (Not found.)

Aside from Felipe Segundo and Juan Carlos Gómez, the dead man in living room identified by Morales as Abel Salas, a farmhand. Deaf Mute Farías's body also found; he buried Lee Gómez, the pilot Grayson, plus two French Canadians aboard Cessna on the day of the escape.

Aside from personal effects on above, great amounts of American, Canadian, and Mexican currency found on Pilot Grayson and Fr. Canadians.

Morales gave graphic description of murder of Lee by F. Segundo and twins. Lee shot three times; half of face shot off. Almost verbatim from your cassettes received here.

Cocaine and marijuana in barns charred and disposed of in Gulf of Mexico yesterday under army and my personal supervision.

In re bodies in second barn: your lab work on I.D. correct; 3 minor criminals from your area and 2 pilots. No I.D. & checking. Additional records received here from your office in re Flora pawn shop robbery: manager identified remains of automatic rifles in crates came from his store. Am including our tech squad's partial list of I.D. numbers on weapons at end of this message.

Sneakers worn by shooter: New Balance. Tire tracks found on side of road next to fence: Mexican Goodyear—Oxo.

Synthetic fiber (navy blue) on barbed wire similar to synthetics used on jumpsuits, leisure pants, etc. What we call *dril*.

Gómez ranch house set on fire two days ago; the day El Barco Zaragoza and the albino Enrique Salinas died. Report from Fed Intelligence: nothing to tie Góngora and Espinel families to subsequent arson. Vandalism suspected but no proof as yet.

Nothing to report from *casas de cita*.

No news on whereabout on missing twin. El Barco Zaragoza left money and property to Enrique Salinas's family. Eduardo Salinas, albino's son, no longer living in Barrones. He and widow moved away a week ago. Whereabouts unknown. Is he of interest to us?

Good question, thought Peter Hauer.

The usual red wax with the Mexican eagle seal was followed by Lu Cetina's illegible signature, a rubric.

Hauer barely glanced at the serial numbers of the stolen automatic weapons, initialed the fax and placed it in Buenrostro's in-basket.

He poured himself some limeade before calling the widow Grayson. The answering machine came on with a message to wait for the beep. As soon as Hauer identified himself, the widow Grayson came on the line as she cut off the monitoring device.

"This is Laura Castañón de Grayson, detective. How are you?"

Hauer asked if he could come by for a few minutes. After a slight pause on her part, she said yes, and that she looked forward to seeing him again.

He picked up his poplin jacket from the clothes rack, called in the desk sergeant and told him where he was going.

"Contreras, tell the chief inspector he's to remind Southwestern Bell that we need a record of every call Mrs. Grayson's made or received for the last six weeks. Tell him to call Director Cetina in Barrones if any Barrones numbers appear on the list of telephone calls."

On his way to the parking lot he thought on some questions to put to the widow after he told her of her husband's death.

The dope at the yacht party. Did she know the twins? How long? How well? Who had called them to the party? Who made the purchase? He left the parking lot and drove toward Washington and Third, the widow's address. The three-bedroom, two-car garage told him nothing. Paved driveway, cedar fence, air-conditioning units for each room. The usual overpriced, brick veneer "you pay for the trees and the safe neighborhood" gimcrack of a house . . .

Maybe, he thought, maybe she's the key to the remaining twin. In what way, Hauer did not know yet.

ii

Hauer knocked on the door, waited some five seconds, and knocked again, harder this time. He waited another five seconds, was about to knock a third time when he heard steps coming to the front door.

Laura Castañón de Grayson, now, thought Peter Hauer, *viuda de* Grayson, opened the door slowly and smiled. Drinking, said Hauer to himself. She smiled again, gave the door a slight push and led Hauer into the living room. Not cheap furniture, he noted, merely uninspired.

No, no coffee, thank you. He watched her closely. Was she focusing? Was she able to do so? Doesn't smell of liquor, though. Stoned? He tried to look at her eyes but they were hidden under eye shadow and fake eyelashes. Attractive enough–she doesn't need all that junk. He realized his mind was beginning to wander and said, "Mrs. Grayson, I've some bad news for you."

Before he spoke again, Mrs. Grayson brought a tissue to her face.

"If it's about my husband, I know. I didn't want to believe it, but José Antonio Gómez called here last week and told me so himself. It was a tragic accident out in the Gulf and our Mexican insurance agency is investigating. I'm surprised the police didn't know."

This knocked Peter Hauer for a loop. What story had the Gómezes cooked up for her? he wondered. She admitted she was wrong for not calling the courthouse, and yes, she meant to tell him, Detective Hauer, about it the last time he had called. She was afraid to admit to him she had done a couple of lines at the yacht party. She didn't want to involve anybody else. But no, she didn't have a problem with drugs.

It's the medicine, she explained. It's made her dizzy, although it was supposed to relax her and regulate her sleeping.

"I haven't done much of that since my husband disappeared."

The name of the doctor, asked Hauer. She looked at the floor and for a moment seemed to him as if she were about to faint. "I, I got them in Barrones. I don't need a prescription over there."

Hauer said nothing.

She blew her nose, threw away the tissue, and took a fresh one.

"I'm okay, really. What do you want to know?"

She didn't ramble and seemed to be in control. The twins were at the party early; they left to make a purchase for the Gilberts, and returned later. No, that wasn't right. Only Juan Carlos came back.

They were paid American dollars. She didn't know how much was bought. Juan Carlos left after that.

Later, much later, although she didn't know the exact time, she saw him and his brother again. Out in the parking lot.

Her husband had introduced the twins to her at a dinner club across the river. And yes, she'd met their father, too. About the time his brother Lee had broken out of the Belken County jail.

Hauer finished writing his notes and asked: "Who called the twins to come to the party?"

She didn't know. The Gilberts, maybe. The twins were there, they left, and then they came back. Suddenly she asked, "Do I need a lawyer?"

Hauer explained she wasn't being charged with anything. He was making an inquiry, and she was being helpful.

In that case, she said, she'd known them for over a year. When her husband started flying for the family. Of course he flew for others, mostly fishermen, but since the Gómez ranch is so close, there was more money in flying equipment, machine parts, that sort of thing, than for flying fisherman out to La Pesca for a week at a time.

Had she heard from the twins since the night of the party? No. She was sure of that. She'd been under medication since she learned of her husband's death, but no, not a word from either twin. Hauer closed his notepad and thanked her.

Well, he thought, the telephone records would show if she were telling the truth.

Before leaving, looking idly around the room, he said, "The Mexican authorities made a positive identification of Mr. Grayson. I'm sorry."

At this point, she picked up two photographs. "My son," she said. "He lives in Murfreesboro, Tennessee, with my first husband."

He noticed other pictures scattered around the room.

She led him to the door, they shook hands, and Hauer walked to his car. She told the truth, said Hauer to himself. But not the whole truth, he added.

He drove back to the courthouse.

THIRTY-SEVEN

Buenrostro pushed the Lee Gómez file one side and thought back a scant three weeks: the escape, the betrayal by his own brother, the deaths of the pilot Grayson and the two French-Canadians. That, he said to himself, had been the beginning. Throw in the two men at the parking lot and young Daniel Varela, the driver of the Silverado. The Quevedo brothers escaped death only because Lu Cetina waited them out at the Flamingo instead of rushing in; California commando style, she called it.

But it didn't end there, he thought. Now, Felipe Segundo was dead, as was one of the twins. And no idea where the other one had gone off to. Then there were the South Americans, the deaf-mute, the ranch cook, the hijackers at the pawn shop plus the pilots. At this point, he stopped thinking. He called the desk sergeant.

"Contreras, any uniforms out there?"

"Yessir, Baus is here."

"Send him in." Buenrostro took the thick file and re-tied it with some fishing cord. He then wrote a note to Executive District Attorney Gwen Phillips, and placed it on top of the file. When Baus came in, Buenrostro handed him the file, with instructions to hand-deliver it and the note to Gwen Phillips. After this, he got up from his chair and lazily stretched himself as he walked to the east window. He leaned in front of the air conditioning unit for a few seconds, poured himself a cup of coffee and stared out the window in the direction of the Gómez ranch.

He shook his head. Something was twirling around in there, something about the case, about the Gómezes. It bothered him that he couldn't remember, and he frowned. He took another sip and went into deep thought.

Staring at the parking lot, his thoughts came back to the getaway and to the diversion at the cafeteria parking lot. There had been a second diversion, he remembered. The robbery at the pawn shop. This had been followed, perhaps coincided, with the fire at the liquor store.

What was missing? Lu had contacted Lee's and Felipe Segundo's wives and both hung up on her; they wanted nothing to do with either man. And, oddly, nothing to do with the twins. This was strange. Most Mexican families would do anything to keep in touch; not in this case, though. Was he missing something?

What was it Lu had said? Lee's wife didn't even bother to come to the phone. She had a maid do it.

The phone rang; desk Sergeant Contreras said District Attorney Valencia's secretary was on the line.

Not now, he said to himself. He walked to the front desk and told Contreras to relay a message: The chief inspector just stepped out and would return the call as soon as he got back. Contreras looked at his chief for a moment then passed the message on to the secretary. Buenrostro stood by Contreras's desk and asked for Hauer.

"At the dentist's, Chief."

Buenrostro sat down on his desk. Who profited from all this? The cocaine and the other drugs had been ruined and later dumped into the Gulf. The money remained in the Texas banks, and if the feds could prove the money came from drug profiteering, that was it for the Gómez family as far money was concerned. Who profited? Well, the Salinas family. Would revenge would be profit enough?

The big-time smugglers for northern Mexico, the Espinel and Góngora families? They'd need new middlemen to transport the product from across the river and then to guide it on through to Houston, Dallas, Chicago, wherever. They'd find someone. Somebody was always willing to take a chance to make big, big money all around.

That would be Lu Cetina's problem. He returned the coffee cup to the table. My troubles, he thought, would begin soon after that. In thirteen years, two or three murders had always preceded or followed the bigger shipments. He suspected it would be worse the next time.

Whatever was bothering him would come out sooner or later, he consoled himself. Yeah, he thought, at two or three o'clock in the morning. He decided to forget all this, and began looking forward to a four-day weekend of Gulf fishing with Sammie Jo and Sam and Edna Dorson.

Clearing some of paper on his desk, he noticed a Belken County memo in his in-basket. There, written in Peter Hauer's neat handwriting, was a carbon-copy notation of his various visits to the widow

Grayson. The latest date went back to three days ago, when Buenrostro had authorized Pete to see her and tell her the truth about her husband. His body, in a sealed casket, had been returned to the Texas side soon after.

Initial meeting widow Laura Castañón de Grayson at Court House: Husband, a pilot, missing; on trip to Mexico according to airport's copy of pilot manifest .

First visit to Mrs. Grayson's home. Reported no news on husband. Still working on the case, etc.

Second visit. Widow thought I'd come to see her in re her husband. Explained purpose of visit was the yacht party. She knew everyone there. Admitted using drugs that night; no idea who sold them to the yacht owners. Sellers drove a white pickup. No idea of year, brand, make, etc.

Her husband had delivered machine parts for the Gómez family for years. Had met Lee and Felipe Segundo Gómez; and she and her husband visited the ranch a couple of times for parties and such. Knows twins.

Note: Did not inform her of husband's death as per Chief Insp's instructions.

Peter Hauer, ever the meticulous one, had appended another sheet of paper:

Third visit: Broke the news to the widow Gr. Not surprised when informed of death; said she was expecting the worst. Offered usual County's help in bringing body back to Texas. Stayed for coffee.

Up-market furniture but cheesy. Various pictures of son in living room; boy's picture in teens and early twenties? Lives with first husband in Tennessee.

Admitted knowing twins for over a year. They supplied coke at Gilbert's yacht party. Claimed embarrassment. Not as good a liar as she thinks.

Hauer's initials followed this last entry.

Buenrostro thought for a minute. Dorson and he had known the twins since their childhood. Do Peter Hauer and Ike Cantú know them by sight, he asked himself? Where am I going with this? He went to the Varela file and looked for the photos of young Varela and the twins; he laid them on Peter Hauer's desk. After this he called Hauer at the dentist's office.

"A couple of questions, Pete. Have you ever met or seen the Gómez twins, and did you get a look at the snapshots of them with Daniel Varela?"

Hauer thought for a few seconds and said, "Never met 'em, no. Saw the snapshots. Not very clear, were they? Is it important?"

Buenrostro again said he didn't know. It was just something that had been bothering him for a few days.

"They're on top of your desk. Look at them when you come in. One last question, Pete. You reported seeing pictures of her son in the living room."

"All over the place. Five to seven, eight, maybe. Lives up north, she says. Is that it? I'm holding up the dentist here."

"Come back to the office when you're through. I may have something for you."

Buenrostro hung up as Dorson and Cantú walked in.

Before Cantú reached his desk, Buenrostro asked: "You ever meet the Gómez twins, Ike?"

Surprised by the question, he hesitated for a moment and then said no, he'd never met them. Buenrostro then asked if he'd seen some snapshots of Daniel Varela and the twins. This time, Cantú said, "Sure, when his mom and sis came in. I interviewed them and they left the photos here and we made copies for us. We lose 'em?"

Dorson stepped in: "No, there they are, Ike, on top of Pete's desk. What's this all about?"

"Something Pete wrote in his interviews with the Grayson woman. Finally admitted doing dope at the yacht. She said she'd seen a white pickup at the parking lot that night, but she didn't know the young men who sold them the cocaine."

An inquiring Dorson said, "So?"

"Well, she was lying. She later volunteered she and her husband and the Gómezes had a social relationship. She knew Lee, Felipe Segundo, and the twins. It's all there in Pete's notes."

Dorson again said, "So?"

Buenrostro answered evenly: "She lied about not knowing the twins, then she told Pete she did."

Dorson said, "Not much there from what I can see."

Buenrostro nodded slowly and then said, "I think there's a connection, and the yacht party is it. We can place the twins there; she said they sold the dope to them out of a white pickup, remember?"

Dorson waited for Buenrostro to go on.

Ike Cantú said he didn't see the connection.

"It's the yacht party, none of the partygoers knew them. So, how did the twins get invited there, to the parking lot?"

"Somebody called them," said Ike Cantú.

"And your candidate is Laura Grayson," said Dorson, flatly.

"Pete caught her in a lie. Read Pete's last interview." With this he passed Dorson and Cantú the file.

THIRTY-EIGHT

i

Buenrostro went into his office and served himself a second glass of iced limeade; he added some extra ice cubes and stirred the glass with a pencil. Five minutes later Dorson and Cantú walked into his office.

Dorson: "You have to have known the twins to identify them from the snapshots. I knew them, of course, but I think I filled them in mentally when I first saw them. Ike here didn't know them and could barely make them out."

Ike Cantú said, "At any rate, when I first saw the snaps, I focused on Varela."

Buenrostro nodded and said, "I think that's what Pete did. We were interested in Varela because he was missing, and then we concentrated more on him when the Quevedos gave us the information.

"Here's what we're going to do: Ike, take an unmarked car and keep an eye on the neighborhood. Sam, call the widow and say you're going out there for her protection. We need to see those pictures. She balks and you arrest her. Charge her with obstruction if she doesn't cooperate."

Dorson: "The photos that important?"

Buenrostro nodded. "I think it's the Gómez twins. Or one of them, anyway."

"Good Lord."

"Yeah. We'll see."

As soon as they left, Buenrostro typed a brief update for the district attorney and went upstairs to Valencia's office. He loosened his tie in the elevator.

"Thank you, Chief. You know, I think we ought to charge our overtime to the Mexican police for all the good work you and your men did."

Buenrostro didn't say a word for a moment. This always made Valencia nervous. Buenrostro let him off the hook: "Tit for tat. They help us, we help them."

"Yeah, well, our taxpayers don't know how hard we work in this office."

"Kenny Breen can usually come up with some good press release. Trouble is, the remaining twin is still missing, and that puts a crimp in Lu Cetina's finishing up the case."

"She any good, Rafe? I mean, she's a woman, and Mexicans are pretty macho-men when it comes to having a woman for a boss, right?"

"Well, Reynosa's not forty miles away from Barrones and they've got a woman mayor. And she's not even a member of PRI."

"Really?" said an incredulous Chip Valencia.

"One of the founding families. She's an Avallaneda."

"I'll be damned. Well, anyway, it was a solid report. You'll keep me informed, right? I'm due to meet with the Commissioners' Court in half an hour. A budget battle." He grinned.

On his way to the elevator, Buenrostro thought: An easy man to please.

Peter Hauer, back from the dentist's, walked in, hung his jacket over a chair, and sat at his desk. Buenrostro entered through the side door, went to Dorson's desk and handed Peter Hauer the snapshots.

"What am I supposed to see?"

"Look at the twins, not at Daniel Varela. Seem familiar?"

Hauer shook his head. "I need a head shot. What am I looking for here? I mean, they're not clear enough."

"That's okay, Sam's bringing in some others in a bit."

The phone rang. Gwen Phillips came on the line and said, "Sorry to bother you, handsome, but my boss is lining up votes upstairs for a budget increase this very minute." Buenrostro pressed his lips and waited a few seconds before saying anything.

"You there, Chief?" asked Gwen.

"I'll talk with Judge Garza, Gwen. I don't want you to get into any trouble." He thanked her and hung up.

Ten minutes later, Dorson and Cantú walked into the squad room, and Dorson tossed a brown envelope on top of Hauer's desk.

Peter Hauer pulled out several four-by-six photographs. He looked at them for a few seconds and then turned to the snapshots again. "What are we looking at here?"

"We're looking for a connection, Pete. Those are the photos you saw at the widow's, right?" Dorson, quietly.

"Yeah, sure."

Dorson and Cantú spoke at the same time: "That's José Antonio and Juan Carlos."

Hauer let out a soft whistle. "The survivor and his deceased brother."

He looked at Dorson.

"One and the same," said Sam Dorson.

"She had them both as lovers?" asked Hauer, incredulously.

Buenrostro rubbed his nose. "It's a hunch, but the twins are a twisted pair. She used the Tennessee story to throw you off."

Hauer said nothing. He looked at the pictures again, then said, "I think she's nuts."

Buenrostro checked his watch, and mentioned the Commissioners' Court meeting. After a while he said: "She's connected now."

Dorson agreed. "And she's heavy into dope. I think she's losing it, guys." Buenrostro left for the budget meeting upstairs.

ii

At seven that same evening, Judge Garza called Buenrostro at home to tell him that Valencia's motion for a budget increase had been tabled.

This would give the Commissioners' Court an extra two weeks before the motion could come up again. He, the judge said, would appreciate help from the *Enterprise News* to publicize Valencia's plan for increased firepower and unnecessary spending of tax money.

Buenrostro said he'd call Peter Hauer, who had established a working relationship with Marcia Ridings, the paper's editor. With this they both hung up. Buenrostro called Hauer at home and left a message on the answering machine.

Saturday morning, at six o'clock, the sun shone brightly against the cloudless summer sky as Buenrostro and his wife finished packing for their weekend fishing trip with the Dorsons. Tugging at the luggage rack one more time, he went inside and called his in-laws. Noddy Perkins had recovered remarkably from his hospital stay, and was already once again logging in twelve-hour days at the bank.

The old man's voice came on and Buenrostro heard the click of a second line being picked up. Would he and Blanche want to come along? The twenty-two-footer was packed and ready to go, said Buenrostro. All he and Sammie Jo had to do was to drive by and pick them up.

Noddy Perkins hesitated briefly.

"Leave the bank, Noddy. It'll be there Monday morning when you get back. Sam and Edna Dorson are coming along too."

At this point, Blanche came on the line and said yes, to please come by. She'd pack a few things.

An hour later, at seven-thirty, Desk Sergeant Contreras waited for his replacement, Art de la Cruz. He glanced at his watch as the door opened. A man in a brown uniform came in and delivered a package.

"UPS, sign here."

Contreras signed and took the package. "Looks like a video," he said to the delivery man, who had already walked out the door.

Contreras placed the package in the right hand drawer, and locked it. He then made a note of the delivery for Art de la Cruz, who did not walk in until thirty minutes later. Late as usual, sighed Contreras. He was out the door and on his way to the parking lot before de la Cruz had a chance to say anything.

Thirty-nine

i

At one-thirty a.m., five hours after the video had been delivered to Homicide, four firemen at the Klail City branch station on Cooke Boulevard sat playing a game of Hearts when a citizen called to report a fire. "Come quick," the excited voice said. "If you don't, the whole neighborhood'll go up in flames. Come on, hurry it up, get a move on."

A senior sergeant asked for the address as the rest of the night crew climbed into their gear. The doors housing two fire engines opened up at the press of a button.

It was the widow Grayson's house, not ten blocks away, and the fire engines arrived there in eleven minutes; by the time they had hooked on the water mains, three minutes later, the two-story house was in ruins.

A middle-aged man came running to a group of firefighters and said, "My name's Ed Booth. I'm the guy who called. Look at that house. Jesus."

The fire chief, an old hand named Eddie Valent, said, "Why didn't you call earlier? Look at the place."

"No, you don't understand," said Booth. "The fire just started a few minutes ago. The wife and I were up watching television. Then, a big explosion, and then another. I called you guys right away, and then boom! another explosion. Three, maybe four in all, and look at that house."

During this, two television crews showed up and began setting up their equipment. A cameraman looked around, bored. "No flames," he said to the announcer, who nodded and thrust a microphone to a passing firefighter.

The man turned away and said, "Talk to the chief, I'm busy here."

Some firemen stood hosing down the sides, roofs, and yards of the neighboring houses while others directed their water hoses at the charred remains.

Booth was right, the house was gone. Fire Chief Valent compared notes with his second-in-command, Jim Villegas, another seasoned firefighter.

"An all-electric neighborhood, right, Jim?"

A nod from Villegas, who then said, "Explosions in an all-electric house with no natural gas." He looked at Chief Valent.

A younger firefighter ran up and said, "Found two five-gallon cans back there. Looks like army surplus cans. I'd say they were blown out of the house, chief."

Valent then said there might be others since there were four explosions in all. Jim Villegas was writing down his notes when another firefighter came up: "There's a badly burned body, chief. A woman. All curled up."

Before Valent went to see the body, he said, "Save those cans for fingerprints. Don't touch anything. I'm calling the chief inspector."

A sleepy Art de la Cruz answered the phone. Twenty minutes later, Hauer and Ike Cantú drove up. Fire Chief Valent told them of the body, then said they would have to wait a while before they could look at it. His arson squad, he explained, was poking here and there inside the house and having a time of it, since the roof of the second story structure had crashed down on the living room.

"That body ain't going no place anyway," said Valent. "One of my boys found two army gas cans. There might be others and that would explain the heat, the speed of the fire, and the explosions."

A sudden gust of wind, plus the force of the water, caused more ashes and smoke to fly around; the smoke grew thicker. The detectives moved to behind one of the fire engines.

"Where's your boss?"

"Went fishing early yesterday," said Cantú, "but I imagine he's on his way back by now."

"Hey," said Valent, "this may not be a homicide."

Hauer and Cantú looked at him and said nothing.

ii

Buenrostro and Dorson were back in the office by eight o'clock that morning. A county patrol car was waiting for them by the time they walked down the marina.

"The widow Grayson's dead," Peter Hauer said, unemotionally.

Just then the phone rang and Hauer turned on the amplifier. It was Fire Chief Valent: "You all can come over now. It was arson, all right. Found us a fourth can, and there may be others.

"That was fierce heat in there, detective. Gasoline'll do that. I just called Dr. Dietz at the crime lab and he's on his way over here too." With that, he hung up.

Hauer turned off the amplifier and Buenrostro said, "Take Ike with you, Pete. Sam and I'll see you there."

Dorson and Buenrostro sat in the squadroom in silence. They'd worked together for fifteen years, and talk in the courthouse was they could read each other's minds. After a few minutes, Dorson reached over to Hauer's desk, picked up the phone, and said, "I'll call Lu and let her know about the fire." He dialed the Barrones number and left a message.

"Sundays," he said, and shook his head.

Buenrostro then walked to the refrigerator and took out two bottles of beer. They sat and drank without speaking. Buenrostro looked at his half-empty bottle and ran it down the drain. Turning to Dorson, he said, "José Antonio crossed the river and set the house on fire. Why would he kill her, though?"

Dorson shook his head. After a while he said, "The Gómezes should have been Hollywood producers. They like to do things in a big way."

Just then, the phone rang again. It was Henry Dietz calling from the fire scene with a preliminary report. Dorson turned on the amplifier as he finished his beer. Dietz's raspy voice came on: "She committed suicide, guys. Used a big gun.

"We found the remains of a camera tripod, but we haven't located the camera so far. Two leftover pizzas in the fridge, not much else. No idea what women eat when they live alone," Dietz said in wonderment. "And you can forget the clothing and other personal stuff, one of the gas cans was emptied all along the walls on both floors. Whoever it was wanted to make sure the house and the woman went up."

He stopped suddenly. "Why is the name Grayson familiar?"

Dorson explained and then Dietz went on. "Remember seeing pictures of Dr. Goebbels in the Bunker after he and the family were burned? Same condition as the woman. Curled up, unrecognizable.

We'll check on the teeth, though, that ought to do it." Dietz said he'd call later.

Goebbels, thought Buenrostro. He thought of Magda Goebbels and the children. That was a picture he remembered from his junior-high days. What a thing to show kids at that age, he thought.

"Suicide," said Dorson, and Buenrostro nodded.

A moment later, Buenrostro said, "Henry mentioned a tripod and a possible camera. Probably one of the hand-held ones and may have been removed prior to the fire." He stopped, looked at Sam Dorson, and then said, "Prior to the fire, but after the suicide."

"An assisted suicide,' said Dorson. "Like that doctor up north, in Detroit or Milwaukee. He's got an Armenian name, I think."

"Those are being called mercy killings. This has the earmarks of the Gómez family."

Dorson looked up from the floor and said, "Fingerprints on the gasoline can. Let's hope they're on file."

With this they drove to what remained of the house that had once belonged to the late Laura Castañón de Grayson.

iii

Ike Cantú and Peter Hauer stood in the shade of a stubby palm tree talking to a man in the black uniform of a fire captain as Dorson and Buenrostro pulled up. Presently, Henry Dietz joined them.

Dietz and an arson specialist agreed it was arson. A fourth can had been found embedded in the hollow cement blocks of a homemade barbecue grill in the patio. The arson specialist said the first thing to go were the walls of both floors. They'd been lined with gasoline and then, whoever set the fire had thrown the fourth gasoline can on the stoop between the kitchen and the outdoor grill.

"With that much gasoline around a match or two would do it."

Ike Cantú asked, "How much time would it take to burn the house down?"

Chief Valent came up and said, "Three bedrooms, two baths, kitchenette, family-living room, den, with adjoining two-car garage and twenty gallons of gas? Twelve, fourteen minutes. Between the time of the call to the branch station, the short drive out here, all that took twelve to fifteen minutes. By the time the crews got here, in those fifteen minutes, the house was gone. This is brick veneer. Your regular overpriced rat trap in a fancy neighborhood."

Dietz cut in and said no bullet had been found yet.

Buenrostro nodded and said, "Sam, you, Pete, and Ike talk to the neighbors. Anything else, Henry?"

"Waiting for prints from the cans." Dietz looked at his watch and asked Buenrostro for the cell phone. "I'll call the lab."

Buenrostro asked if he could look at the body and was led there by a firefighter. A few minutes later Henry Dietz called out: "We've got a match from the prints Lu Cetina sent us here three weeks ago. They belong to José Antonio and Juan Carlos."

Buenrostro nodded and tried to keep out of the way. "Floor's still warm."

The firefighter said, "Gasoline. We'll be watering here for another six hours and then leave a crew to see it doesn't flare up again."

Forty

Noon Sunday. After a quick lunch, the Homicide section met in Buenrostro's office. Cantú dragged his chair from the squadroom, Dorson sat on the window seat next to the air conditioning unit overlooking the parking lot. Hauer sat in Buenrostro's chair, and Buenrostro as usual leaned against a filing cabinet. He motioned to Dorson to begin.

"You've all read Dietz's report and those of Chief Valent and his people. Nothing I can add to that except to remind us that José Antonio Gómez is very much alive.

"Most of the people in that neighborhood use the weekends to go to Padre, to Barrones, or somewhere else in the Valley. Most of them are in their second marriage and they're DINKs."

Buenrostro asked, "What's that?"

Dorson said, "Double Income, No Kids. That's what they call themselves. DINKs. There are four houses to a block in that restricted development, and they share a huge backyard. The widow, then, had three neighbors.

"Pete talked to a couple named Cornish who went out with friends around seven. Earlier that afternoon, around five, Mrs. Cornish said she saw a white pickup in the driveway. Her husband said it was a white Jimmy. They'd seen it in the driveway off and on for some two or three weeks. He hadn't seen it parked there for a week or so until it showed up again yesterday afternoon.

"They first saw it at three p.m. when a young man got out and brought some pizzas into the house. The widow opened the porch door and walked in with him. Cornish says he'd seen the youngster before.

"The Jimmy was still in the drive way when the Cornishes left for dinner at seven. They didn't get home until two-thirty a.m. and then drove like hell the last six blocks when they saw the cop lights and the EMS vehicles."

Cantú read from his notes: "I talked to the Dowlings. They live at the other end of the block. Dowling owns a green Jimmy, and he said the white one at the driveway was brand new. He last saw it at nine o'clock when they drove to Barrones for dinner with friends. They got back around three a.m. and missed most of the excitement.

"The people in the fourth house have been gone for a week according to Dowling. I checked and found the verandah full of newspapers. That's it for me."

Buenrostro said, "I checked the desk sergeant's log for Friday night. The firefighters got to the house eleven minutes after the call. That jibes with the time that Valent entered in the report."

The light on line three blinked once and Hauer picked up the interoffice call. "Yes, what?"

Desk Sergeant Contreras said, "I need to see the chief."

A few seconds later, Contreras walked in, shaking his head. He looked at Buenrostro and said, "Chief, this package came by UPS yesterday morning before shift change. I logged it in, but de la Cruz didn't read the log, I don't think. It's addressed to you, see? I came on again at seven this morning, and that's when I saw the package hadn't been delivered. Sorry, Chief."

He held it out and said, "Looks like a video, don't it?"

Buenrostro took the package and opened it. He turned it around a couple of times and said, "Needs rewinding," and then tossed it to Dorson. Hauer then told Contreras to hook up a VCR, and Cantú went out to the squadroom to wheel in the television set.

Buenrostro told Contreras, "No calls."

Hauer turned on the set and placed the tape in the VCR to rewind the video. While they waited, Buenrostro took a chair alongside Dorson and Cantú. After the rewind, Hauer pressed the play button and went back to Buenrostro's desk.

Laura Grayson and José Antonio Gómez sat side by side, facing the camera. She picked up a pizza box, went off-camera, and came back with a bottle of red wine. They spoke during this time, but there was no soundtrack. Gómez took two glasses from a cabinet, and she poured for both of them. She smiled and kissed him on the cheek, and he seemed to pull away a bit. They then toasted each other, and the widow went off-camera again. José Antonio looked at the camera and raised his glass, as if toasting his audience. Standing up, he reached behind him and drew out a handgun. He smiled again, pointed the gun to his left temple, and laughed.

He then sat by an end table and laid the gun next to a flower vase. Soon after, the widow reappeared again, naked. She began to undo Gómez's clothes. He stood perfectly still. She then took off his shoes and brought him to his feet. First, she unzipped his fly, undid the belt, and pulled his trousers down. She then removed his underwear.

Naked, they walked to the camera hand in hand, did an about-face, and stood by the sofa facing the end table. She then knelt down, looked into her purse, and undid a small baggie. Using a playing card, the queen of hearts, she measured out four lines of cocaine on the table. This time she stared at the camera and, using her middle finger, she flipped off her unseen audience. José Antonio laughed and did the same.

Each one rolled a one-hundred dollar bill and did a line apiece. They then embraced briefly, before she went down to his penis. The twin laughed, pushed her away, and began masturbating. At the same time, the camera showed the widow doing her second line. Finished, she leaned toward the table, grabbed the gun and made love to it. She kissed it, took it in her mouth, and then placed it on the black-haired vee between her legs. She stared at the camera the entire time and smiled dreamily. Gun in hand, she opened her arms, walked to José Antonio and kissed him lightly on the lips before she fell on her knees again. She tried to draw him to her and laughed at him as he tried to pull away.

Struggling now, he pushed her off. Looking slightly puzzled, the widow Grayson grabbed the gun and pointed it at him, and then began to laugh as José Antonio Gómez began to masturbate again.

It looked like a ritual, something done before, rehearsed; choreographed, even.

Suddenly, she goose-stepped to the sofa, back to the camera with the gun at her side. She then knelt with her back to the camera, placed the gun in her mouth, took a deep breath and pulled on the trigger. Her brains splattered on the sofa, the floor, and on the table, which toppled over.

At this point, Hauer exclaimed, "God," and Ike Cantú jumped out of his chair. Buenrostro and Dorson exchanged glances briefly but said nothing.

On the monitor, José Antonio Gómez shrugged and remained sitting for a few seconds. He looked at the widow with little interest or emotion. He looked at the camera and shrugged again.

Suddenly he got up, dressed quickly, and walked out of camera range. A short while later, he returned, wet his fingertips, and picked up some of the cocaine on the carpet and swallowed it. Taking a deep breath, he went off-camera again. He then brought back two five-gallon cans, then a third. He was back a few minutes later with a fourth can and looked at the camera again. Smiling at the widow's body, he kicked her sharply in the head.

He looked down for a second and then kicked her in the side. This caused her body to turn around, and she lay on her back, whereupon he kicked her in the rib cage. He then wiped his forehead and reached into his shirt pocket, from which he drew a cigarette lighter. Smiling once again, he tossed the lighter up in the air and caught it as he walked toward the camera. The video clicked off. The squad room fell silent for a moment.

Hauer was the first to speak. "Well, what the hell was that all about?"

A disgusted Cantú said, "Maybe a shrink ought to see this," and looked around the room for confirmation.

Buenrostro went to the VCR, put the tape on rewind and waited. Peter Hauer said, "This is the first time I've seen someone shot. I mean, someone I know." He stared at the floor, shook his head, walked to the middle of the room and stood there with his hands in his pockets.

Buenrostro said, "It looked like a game, didn't it? Something they'd done before, except that this time there was a round in the chamber. Little son-of-a-bitch planned it all along. A judge and jury would rule it murder."

"In the first," said Sam Dorson.

The four detectives again fell silent until Cantú said, "Well, he showed us the gasoline cans, the lighter . . ." He stopped at mid-sentence and looked at the floor again.

Hauer said nothing. He stood by the air conditioning unit and stared at the nearly empty parking lot.

Dorson stared at the blank television and shook his head. He removed the cassette and returned it to the case which Buenrostro handed him.

Hauer broke the silence. "How did he cross over to this side of the river that many times? The Cornishes and the Dowlings have seen the Jimmy off and on for two or three weeks now." He stopped for a moment, seemed to have made his mind up about something and said, "I'm calling Art Styles. He was supposed to have men posted at all the bridges."

Dorson broke in and said, "He and the Jimmy could've been here most of the time. Remember what the neighbors said."

Hauer ignored that and called Immigration. "It's me, Art, we've got witnesses here who've seen the Gómez white Jimmy at a driveway for some two or three weeks now. What the hell's going on?"

Silence. Styles coughed, recovered himself, and said, "If my people say they haven't seen it, then that vehicle hasn't crossed to this side of the river, period."

Peter Hauer waited.

"Try this," Styles said, "maybe it didn't cross the bridge from or to Barrones or any other border town. Maybe it's been in a parking garage in Klail all along. Hell, it could've been anywhere."

Peter Hauer lost his patience and said, "Bullshit."

Buenrostro then asked for the phone.

"It's me, Art."

Buenrostro briefly explained the situation. This seemed to mollify Styles, who said, "You know, Rafe, it's just possible that the twin didn't cross over at any time. That he kept the vehicle on this side of the river. They're not dummies, you know. Anyway, we've checked no less than a dozen white Jimmys and many of those are repeaters, which is only natural since people cross over all the time. But your people's Jimmy? No, sir."

Buenrostro thought on that for a while before speaking.

"Here's Pete."

Peter Hauer apologized to his old friend, who once again asked if they'd see each other at the St. Joe's reunion. When Hauer hung up a few minutes later, he spoke quietly, evenly: "I've known Art Styles since kindergarten, and this is the first time I've ever been angry with him. I lost it, that's all. There's no excuse for it." He picked up the phone, called a local florist and ordered a dozen roses for Styles's wife.

Buenrostro spoke up and said, "Art may be right. Maybe José Antonio took cabs across the river or drove another car, something. If so, he parks the car in the garage or in the driveway, out in the open."

Peter Hauer said, "It's not my day, and I'm most probably not thinking straight, but the last time I talked to the widow, I had the feeling she wasn't alone. That there was someone else in the house."

For his part, Dorson said, "I saw her last when I picked up the photographs. Now that I think of it, she may have been on something even then. But I probably got that from the video, not a professional assessment, I must admit . . ."

And he broke off.

Buenrostro said simply, "I'm going to the lab, and I'll fax Lu Cetina's office, give her the news. It's Sunday, go home."

He stood by the door and waited for the squad to leave his office before going to the lab to see Henry Dietz.

Forty-one

Two weeks later, the third hurricane of the season stalled in the Gulf, and the Valley sweltered under the heat and the humidity. The heavy rain squalls brought occasional relief as the lower Texas Gulf Coast braced itself for a predicted landfall anywhere between Corpus Christi and La Pesca, in the state of Tamaulipas.

Sammie Jo Buenrostro listened with mild interest to the weather report and switched off the set before the next commercial. She looked out the window and watched as the rain fell off and on. She then walked into the living room, where Buenrostro put the finishing touches on a balsa-wood model of a Messerschmidt 109. As Sammie Jo watched her husband, the phone rang and she answered it.

Buenrostro looked up as Sammie Jo said, "It's Lu. A bit excited, I'd say."

Almost breathless and with a sound of relief at the same time, Lu Cetina said, "We've located José Antonio, Rafe. He's at one of the *casas de cita.*"

He checked his watch: ten twenty-five.

"Be there in thirty minutes."

He hurried to the bedroom closet and got out of his pajamas. "Lu's got José Antonio holed up in a house in Barrones. Call Sam, tell him I'll pick him up in five minutes."

Buenrostro pulled into Dorson's driveway, and they were soon on their way while Dorson called Lu Cetina's office. He was told to drive to the old bridge, where she would be waiting for them. Twenty minutes later they crossed the river, and Buenrostro drove straight to the main Customs office in Barrones.

"He's at the Salón México, on seventh, right next to The Submarine Club. He's been on the run since the fire at the widow's two weeks ago. Yesterday, he holed up there, and he's taken over the entire house. He drank and drugged up, and he slept during the day. This *casa* is another Gómez enterprise, by the way.

"He's also holding the house musicians. They play, the women strip, and they go through some kind of dance routine whenever he's awake. He strips too and sits there, toying with a gun while they dance. Two or three hours of this and then it's back to bed. The owner is terrified. Who knows what the kid will do next? She had one of the cleaning women call us in, and this is where we stand.

"I want him alive, Rafe. We need to get this over with."

Buenrostro said, "It's your show."

Moments later, six Jeeps drove up to Customs, and she, Buenrostro, and Dorson got into the lead car. The Jeeps wended their way slowly and proceeded to block the narrow one-way street. The area was secured with uniformed city, state, and federal police. With Lu Cetina leading the way, Buenrostro, Dorson, and the old veteran, Elizondo, walked to the front gate and then were led in by the woman who ran the *casa de cita.* Six *federales* followed them and stationed themselves in the first floor's hallway, guns drawn.

Quietly, the woman and the four detectives reached the second landing. String music came from down the hall.

"In there," she whispered.

The woman pointed a highly polished index fingernail toward some heavy, wine-colored velvet curtains. "He's got the gun with him. I think he may have overdrugged himself this morning. He slept later than usual, and then, when he paid off the supplier this afternoon, he said he wouldn't be needing him anymore. He also said he would kill anyone who tried to leave."

Buenrostro and Dorson looked at each other.

"Señora Directora, I've got six girls in there with that crazy man." After a while, she whispered, "The Gómezes own this house and the Salón del Rey over on Abasolo."

Lu Cetina looked at her and nodded.

"Three *casas* in all. Judy's, too." the woman whispered.

The soft music stopped for a second and José Antonio Gómez's voice rose: shrill, nervous, and threatening at the same time. He was yelling at the musicians.

"Toquen esa música, cabrones. Ya, ahora mismo, ¿se les paga en dólares americanos o no? Tóquenle."

Elizondo drew out his gun, as did Lu Cetina, who motioned to the woman to go downstairs. As the two Mexican detectives made their way across the hall toward the velvet curtains, Buenrostro and Dorson followed close behind. They were unarmed.

Signaling to Elizondo, Lu Cetina pulled gently at the curtain and peered inside.

José Antonio Gómez, naked, gun in hand, was slithering around the women. He rubbed the gun against them, giggled, and hummed whatever the musicians were playing. The women, as if in a trance, danced slowly to the Mexican *boleros.* Whenever the music stopped, Gómez pointed his gun at the musicians, and once again the women rose and began to dance.

Lu Cetina motioned to Buenrostro and Dorson. They took in the scene and then, suddenly and with surprising agility, old man Elizondo entered the room and knocked the gun out of José Antonio Gómez's hand. Surprised momentarily, young Gómez reacted by whirling and backhanding Elizondo across the jaw. At the same time, Lu Cetina pointed her gun at José Antonio Gómez, who now held Elizondo's gun. They faced each other for an instant. He kept the gun pointed at her and then, with a disarming smile, turned the gun toward himself, and shot himself above the left eye. The force of the blast blew him backwards and into the arms of a surprised violinist.

The prostitutes didn't hesitate for a second. They dashed out into the hallway, screaming and crying, while the musicians, as if hypnotized, stood in place until they saw José Antonio slumping against the bloodied wall and on to the floor. Suddenly, they too scampered through the curtain and down the hallway.

Lu Cetina, sweating heavily, swore as she holstered her gun. She then looked toward Elizondo, who had recovered and was now attending to José Antonio.

"He's alive," said the old veteran. "Lost an eye, but he'll live."

Lu Cetina took Elizondo's cellular and called the Green Cross–the Mexican EMS–which was waiting downstairs. Suddenly, the six uniformed *federales* dashed in, guns at the ready.

They immediately turned around and began to keep away a crowd of women which was beginning to form.

Once outside, Lu Cetina said, "Elizondo says the kid'll live."

"You took a hell of a chance," Buenrostro said evenly.

"Elizondo's a good man, isn't he?" she asked.

Dorson said, "He took a whack, all right."

In a disconnected voice Lu Cetina said, "I was afraid of this. After he got rid of the widow, I somehow sensed he'd do that, try to kill himself." She sounded tired, relieved, and disappointed at the same time. "Will you look at this uniform?"

"You did a good job, Lu," said Buenrostro.

She nodded for a moment and, as they approached her car, she looked steadily at the two detectives. "Who killed the people out at the ranch, Rafe?"

"Eduardo Salinas."

"Would you have told me if I hadn't asked?"

Dorson stepped in. "Ask a policeman."

Puzzled, she asked, "What's that?"

Sam Dorson, smiling, sang out:

"Every member of the force
Has a watch and chain, of course
If you want to know the time,
Ask a p'liceman!"

Lu Cetina laughed her throaty laugh, and said, "That's a silly piece, what's it from?"

"I don't know," said Sam Dorson.

"We'll need to be going back, Lu."

As they walked to her car, she turned to Buenrostro and said, "I imagine we'll get this sorted out in time. José Antonio and the widow were lovers, right?"

Buenrostro looked at Dorson, who said nothing.

"Well?" She looked straight at Buenrostro.

"Both twins, Lu. They also kept her supplied with dope. The parties at the yacht turned out to be regular affairs."

The three rode in silence to the Barrones customs office. As they left the car, she said, "We'll get Eduardo Salinas, Rafe."

"Shouldn't be too hard. Good night."

Half an hour after that, Buenrostro dropped off Sam Dorson. With his hand on the door handle, Dorson said, "After all these years, Brother William Paul is retiring. He'll announce it at next week's reunion."

"Thirty years to the Church," Buenrostro said. "A good man, Billy Paul Green."

He backed out of Sam Dorson's driveway slowly and turned sharply in the middle of the deserted street. As he did so, he felt the familiar twinge in his left shoulder. He paid no attention to the pain and a few minutes later pulled into his driveway. The lights were on in their bedroom, and the time was twelve-thirty.